WITCI

A Blood Rev

Crystal-I

Witch's Net : A Blood Revelation Novel
By Crystal-Rain Love
Copyright 2013 Crystal-Rain Love

Prologue

He walked along the harbor, a fine mist of water blowing up from the bay to caress his skin, renewing his tired senses. He should go home. He knew he had a woman and child who needed him there, but still... something called him. Something stronger than his sense of duty.

He breathed in the salty water scented air as he scanned the area, searching for whomever or whatever it was that beckoned him, but the source feeding his curiosity remained hidden, as it had been doing for the past several weeks.

It ended tonight. He couldn't take any more. The dreams, the night sweats, the strange music that popped in and out of his head at random, the voice which seemed to stroke him intimately, inducing hard-ons at the most inconvenient times. The sense he was doing something wrong to his girls although he hadn't actually *done* anything. But he'd thought about it. The voice in his head made damn sure he thought about it.

He continued forward, ignoring the suspicious looks he received from the fishermen out working in the wee hours of the night, or morning, depending on how you looked at time. He realized what they had to see, the wild look in his eyes, the hair that had been left in spiked tufts from where he'd dragged his fingers through it a thousand times. He was strung out on a drug he'd never even touched. He didn't even know what it was but his craving for it was fierce.

A hand gripped his arm and he jerked around to see an old fisherman with a scraggly white-flecked beard shaking his head at him. "Don't go to her, boy. I've seen too many of you young ones leave with her and not come back," he cautioned.

"Who?"

A feminine chuckle caught his attention and he turned his head to see a woman bathed in moonlight, her hungry gaze locked on him. Tall and sexy with long dark hair and a body women would pay to have. She laughed again and he swore he heard piano keys being struck.

"Go home, young man," the fisherman warned him again. "You're not the first that's come down by the water searching for something, all wild-eyed and desperate. They leave with her and they don't come back again."

He heard the man's words but they had no effect on him. He couldn't pay any attention to anyone else while she stood there in a long, slinky champagne-colored dress gloving her ample breasts, slender waist and full hips like a second skin. Her red lips were full, her midnight eyes luminous behind thick lashes which she batted coyly as she opened her mouth again and sang an aria which sent shivers down his spine.

"She sounds like an angel."

"That's no angel," the fisherman said but he paid him no attention.

The woman crooked her finger, instructing him to walk the few feet that would bring them together and he had no power to resist her call. She smiled as he approached and although something predatory lurked in her gaze he couldn't turn back. She reeled him in like a fish on a hook.

She smelled of the sea, of salt and fish and ocean breezes. The dark color making up her irises seemed to swim inside her eyes and the lips she touched to his were cold and clammy, causing him to jerk back long enough to remember he had a woman at home, a woman who was warmth to her coldness.

"She's not right for you, lover," the woman whispered, her strange melodic voice blowing out like wind. "If she were, you wouldn't dream of me."

He started to deny her remark but she started to sing again and all images of his woman were dispelled from his mind, replaced with images of him and the strange woman with the beautiful voice. They were naked, entwined together as they swam in the sea, mating in the water as a group of fish swam nearby. He saw them on the beach, the sun glistening off their exposed flesh as she did things to him he wouldn't have the guts to ask of another lover. And she did them well.

"Who are you?"

She smiled, turned, and started to walk away, her voice wafting back to him as she sang a song with no words. It pulled him to her.

It came back to him that he had a woman at home, one who had given him a child and had been there for him more times than he could count, but he couldn't stop following this woman. Her song stroked him like a phantom hand, bringing him to the brink of orgasm but holding him in check so he couldn't topple over the edge. The pressure kept building and he wanted desperately to release it.

"What she doesn't know won't hurt her," the woman called back to him as she led him inside a dark building quite a distance from where he'd met her.

That's right, he thought, following her to the center of a dark room. She stopped, pivoted and licked her lips. Damn, she was fine. Just a little taste was what he needed and he'd never see her again. Nobody would know a thing.

"Good work, love," a rich, masculine voice said from behind him and he felt a vise-like grip on his shoulders seconds before white-hot pain seared the flesh of his neck.

Malaika jerked into a sitting position, sweat drenching her body as her heart tried frantically to burst from the wall of her chest. She gazed down beside her and saw the small child who had crawled into her bed during the night. Her light brown head rested peacefully upon her father's pillow as she held her favorite teddy bear close to her chest.

"Oh, baby," Malaika whimpered as she smoothed a hand over her sleeping child's braided hair, knowing the girl would never see her father again.

She'd just seen him die.

ONE

Jonah waited for the barricades to be parted long enough for his car to be allowed through and pulled the vehicle to a stop outside the building.

The murders had started a month ago, on the first day of the year. The calls were the same, either someone reported hearing a person screaming horrifically or they'd get a call of a body found, the throat and most of the chest torn to pieces, bite marks all over. And nobody ever saw a thing so they had diddly-squat to go on.

He glanced over at his partner, Veronica "Ronnie" Reilly, and she shook her head before opening her door. They both knew they wouldn't find anything except a torn body. No fibers or blood coming from any source other than the victim, no footprints, no witnesses. Nothing. Multiple bodies had been found weekly for the past month, but they didn't have jack when it came to figuring out a suspect or motive. A month wasn't a long time, but with ten bodies found during that period, something should have stuck out by now.

He stepped out of the car and looked at the foreboding building closed off with crime scene tape. He'd grown tired of finding bodies but no answers, and of his fears that whoever or whatever was killing these people wasn't human, not even a normal animal. He wished he could go back in time before he knew the truth about what lurked in the night... before the night he'd been hung on a wall by a demon-possessed man, kept captive in a basement with a vampire.

Ronnie stepped in front of him, saying something but although her lips moved, he didn't pick up any sound. A strange feeling, a buzzing electricity, tingled along the back of his neck, drawing his attention to the crowd which had formed outside the police barrier. The faces of onlookers blurred together as he scanned the mob, his gaze passing over all but one. She stood near the front, her familiar face stricken with despair as she stared at the building.

"Hey Joe, you with me?"

Jonah turned back toward his partner, who was looking at him curiously. "Ten o'clock in the crowd, light to medium-skinned African-American female, cornrowed hair pulled back into an afro-puff, pink sweater, nice body."

"Nice body? Is that a professional assessment or are you just jonesing?" Ronnie quipped as she cast a covert glance in the direction he'd given. "Shit. Yeah, I recognize her," she said, turning her green gaze back to his. "She was at the last scene and if I'm not mistaken, she may have been at the first one."

"What do you think?"

"Killers often come back to view the aftermath."

"You really think she could have killed these people?"

"Stop thinking about the nice body, Joe, and use your cop head."

"I am," he said, a little anger mixing in his tone. "Think about the carnage we've found so far. Throats torn out, bodies ripped to shreds like they'd been attacked by animals. Bite marks from something eating their flesh. You really think she could have done all that?"

"Somebody had to do it, no matter how unbelievable it was."

Yeah, and I'm betting that somebody couldn't stand in pure daylight, he thought to himself, wishing his partner knew the things he knew. It would make things a lot simpler. "I just don't see her doing it. She's barely four inches over five feet. Some of these vics were big guys."

"She could have had help."

True. She could be just like the man who'd hung him on a wall, she could be a devil-worshiping psycho. With the devil in your corner there was a lot of sick shit you could do.

"One thing's for sure," he said with an air of certainty, "there has to be a reason behind her being at multiple crime scenes."

"Shall we find out that reason?"

"I think we shall," Jonah decided as he gestured for Ronnie to precede him to where the young woman stood with the rest of the crowd beyond the barricade. He studied her harder as they made their approach, taking in her smooth skin, cute little nose and full, juicy lips. Her chest was a little on the small side but he'd always been more of a butt man himself, and she definitely filled out her low slung jeans which showed off a flat, toned stomach and trim little waist. She was attractive but his focus wasn't on the pretty face or great body, it was on the anguish he saw in her caramel-colored eyes as she stared at the building, oblivious to the fact she was being honed in on by two homicide detectives. She was definitely connected to the case in some way. What a shame it would be if he'd have to put a bullet in that pretty little package. The thought of causing her pain twisted his gut and tugged at his conscience. Jonah frowned at the odd reaction.

As they got closer he realized she was speaking softly and upon closer inspection he was surprised to discover she was praying, which knocked out the idea she was working with the devil. The fact she stood in broad daylight without the slightest visible hint of discomfort told him she wasn't a vampire either. Then it hit Jonah that he was becoming more like his brother, Jake, searching for evil in everyone he crossed.

They came to a stop before her and he cleared his throat, drawing her attention but before he could speak she let out a startled cry, her eyes growing wide as she looked directly at his partner. Ronnie looked at him in confusion and he shrugged, not understanding the young woman's response either.

"I'm Detective Porter," he said after an awkward moment with the three of them just staring at each other passed, "and this is Detective Reilly." He paused long enough to motion for the officer standing nearby to move the sawhorse before the woman just enough to allow him to guide her past it, his hand under her elbow. He was struck again by familiarity but wrote it off to having spotted her at other crime scenes. Just how many had she been at? All of them? The woman in question didn't utter a sound, too focused on staring at his partner with a strange intensity in her eyes. She looked frightened out of her mind. Jonah shared a baffled look with Ronnie and continued speaking. "We've seen you before, outside of another crime scene. Is there something you'd like to tell us?"

She licked her lips, then chewed lightly on the bottom one as she redirected her gaze toward the building once more. She shivered visibly before turning her attention back to Ronnie. "You can't go in there."

Ronnie and Jonah shared a look before she asked the woman why she would say that.

"Just trust me. You can *not* go inside that building." Her voice shook and something about it raised red flags in Jonah's gut. She was too adamant, too horrified.

"What do you know that we don't?" he asked her, ignoring the look he received from his partner, who undoubtedly believed the woman was a loon. Ronnie didn't know the things he knew, though. She hadn't had the experience of being big brother to a vampire hunter. Jacob Porter had killed vampires, witches, vengeful spirits and things Jonah didn't even want to know about. And he'd taught Jonah that when your gut was screaming at you that something abnormal was up you'd damn well better listen to it. And right now his gut was outright screeching.

"Detectives!" A young uniformed cop with reddish brown hair and a deep tan approached them, his scowl giving away the fact he was eager to get things rolling. "The M.E. is here and he's anxious to get the body in the lab."

"You can't go in there!" The woman shook, her eyes blazing with determination. "You'll die if you go inside that building!"

"Is that a threat?" Ronnie asked, her tone cool and deadly.

"No," the woman responded, taken aback.

"How do you know she'll die if she goes in there?" Jonah asked, raising a hand to silence Ronnie before she could criticize him for being taken in by the woman she obviously thought was a nut-job.

She looked directly at him for the first time and he felt drawn in by her caramel colored eyes and for a moment his mind was filled with images he had no business thinking about while questioning a possible suspect at the scene of a crime with some poor soul's body decaying nearby. "I just know it. Keep her out of there."

"This is nonsense," Ronnie exclaimed irritably as Jonah found himself getting lost in the woman's gaze. "Let's see some ID."

"Why?"

"Because we're taking you in for questioning. ID, now!"

The woman reached into her back pocket and took out her driver's license, handing it to Ronnie with a trembling hand. "I've done nothing wrong."

"Except threaten my safety and hang in one crime scene crowd too many, Miss Jordan," Ronnie replied, glancing at the ID before handing it to the officer who'd recently approached them. "Detain Miss Jordan, please." She turned toward Jonah, annoyance clearly displayed in the lines of her bronzed face. "Let's go check out that body so the M.E. can do his stuff."

"No! You can't go in there! Please!"

Jonah stared at the woman as she yelled out her warning, tears filling her eyes. She didn't even know Ronnie, yet she was adamant something was going to happen to her if she set foot in the building and whatever it was terrified her. Jonah's gut told him she knew what she was talking about.

"Hey, Ronnie, stay back while I go in," he suggested as they neared the door which would lead them into the abandoned warehouse.

Ronnie turned to look at him, clearly bewildered. "Oh come on, Joe, don't tell me you're listening to that woman! What do you think she is, some sort of psychic or something?" She managed to look amused and irritated at the same time which made Jonah feel like a damn fool but he knew stranger people than psychics walked among them.

"It's been known to happen before."

"What?"

"Deja Vu, Nostradamus, hair raising on the back of your neck when—"

"Jonah Porter! Have you gone crazy?" Her question came out as a harsh whisper as she drew closer to him, careful to avoid being overheard. "I know the creep who got the jump on you believed he was Satan's little helper but that stuff isn't real, neither are psychics. You know this, Jonah." She backed away, satisfied she'd gotten her point across and turned toward the building. "This place is crawling with cops. Nothing is going to happen to me."

Unable to think of anything he could say to his mule-headed partner to convince her that her life may be in danger, anything that wouldn't make him sound like a quack, he gave in and followed her inside the building. He'd just have to stick to her like glue in case something bad did pop off.

The stench hit them as soon as they set foot in the door. The victim had been murdered in the center of the first room. Like the others, his throat was torn out right down to the bone and a huge cavity rested in his chest. The M.E. squatted over him, peering closely into the cavity.

"Looks like his damn heart's been munched on," he said, glancing at Jonah and Ronnie as they neared the body.

"That's a bit different," Jonah commented, pulling on a pair of latex gloves before squatting on the other side of the body, so close to Ronnie their hips touched. She looked at him with narrowed eyes, then rolled them, realizing what he was doing and thinking it was stupid. Jonah didn't care. If his partner was in danger he was staying by her side whether she liked it or not. "The bite marks look the same," he added, pushing aside a piece of fabric to reveal one of the marks on the man's abdomen.

"The same damn bite marks that I can't identify," the gray-haired medical examiner, Hank Bonner, grumbled. "I've sent digital photos to colleagues all over the states and to a few overseas. Not a one can identify what type of creature would leave these imprints."

Jonah studied one of the bite marks, observing what had been eluding the M.E. The print left behind indicated that what or whoever had eaten off of the man had a jaw like a human but with far sharper teeth. Some of the other marks were closer to looking like that of a wild dog or a coyote. It was as though the killer was both man and animal, or a man who allowed his pet to feed on the bodies of his victims.

"I just can't understand the lack of blood," Ronnie muttered. "These vics should be lying in pools of it but it's as if it nearly all got sucked out of them before they were fed on."

"Maybe it's a sloppy copycat you've got on your hands," Bonner offered, referring to the last serial killer case Jonah and Ronnie had worked. Carter Dunn had been using a blood-thinning agent and a machine to bleed his victims dry before dumping them in parks with what looked like fang holes in their necks. "And Carter Dunn's brother hasn't been captured yet."

"No, this is different," Jonah said, not bothering to add that Curtis had been captured, just not by the police. Jake had taken care of him, which probably meant he was dead. "These vics are being eaten off of. The Dunns didn't do anything remotely like that."

"Plus, Carter Dunn only killed females," Ronnie interjected and although Jonah knew that was incorrect he remained silent. Nobody needed to know how much he knew about Carter Dunn or how he'd retained that information. Hell, he wished he could forget it all.

"This poor guy appears to have been killed the same way as the rest of them," Ronnie concluded. "Do we have an ID?"

"His driver's license gives his name as David Johns," a nearby officer stated. "He lived on the other side of town."

"Thanks," Ronnie said. "Were you first on the scene?"

"Yes, Detective."

She rose to question the officer while Jonah remained crouched by the body, wondering what the hell had gotten hold of the unfortunate man. Most of the victims were male and two of the three female vics had turned out to be lesbians. It could mean nothing at all or it could mean everything. They'd come from all areas of Baltimore, different incomes, different professions. The only thing they seemed to have in common was a possible attraction to women, so maybe a woman was luring them to their death.

Jonah shook his tired head, knowing he was grasping at straws. The other female vic, Joanne Wilson, was a married mother of three and how did he know that any of the males weren't gay just because it hadn't showed up during the investigation yet? He needed to quit thinking of what-ifs and find something concrete.

He stepped back as the victim was zipped into a bag and put on a gurney, guilt coursing through his body. How many more had to die before he even got a lead?

He looked over at Ronnie as the M.E. left, and started. The only person left in the room with him was the crime scene photographer who was busy packing up his equipment.

"I've taken pictures of the body," the photographer said. "I didn't see any blood splatter anywhere but I can stick around in case you find something that you want photographed."

"Where's Ronnie?" Jonah asked, wondering why the photographer even thought he could leave without being dismissed. He'd worked with the guy before and knew he knew the drill.

"The detective went to investigate other areas," the photographer said, peering out the window.

A cold chill ran the length of Jonah's spine as he recalled the woman outside's warning. Shit. Something was wrong here.

He ran through the lower rooms of the warehouse searching for his partner but each dusty room turned up empty. Then he heard it, a yelp and the sound of something slamming hard against a wall above him. He found the stairs and ran up them toward the sound, with his heart in his throat.

He reached the top of the stairs and stilled as crazed laughter rent the air. "What the hell?" he whispered as he followed the sound, entering a room to find Ronnie pinned against the wall by the same cop she'd been talking to earlier.

"Put her down," he said after aiming his gun at the man's back.

The cop turned, his face distorted. His eyes glowed yellow and his nose and jaws had elongated into a muzzle filled with sharp teeth which were on full display as he snarled at him.

"Looks like we found what's been eating these vics," Jonah said, purposely keeping his voice calm so Ronnie wouldn't freak out any more than she already was. Her eyes bugged out of her head as tears drenched her cheeks, a scream caught in her throat. The poor woman was about to piss herself which really ticked off Jonah. He'd seen the woman stare death in the eye and not even flinch. Despite the fact she was a total hard-ass with very little sense of humor, he'd built up a great deal of respect for her. This beast was going to die for terrifying her. "Put her down, mutt."

The beast snarled at him, tightening its clawed hand around Ronnie's throat until she bled. "You should fear me, human."

"You should fear *me*, bitch."

The beast snarled, then chuckled. "Stupid human with your little gun. You know nothing about dealing with my kind."

"That's where you're wrong, you ugly bastard. I was taught by the best." Jonah pulled the trigger, sending a silver-coated bullet into the beast's chest.

It screamed, its cry sounding like awful, high-pitched laughter as its chest started to burn from the silver. Jonah aimed his gun at the thing's head but it moved too fast, using a massive claw to rip through Ronnie's body as it fell with her to the floor.

"No!" Jonah screamed as he lunged for it, but he was grabbed by behind. With two claws digging into his shoulders he couldn't get off a shot.

He was flung against a wall, his head cracking against the wood so hard stars flew before his eyes. It took a moment for his vision to clear and when it did he came face to face with another snarling beast, this one wearing the photographer's body.

He managed to get one shot off before his gun was swiped from his hand but it was a good shot. The bullet hit the beast dead center in the heart.

He looked for Ronnie and found her holding her radio to her mouth, desperately trying to call for back-up, but she couldn't speak. The wound to her throat was too bad. The beast-cop dragged her across the floor, trying to leave with her. No way in hell was that going to happen.

Jonah located his gun and quickly scooped it up, pivoting just in time to see the beast running toward him as below them chaos erupted. Ronnie may have not been able to speak but the police outside had heard enough over the radio to discern they were in trouble.

Jonah knew he had to kill the damn things before they could kill anyone else. The other cops wouldn't know what to do with them and would only get in the way.

He fired off a shot, hitting the beast in the chest, momentarily dazing it so he could get closer. While the beast was trying to recover from the silver shot burning its insides, Jonah got close enough to ram his gun into the beast's mouth and blow out the back of its head.

He watched as the beasts' bodies went back to normal, transforming to look like humans as the police rushed the upstairs of the warehouse. A pair of cops yelled for an EMT as they dropped to their knees beside Ronnie's bloody body and the police chief stepped into the center of the room, standing over the body of the dead cop. "What the hell happened in here?" he asked as he looked between the two bodies then raised his icy gaze to Jonah.

Clueless how to explain it all, Jonah shrugged. "I honestly don't fucking know."

Ronnie was in critical condition but alive. Her throat was seriously damaged but with time and medical care she would be able to speak again. Whether or not she'd ever overcome what she'd been through, Jonah didn't know.

He cursed as his brother's phone went unanswered again and thumbed the END button on his cell. What the hell had happened? He knew about shifters, sure, but the one was a photographer he'd worked with before. There was no damn way that man had always been a shifter and even if he was recently turned it just didn't add up. Jonah's gut churned so hard he thought he might throw up. Something was seriously wrong with this whole scenario and for reasons he couldn't explain he still couldn't shake the idea that it had something to do with a woman. His mind went back to the woman outside the building. How could she have known what would happen? She had to be psychic. There was no way she could be directly involved with those beasts. She'd tried too hard to warn Ronnie. Or maybe she'd just wanted it to seem that way... Jonah shook his head, too tired to think straight. Where the hell was Jake? He needed him.

"Porter!"

He looked up, cringing slightly as the police chief entered the waiting room. He'd been raked over the coals enough for one night and still hadn't thought of any logical reason to give the chief about what had happened.

"She wants you," he said, nodding his head toward the hall.

Jonah nodded and quickly passed the chief, feeling the weight of his assessing stare boring through his back. He'd already been found nearly beaten to death inside the home of Carter Dunn, the killer's body a charred pile of limbs, and now he'd been part of a shoot-out that made no sense, his partner seriously messed up. Too many crazy things that he couldn't logically explain were happening to him and he could just feel the mental evaluation coming. Hell, one more weird thing and he might be asked for his badge.

"Hey," he said as he closed the door to Ronnie's room behind him and stepped over to the side of the hospital bed.

She looked awful. Her neck was braced and heavily bandaged, all the wounds along her body bandaged and tubes and wires were attached to her nose and chest. Despite her natural deep tan she was a sickly white.

"I guess you're trying to wrap your mind around what happened tonight."

She stared at him, her eyes watering, and anger surged through him. He and Jake may have made jokes about her hard-ass mentality, even quipping that underneath her skirt hung a set of steel balls, but she was his partner. Nobody made her weak on his watch.

"They're dead, Ronnie, and if there's more of them I promise you I will kill them all."

She reached for the pad of paper next to her bed and Jonah grabbed it for her, handing it to her along with a pen. She scribbled quickly and showed him the pad.

WHAT WERE THEY?

"Shifters," he answered, figuring she'd be the last person to call him a loon now. "I know you've always thought my brother was a psychopath but the truth is he's the way he is because he has devoted his life to killing things like what we came face to face with tonight. Evil is everywhere. Vampires, shifters, witches, demons, you name it. It's not all stories."

She scribbled on the pad again.

CARTER DUNN?

"Demon-possessed. He used the blood he extracted from the victims to feed a vampire whom he extracted blood from in an attempt to create a serum which would give him immortality without actually becoming a vampire. And trust me, you don't want to know what really happened in there that night. I'm just lucky I survived, that my brother found me in time."

She closed her eyes, allowing a tear to fall before scribbling more on the paper.

MILAIKA JORDAN. HOW DID SHE KNOW?

Jonah sighed in frustration. "I'm guessing she's psychic. When the police on the scene were notified there was something going down inside she used the commotion to her advantage and got away but we have her driver's license. I'm heading to her apartment tonight. I wanted to make sure you were alright first."

BE CAREFUL, JOE. I DON'T HAVE FAMILY. YOU'RE ALL I GOT, KID.

He smiled at the woman who was barely pushing forty-five, but insisted on treating him as if he were a baby compared to her. "I've been trained by the best hunter in the world, Ronnie. You just focus on getting better so we can get back to kicking ass together."

The look in her eyes said it all. Regardless of how well she healed, after this she might not ever set foot on a crime scene again.

Malaika closed the toilet lid and rested her head on the cool surface as she flushed away the purged contents of her stomach. She knew better than to relax for long, knowing the minute she closed her eyes she'd see it all over again. Strange beasts feeding on dead bodies.

She shuddered as she forced herself to stand and rinse her mouth out with water from the bathroom sink. As she brushed her teeth she saw the creatures' elongated fangs in her mind's eye. What was happening? She'd always had visions but nothing this grotesque. And the scariest thing of all was that she knew every vision she'd ever had was caused because somehow, she or someone she knew was involved. And these visions had started the night Craig had died.

Craig couldn't be involved, he just couldn't. He couldn't be a part of something so horrific. He was a victim, just like the others. Maybe that was the tie. Through his death, she'd been connected to the killer. But how would that explain sensing him at the sites?

She jumped as someone pounded on her front door. Quickly, she received a picture of the male detective in her mind. Great. She so wasn't in the mood to deal with the homicide detective's questions, regardless of the fact he'd seemed to listen to her at the crime scene earlier, not just with his ears but with his mind.

He knocked again and she rushed down the hall to reach the door before he made more noise. Her baby girl hadn't slept well in weeks, dreams of her daddy plaguing her during the night, and she sure wasn't going to let this man wake her when she seemed to be resting peacefully.

"Stop banging on my door before you wake my kid," Malaika snapped, swinging the door open. "Do you know what time it is?"

The detective arched a brow, flashed his badge, and stepped into her apartment, uninvited. "Do you always open your door this late at night without checking who it is first?"

"I knew it was you."

"How's that?"

"Peephole," she said irritably, her mood growing darker as he looked at her suspiciously, giving her the sense he knew better. "How's your partner?" she asked, knowing the woman had been badly hurt but survived the attack she'd foreseen. The aura surrounding the male detective indicated he felt the need for vengeance but wasn't in mourning.

"She's in the hospital, nearly had her throat torn out."

Malaika winced at his blunt answer, having seen that part in her mind's eye. How had she survived? In the vision she'd seen beforehand the woman had been ripped to shreds and consumed.

"How did you know what was going to happen?"

"Gut feeling," she said quickly, folding her arms, wondering if the detective could hear her frantically thumping heart.

"That was one hell of a gut feeling." He surveyed her apartment, his gaze resting on a picture of Deja which was perched on top of the small table before the window. "That your daughter?"

"Yes."

"Cute kid." He smiled a little, easing some of Malaika's anxiety but it came back in full force when he whipped his head around and asked point-blank, "What do you know about these murders?"

Malaika gasped, surprised by the sudden question and more than a little afraid. "I don't know what—"

"Don't, Ms. Jordan. Don't tell me you don't know what I'm talking about or that you just had a feeling my partner was going to be hurt. You were terrified, scared out of your mind and you were dead-on. She should have never went in that building and you knew it because you either knew the men who attacked her—"

"Men?"

Malaika tightened her lips together when she realized she'd spoken out loud. The look the detective gave her caused her to shiver.

"Men, Ms. Jordan, but they weren't normal men, were they?"

She forced herself to look him straight in the eye despite the way his intense gaze sent her nerves into a frenzy. "Look, I wish I could help you but I honestly don't know—"

"Are you a psychic?"

The question, presented so abruptly, gave her pause. For as far back as she could remember she'd had the visions. Her mother had told her she was crazy when she spoke of them, said she'd been listening to her grandmother far too much. Due to what her mother considered a harmful influence she hadn't seen her grandmother since she was a child.

She'd learned to keep her gifts secret. The few times she'd tried to clue anyone in to what she could do she was either laughed at, labeled a lunatic, or called a freak.

"Are. You. A. Psychic?" The detective enunciated each word, his irritation and impatience clear.

"Psychics aren't real," Malaika muttered finally, deciding against telling the truth. It hurt too much to see the looks she received after revealing her gift and it had been a hard day already.

"Neither are monsters, Ms. Jordan, but I killed two of them earlier."

She looked at the detective, studied the hard set of his jaw. He was mad, for sure, but not at her although she wasn't doing anything to dissolve his anger. His eyes bore straight into her own, demanding answers, answers she got the feeling he already knew but he needed confirmation. How could he know? And why would he believe her when nobody else ever had? Except her grandmother, who she'd been told was mentally ill.

"Mr. Porter, I wish I could help you but I don't know who is killing these people. I honestly don't."

"We saw you at another crime scene before today. Why were you there? How did you know something bad was going to happen to my partner?"

"I told you—"

"Dammit, lady, I can take you in right now on aiding and abetting charges!"

"What? I haven't done anything!"

"You're withholding information and that's enough. Now unless you want that cute little girl of yours to witness her mama being taken downtown in cuffs—"

"Alright, fine! I have visions. Is that what you want to hear?"

"Is it the truth?"

"Yes."

"Then, yes, Ms. Jordan, that's exactly what I want to hear along with every detail. When did the visions start? Who do you see? When and how often do they occur? What information—" He halted, cocking his head to the side and narrowing his hazel eyes. "Why do you look so stunned?"

Malaika realized her mouth had been gaping and quickly closed it, blinking away her momentary shock. "That's it? You're not going to ask me if I'm running a con or call me crazy, ask if I'm on any medications or should be?"

"Why would I do that?"

"Because it's what people tend to do after I make the mistake of revealing the fact I can sometimes see things before they happen."

"Well, Ms. Jordan, in my line of work I've come to realize that people as a whole are stupid, not to mention blind to anything they can't rationally explain. Hell, there was a time I would have thought psychic abilities were bull if you want to know the truth, but I've been through things that..." He laughed, little mirth coming through the restrained sound. "Trust me, honey, I've seen things that make visions seem like nothing special at all."

"You have to believe me, Mr. Porter, I don't have any involvement with any of this."

"Yeah, I kind of figured that out when I heard you praying outside the building," he said with a grin, "and call me Jonah, please. Now, I need you to trust me and tell me everything you know, even if it seems insignificant."

"What?" Malaika placed her hands on her hips, indignant. "If you didn't suspect me of anything, why did you threaten to arrest me?"

"To get you talking," Jonah said, his smile broadening. "I figured the fastest way to get you to admit to your ability was to scare the hell out of you. Now that I've accomplished that, I need you to tell me everything."

"Well, that could take a while," she muttered, a few residual sparks of anger still flaring. She realized to her shame that she'd be madder than hell if not for the fact the detective was so damn attractive. He stood a little over six feet tall with a lean build and a handsome face. He wasn't movie star gorgeous but there was something about him that made a woman take notice. The air of authority about him certainly didn't hurt his overall appeal, nor did the dark hair which tended to fall over his brow, giving him a bit of boyish charm despite the ruthlessness she could see hiding in his eyes. Beautiful hazel eyes, she noted, a little more brown than green.

What the hell was wrong with her? Craig, the father of her child and love of her life, wasn't even decently buried—may never be, considering he was most likely eaten alive—and she was checking out the detective? What kind of woman was she?

"Ms. Jordan?"

Malaika blinked, chasing away her wayward thoughts to look at the man who was staring at her curiously. "I'm sorry, it's been a long day, but I guess I don't need to tell you that." She chuckled a little, the sound forced, as she gestured for him to take a seat among one of the barstools sitting before the long counter which bisected the small living area from the even smaller kitchen space. "Would you like a drink? I have Coke, sweet tea or grape juice. I'm not much of a coffee or alcohol drinker."

"Sweet tea sounds great," he said, situating himself on one of the barstools facing into the kitchen area as she reached into the refrigerator with shaky hands. I'm just nervous because he's going to question me, she told herself, not because he's *fine*... and a seemingly decent guy who didn't laugh at me or call me a freak when he discovered my ability to see events from the future.

"Where would you like me to begin?" she asked as she poured him a glass of tea and slid it toward him.

His long, tan fingers encircled the glass and she watched in rapture as he lifted it to his mouth and swallowed, the action drawing her attention to his soft-looking lips. Damn. If only her mother could see her now. She cringed at the thought, knowing exactly what her mother would say. *"Well, I guess it's not enough you gave your body to one worthless white man without so much as a ring on your finger and had a child with him but now you're looking for another white plaything to help you forget what you are. What? Your black brothers aren't good enough for you? Or you think you're too good for them? I just don't understand you, girl, you are an embarrassment! If only your father were still alive..."*

Malaika cringed, hearing her mother's words drilling through her head with clarity. Oh, yes, she knew exactly what her mother would say if she caught her looking at the detective, licking her lips with lascivious thoughts crawling through her mind.

"Thanks," Jonah said as he placed the glass on the counter before him and watched her intently. "Start from the beginning or wherever makes logical sense to you. I'm not an expert in the field of..." he struggled for a word but not in a way which made her feel embarrassed as if he were belittling her ability, "psychic matters so you just tell me what you know whether it be something that came to you in a dream, vision, whatever."

Malaika nodded, resting her elbows on the counter, the memory of the first dream chasing away all lustful thoughts from her mind as the images chilled her to her core. "Sometimes I have dreams that are actual visions. Sometimes a vision will hit me out of nowhere regardless of whether I'm awake or not, or engaged in physical activity. The first vision came to me while I slept. There was... a man," she said after a long pause, deciding not to reveal Craig's identity. She didn't know why but the thought of doing so frightened her. Shaking it off, she continued. "The man felt a pull to a woman and there was music, a voice singing to him."

"In his mind?"

"Yes. Only he could hear it. It had been coming to him for a long time, growing stronger each day until he reached the point he had to find it. He had to know who the woman he sensed was." Malaika bit back anger, for the hundredth time wishing Craig had been stronger but there was no point being mad now. He was gone. He'd gotten more than any man deserved for straying.

"He was being pulled by her voice, down by the Inner Harbor area. He passed quite a few fisherman and then she was just there, standing in the glow of moonlight like an angel or something but she was too... *dark* ... to be described as an angel."

"What did she look like?" The detective leaned forward, his eyes gazing into her own with an intensity bordering on desperation.

"Long dark hair, perfect body. Hispanic, I think. Very beautiful, almost too beautiful, you know? She was... unreal."

"Like she could have been projecting herself as every man's dream?" the detective asked, frowning as though surprised by his own words.

"Yes! That's exactly it," Malaika agreed. "She seemed like an illusion. Oh! And there was an old fisherman there. He told him not to go to her, said he'd seen many men go to her and never come back again, but he didn't listen. His mind was filled with images of him and the woman, disgusting images." Malaika shuddered as the disgustingly perverse images rolled through her mind. She hated the woman more for those images than anything else. She'd not only taken her child's father from her but she'd left behind those awful images of them together for her to see over and over again, ruining her view of the man she'd wanted to marry.

"It's alright, Ms. Jordan, you don't have to go into graphic detail of those images if it bothers you, but were they sexual or are we just talking graphic violence here?"

Malaika blinked, bringing herself back to the present. "I'm sorry, they were just so disgusting they shock me every time I recall them. They were sexual but... ugh, I'm no prude, Mr. Porter—"

"Jonah."

"I'm no prude, Jonah, but these images were just... foul. I couldn't believe that he... that any man would be turned on by seeing those things."

Jonah nodded, his brow crinkling in thought. "I'm sorry your mind was invaded with that. Can you tell me what happened next?"

"Oh. Yes, sorry. He didn't listen to the fisherman. He followed the woman and I can't tell you where, I honestly couldn't tell where she led him to. They walked into a dark building and she turned around. Then a deep male voice told her she'd done a good job and there was this horrific pain in the man's neck and... that was it. I woke up, knowing the man had just been killed."

A vengeful little part of her battered heart said he'd gotten what he deserved for being a lying cheat but her mind told her jealous heart to shut up. He'd been enthralled by the woman's voice more than her beauty. He was practically hypnotized. Her mother would say she was making excuses for him, that he'd never been anything more than white trash and she'd been turning a blind eye to it for years and maybe she was a little right. She had turned a blind eye to his faults, let him get away with too much for the sake of their daughter but she knew he'd been more than seduced by the woman, or whatever she was.

She felt warmth cover her hand and jerked, causing the detective to jerk backward as well.

"I'm sorry, Ms. Jordan."

"Malaika. If I'm calling you Jonah, you can call me Malaika," she said, feeling foolish. The man had only tried to comfort her with a light touch on her hand. "I'm sorry. I'm a little jumpy right now."

"I understand, and I really appreciate your help. You've confirmed a part of my suspicions."

"Suspicions?"

"The victims have mostly been male. Two of the three female victims were confirmed lesbians. I had a gut feeling that a woman was luring them. I don't know why but I did and your vision confirmed it. Would you recognize the woman if you saw her again?"

"Yes." And I'd be more than happy to kick her skanky ass, she thought to herself.

"And the fisherman?"

"Yes."

"Good. If he's seen the woman more than once he could have useful information."

"You honestly believe me? No questions, no doubts?"

"You have a gift, Ms. Jor—, Malaika. Hell, you have a gift that could save lives." He frowned suddenly. "Why were you at the crime scenes? Have you had visions before each murder?"

"I've had visions..." Malaika allowed her voice to trail off, wondering how she could explain the newer visions without losing the credibility she seemed to have with the detective. "They don't make any sense. I know they're related," she said, not bothering to tell him she knew this because she sensed Craig in them, "but they're beyond weird."

"Weird, how?"

"I see the silhouette of the woman in some of them, she's doing her whole luring stupid horny men to their death thing but then it changes and I see these beasts. They're like wild dogs or wolves or something." She stopped as the detective jerked, giving her his complete attention.

"Animals or men that look like animals?"

"Animals," she answered hesitantly, wondering if the man before her was a little on the crazy side himself. "Beasts, really. They don't look like anything I've ever seen."

"So you see the men being lured away and then you see them being attacked by wild animals?"

"I see them being eaten by wild animals," she said with a shiver. "And I don't see where they're being led to though I know it's different places."

"Then how do you know which crime scenes to show up at?" Jonah asked, his tone a little suspicious.

Because I feel Craig there, she thought to herself, but didn't voice the words. It made no sense and she knew he was already dead but she just couldn't put his name out there like that. It was bad enough Deja would grow up without her father but to have his name tarnished, somehow involved with this whole mess... No way. She wasn't going there. "I don't know. Just as I don't know why I've only witnessed the men being killed and not the women. I come out of the vision and I get this feeling, this urgency to run toward something. I've been to a few of the sites but each time I'd get there the police would already be setting up barricades. I'm always too late."

"So you never actually know where you're going?"

"Not until I get there. I just follow the feeling... when I can. There's no way I'm taking my daughter near one of those sites."

He nodded his head. "You did see one female victim. You saw my partner."

"A few nights ago I saw her go into that building and..."

"And what?"

"I saw the animals rip her open and eat her alive."

Jonah closed his eyes. "But you didn't see me."

"No."

"Are you sure what you saw was what took place earlier today?" he asked, fear lacing his voice as he opened his eyes to look directly at her.

"Definitely. I know it was at a crime scene and she looked exactly the way she looked today. Same clothes and everything. My visions sometimes aren't exact right down to every little detail. I didn't see you but that doesn't mean it wasn't what happened today. Originally you may have not went in with her, but you believed me. You knew to watch out for her and you did. If you hadn't believed me..." She cringed at the thought of what would have happened if he'd thought her a lunatic like his partner obviously had.

"Thank God I did," he said. "Ronnie's a pain in the butt but she's my partner. I'd take a bullet for her."

Malaika smiled wistfully, wishing she had someone who'd do the same for her. Hell, all she'd wanted Craig to do was be faithful. Had that been too much to ask?

"You mentioned men earlier," she said, breaking free of her reverie. "Men attacked your partner?"

A shadow fell over Jonah's eyes as he answered. "Like you said, your visions aren't exact right down to every single detail but they're damn close."

"Daddy?"

Malaika's heart lurched into her throat as she saw her five-year-old daughter come running down the hall, excitement shimmering in her small green eyes. She reached out to grab her but couldn't stop the little whirlwind before she'd grabbed the leg of a very surprised detective and looked lovingly into his eyes.

"You're not Daddy," she whined, her bottom lip trembling as she realized her mistake.

"Hey, cutie," Jonah said, his tone gentle as he looked down at her. "No, I'm not Daddy. I'm Jonah. What's your name?"

"Deja," she mumbled, turning tear-rimmed eyes to her mother. "I want Daddy!"

"I know, baby," Malaika whispered, scooping the small angel into her arms. "I'll be back," she said over her shoulder as she carried Deja to her room, feeling the detective's stare on her the entire way. The weight of it seemed to be on her ass, she noted with a little thrill of pleasure.

"When's Daddy coming back?" Deja cried. "I miss Daddy! He said he was coming back."

"I know, baby, I know," Malaika whispered as she lay her child in the small bed and pulled the coverlet over her. She kissed her tiny forehead, allowing her lips to linger a moment as she wondered for the millionth time if she should tell her daughter the truth. Her daddy was dead. He'd been eaten.

Taking a deep breath, she pulled away. "Try to sleep, baby. Mommy's got to talk to the detective."

"That man's a detective?"

"Yes."

"Is he looking for Daddy?"

Maybe, Malaika thought grimly, then wondered where that thought had come from. Craig was dead. His body hadn't been found yet, but that didn't mean anything. She'd felt his life slip away. "Go to sleep, Deja."

She turned away from the tears running down her baby's cheeks, sucking in air. She was going to have to tell her eventually. She couldn't allow the little girl to keep longing for a man who was never coming back. Hell, that was advice she should take herself.

She noticed the barstool Jonah had been perched on was vacant as she walked down the short hallway. She entered the living area to find him facing away from her, looking out the window. She hadn't noticed it before, not on a conscious level anyway, but he did resemble Craig. She could see how Deja had easily made the mistake, especially from behind.

"I'm sorry about that," she said, watching him turn. "You kind of do resemble her daddy, the height and hair and all." She was blabbering, she realized woefully. "Do you uh, want another drink?"

"I'm fine," he said, smiling a little. "I don't mind your little girl. She's adorable. Is her father missing?" he asked, his tone showing genuine concern. "She seemed awfully upset."

Ah, the detective and his questions, she thought with a trace of amusement despite her unease. "He walked out that door some time ago and hasn't come back since," she finally said, allowing Jonah to draw his own conclusions. "Do you have all you need from me, Detective? My daughter is kind of upset right now."

"Of course. I'm sorry if she saw me and thought…" He let his statement trail off, giving Malaika a look of apology. "She really is a cute little thing. I'll let you get back to her."

Malaika nodded her appreciation and walked him to the door. He paused in the doorway and looked back at her. "I'd like to take you down to the Inner Harbor tomorrow morning when the fishermen are starting to set out, see if you can find the guy from your vision."

"Sure, that'll give me a whole," she glanced at the clock, "couple of hours to rest."

"I'm sorry. I know it's already late and you've got a small child but time really is—"

"No, I'm sorry," she said, guilt washing over her as she waved away his apology. "That was insensitive of me. People are dying and if I can help prevent another person losing a loved one, I want to. I'm just a little stressed right now."

"Understandably. I know it's too late to call for a sitter. Will it be a problem for your daughter to see me again?"

"No, she was just... she saw you from the back and with you being inside the apartment and all..."

"I understand," he said. "Alright. I'll be back in three hours."

"Detective!" she called as he walked away.

"Jonah," he reminded her, turning back.

"Three hours isn't that far away and you look beat," she commented, noticing the dark rings forming under his eyes. "With all you've been through today with your partner and your job in general... you probably want to get some sleep. Why don't you just lie down on my sofa and take a nap? There's no point driving however far you need to and then driving all the way back here in three hours."

"You sure?"

"Yeah, I mean, what better security could a woman ask for than an armed detective sleeping on her couch?" Sleeping in her bed, she answered her own question, tsking at herself for having such a thought.

"Alright." He smiled as he entered the apartment. "I appreciate it."

"No problem. The bathroom is right down the hall should you need it and you're welcome to the kitchen if you wake before me."

He nodded his thanks and started taking off his jacket as she closed and locked the door behind him. She moved quickly, grabbing a pillow off her own bed and a thin blanket from the linen closet.

She returned to the living area and stopped as she watched him remove a gun from the holster he'd draped over one of the barstools along with his jacket and check the safety before sliding it into the back of his waistband. "I don't want your daughter waking up and finding it," he explained as he turned toward the sofa.

"Oh, that's thoughtful," Malaika mumbled, feeling nervous and tongue-tied at the moment. Had Craig ever made her feel that way just by being near, in a T-shirt which showed he was more muscular than previously thought? She shook her head. She knew one thing, Craig wouldn't have thought to keep a gun away from their daughter. He'd probably have tossed it in a nightstand drawer without a second thought. It wasn't that he didn't care for Deja's safety—he loved the little girl with all his heart—he'd just never bothered to take the time to think what repercussions his actions would cause.

"This blanket is a little raggedy," she apologized as she lay the pillow by the arm of the sofa and sat the blanket on the other end.

"It's fine," he said with a chuckle. "I've slept in far worse conditions, I assure you. Thank you, Malaika."

"Oh, it's no bother." Her insides turned fuzzy as she caught the twinkle in his eyes. "I'll just get the lights for you."

She hurriedly deposited the glass he'd drank from into the kitchen sink and walked back into the living area to turn off the light. The night light in the hallway gave off enough illumination in case he, or Deja, needed the bathroom.

"There you go. I'll see you in about three hours."

"It's a date," he said as he laid his long body down on the sofa.

He was a kind man, Malaika thought to herself as she forced one foot in front of the other, leaving him to rest. For some reason, she found herself wanting to watch him while he slept.

Why was she feeling this? Craig hadn't been gone that long. Because Craig hurt you, she reminded herself, waving away the guilt she felt. Yes, he'd been killed because of it, but that didn't change the fact.

"Why couldn't you keep your dick in your pants?" she whispered as she checked in on her sleeping daughter. She started to walk toward her own bedroom, then changed her mind, opting to curl up alongside her daughter in the small twin bed.

"Why do I still love you?" she whispered again as a tear escaped her eye. He might have been in a trance but there were flashes when he'd remembered her... and Deja. The fact he'd still followed that woman... that he'd been aroused by those filthy images...

Why the hell do I still give a damn at all? She didn't need that kind of pain. He was supposed to have been her man, her rock when she needed one. He was supposed to have helped her raise their child, not leave them to fend for themselves. No, she shouldn't care, not for a man like him. She should care for a man like... Jonah Porter?

He was attractive, smart... held down a good job. He saved people for crying out loud. Yes, there was a man, a *real* man. A...

Ugh, she sounded like her mother, except for the fact her mother would take one look at Jonah Porter and declare him white trash too. Then she'd have to go through *that* whole drama again.

"If I ever find me a new man he'll be blacker than midnight and loaded with money," she muttered, knowing in her heart she'd never love again. It hurt too damn much when it all went wrong. She wasn't going through it again, not even for that irresistibly charming man who was going to give her the biggest orgasm of her life.

She gasped as the vision flashed through her mind.

TWO

Something poked him in the arm. Choosing to ignore it and stay in the hazy little half-sleep state he was in, Jonah rolled to his side and continued with his dream which was becoming more of a fantasy as he slowly started to come awake. He fought against it with all he had. He was not letting go of this dream.

Apparently she'd given him one of her own pillows. The scent of her, cocoa butter mixed with a musky vanilla, wafted from it, teasing him while he slept. No wonder he'd been dreaming of making love to her in her bed.

Sure, there were psycho-mutant-killers on the loose and some woman with the power to lead horny men to their deaths prowling along the Inner Harbor but all that faded into the back of his mind as his dream-self licked Malaika from ankle to collarbone, spending a little extra time in every valley he found in-between. She suckled on his ear lobe as her soft fingers trailed down his back, gliding over his hip as she reached below to grab his painfully hard... Wait. How could she do that and poke him in the eye at the same time?

Jonah jerked his head and woke to see a pair of green eyes looming right in front of his face. He let out a sharp little cry and recoiled in surprise.

Deja jerked back, momentarily scared, but just as quickly erupted into a fit of giggles. "You squealed like a girl!"

He looked at the little girl in pink unicorn pajamas and chuckled. "Yeah, well, do me a favor and don't tell anyone that," he said while covertly looking down to make sure only his dream-self had gotten hard. Now, that would have been embarrassing. "By the way, kid, that was my eyeball you were sticking your little fingers in. Where's your mom?"

"Sleeping. Why were you sleeping on our couch? Did you and mommy have a slumber party?"

Oh, I wish, kid. Damn, I wish.

"No, we're all going somewhere in about..." he glanced at his watch, "twenty minutes so she let me nap on the couch. That way I wouldn't have to drive back here so early in the morning."

"Oh," she said, loosening the death-clutch she'd had on her teddy bear. "I want some fruity tooties."

Jonah just blinked at her, wondering what the hell a fruity tootie was and what she expected him to do about it. Then she wrapped one of her little hands around his index finger and pulled him up. "They're in the cabinet up there!" she said, pointing toward the cabinet over the stove as she guided him toward the kitchen and then left him to climb atop one of the barstools.

He opened the cabinet and took down a box of Fruitie-Tooties, a knock-off of Fruity Pebbles cereal, and preceded to pour her a bowl.

"Why do you have a gun in your pants?" she asked curiously.

"Because I'm a detective and sometimes I need it to stop bad guys."

"Can I touch it?"

"Absolutely not," he answered in a firm voice, grinning as he saw her stick her tongue out at him from the corner of his eye. "Here you go, cutie," he said as he turned and placed the bowl in front of her on the counter.

"Arentcha gonna eat some?"

"Naw, I'm not much of a cold cereal kind of guy."

"Oh, that's right. You're like a cop. You guys only eat donuts."

Jonah laughed out loud, growing more amused as she looked at him in complete confusion, having no idea she'd just insulted him and the entire police force. "Contrary to popular belief, I'm not much of a donut lover either."

"What do you eat then?"

"Well, my breakfast is usually just a cup of coffee," he answered, grinning as she scrunched up her nose at the idea. The grin faded as he glanced around the small kitchen area to discover the lack of a coffee maker. A quick perusal of the cabinets showed he wouldn't even be able to get a cup of instant.

"You think you oughtta go wake up your mom?" he asked as he glanced at the clock, noting the time.

"I'm eating." Deja responded around a mouthful of multi-colored cereal.

Great. He drummed his fingers along the bar, contemplating his next move. Malaika had been in pajamas when she'd opened the door for him, a set of long cotton lounge pants and a T-shirt, so he doubted she'd changed into anything more revealing before going to bed but still he felt uneasy about waking her. He could just imagine how warm and inviting she'd look lying in bed—no matter what she had on—and that wasn't an image he needed ingrained in his mind while working a case he needed her for.

No way was he going near her bed.

On the off chance that she was directly involved with the murders he knew better than to entertain the idea of them getting up close and personal. No matter how good she looked or how innocent she seemed. She had a psychic gift. The only other people he personally knew of with psychic gifts were vampires. She might walk in daylight and pray without being struck dead but that didn't necessarily make her innocent. She could be working with someone. Or she could be some other kind of paranormal villain.

That thought in mind, he pulled out his cell phone and dialed his brother's number. If anyone knew how he was supposed to handle his little psychic it would be Jake Porter, if only the jerk would answer his damn phone. He gritted his teeth as he listened to Jake's call tone, AC/DC's "Back In Black", and was then routed to voice mail.

"Call me, you little prick, before I hunt you down and kick your ass," he growled, irritation getting the best of him.

Deja let out a gasp followed by a loud, "Aww... you said a bad word!"

Grimacing, Jonah disconnected the call and turned toward the girl. "Sorry, hon. I probably shouldn't have said that in front of you."

"Who were you talkin' to?"

"My pain in the a—, my pain in the butt brother. Or his voice mail, anyway."

"Are you mad at him?" she asked, tapping her empty spoon against her full lips.

"Kind of. He hasn't returned my calls and I haven't seen him in a while. I guess I'm more worried than mad."

"My daddy's been gone from home a long time too."

"I heard," Jonah said softly, sitting on the stool next to the little caramel-colored girl. Her green eyes held a sadness so deep it fisted around his heart. "How long?"

She lightly nibbled on her lip, her eyes turned upward as she thought, eventually giving up and shrugging her thin shoulders. "I dunno. I still see him but only when I'm sleeping. He's always gone when I wake up."

"Deja, baby, get dressed."

Jonah looked past the little girl to see her mother in the hallway, leaning with her hip against the wall. Just as he'd suspected, she looked soft and inviting in the morning, all dewy eyed and scrumptious... except for the frown marring her otherwise pleasant face.

"We'll be ready in a minute," she said tersely before spinning on her heel and stalking off.

"Are you sure none of them looked familiar?" Jonah asked as they finished their third trek down the harbor, inspecting each fisherman they'd come across.

"I'm sure," Malaika snapped, her lips thinning into a straight line as she did her best to avoid his gaze.

What the hell was up with that? Jonah wondered for the umpteenth time since they'd set out early that cool morning. He'd brushed off her initial aloofness in the apartment, figuring she just wasn't a morning person, but then the woman had sat rigid in her seat the entire drive to the harbor, looking anywhere but at him. Conversation had consisted of her replying Yes or No to his questions, barely offering any more words than that. Maybe she was nervous, or upset since they couldn't seem to locate the fisherman she'd seen in her vision. Or she could be feeling under the weather. She'd turned a little green the moment they'd gotten within sight of the water. Still, he couldn't help feeling as if she were upset with him directly though he had no idea what he'd done.

"Look, I know it's frustrating not being able to find this guy. We can try again tomorrow morning."

"And if we don't find him then?" she asked, ignoring Deja as the little girl grabbed the hem of her jacket and tugged on it, complaining of tired feet.

"We'll keep looking," Jonah said, scooping Deja into his arms, positioning the little girl so she could rest her head on his shoulder. He frowned at the dark look he received from Malaika and continued. "I can take you downtown to work with a sketch artist if you want. That way you don't have to come down here with me, but I need to speak with this man you saw."

"And if he doesn't exist?"

"What do you mean?" Jonah's tone came out sharper than he'd intended but he didn't feel bad about it. He didn't appreciate being led on a wild goose chase while his partner lay jacked up in a hospital and his brother was MIA. "You said you have visions, see the future. You said you saw this man."

"Just like I saw animals attack your partner but there were no animals," she said, frowning as she looked at where his arm held her daughter. "Sometimes what I see is symbolic, not actual."

"Trust me, that vision was pretty damn close. If you saw someone warning the man not to go to the woman I'd bet a year's salary that it happened." Unless you were lying to me, he added silently, wondering if she was capable of the action. He didn't know her from Adam, couldn't even find anything on her in the records. She'd never owned property, hadn't went to college, hadn't so much as gotten a speeding ticket.

"What really happened in that building?"

Jonah gazed down at the little girl in his arms as horrific visions of Ronnie's attack went through his mind. "That's not a story to tell in front of a small child."

"There's a playground across the street."

Jonah looked toward the direction she indicated and nodded, shifting Deja more securely on his arm as they stepped away from the harbor, closer to the street.

"You don't have to carry her, I can—"

"It's fine," he said as he glanced both ways down the street, making sure it was safe to cross. "I like kids, and this little angel is no problem at all."

Malaika didn't say anything as they crossed the street but Jonah didn't miss the scrutinizing look in her eyes as he set Deja down on the sidewalk and gave her a little tickle before letting her run off to the slides, warning her not to leave their line of sight.

"I'm gonna grab a coffee," he said, noticing the little stand nearby which mostly catered to tourists. "Want anything?"

"No," Malaika responded, again with a one-word answer, and walked over to the bench facing the small playground area Deja was taking advantage of.

Shaking his head, Jonah made his way to the just-opening stand, ordered a coffee and soon found himself sitting next to Malaika on the bench, helping her keep a watchful eye on her daughter.

They'd spent a good amount of time combing over the harbor area where the fishermen started their mornings but it was still fairly early. The area was just starting to come alive, with small stores and cafes beginning to open as early-rising tourists started to trickle onto the street. There were enough that they didn't feel as though they were sitting in the middle of nowhere but not so many that Jonah had to worry about others listening in on their conversation.

Blowing on his too-hot-to-drink-for-the-moment coffee, Jonah cast a sideways glance at the woman beside him. She watched her daughter like a hawk but the rigid posturing of her body had nothing to do with protecting the child. The set of her luscious mouth and hard look in her eyes all but screamed determination, with a hint of anger mixed in. What was going on inside that pretty little head of hers?

"You seem upset, Ms. Jordan. Have I done or said something wrong?" he asked, deciding to be straight-forward and professional. The last thing he needed her to know was that he was actually concerned whether or not she was upset with him on a personal level. In case she wasn't all innocent, he didn't want her to know she could possibly affect his judgment and as much as he wanted to deny the possibility that she could do just that, Jonah couldn't shake the remnants of last night's dream from his mind.

Color flooded her face, turning the light brown color ruddy. "No," she said after careful thought and shook her head. "It's just... I've just got a lot going on in my head right now."

Jonah nodded, understanding. "It must be hard seeing such awful things."

"It is," she responded but something in her tone indicated what was running through her mind wasn't entirely related to the murders. "I shouldn't complain though. You get to see the aftermath in living color. That has to be worse."

"I don't know about that. I don't witness them die, helpless to do anything to stop it." His hand tightened around the coffee cup. "I wish I did have some precognition talent. Maybe then I could save them all, catch their killers before it no longer matters to them."

"It still matters," she said firmly. "You might not be able to see the victims once they're gone but they know what you're doing. Your job makes a difference, not only to the families of those lost or the ones you save, but to all who were cheated out of living. They appreciate what you do."

Jonah cast a glance at the woman beside him, considering the passion he'd picked up in her tone. "Do you see the victims after they're gone?"

Malaika paled, her eyes closing as she lightly shook her head and Jonah knew she'd revealed more than she'd intended.

"I'll be damned. You see spirits."

"Sometimes," she admitted, letting out a sigh as she returned her gaze to Deja, watching the child work her way across a set of monkey bars. "I haven't seen the spirits of the victims in these murders but I've seen enough spirits to know that you're a hero for those whose murderers you find."

"And for those whose killers I don't find?"

"You're only human. The fact you put your life on the line every day trying to bring justice to people you never even knew is more than enough."

Jonah smiled, touched by her sincerity. "Thanks. It truly is a thankless job sometimes. The longer it takes to find a murderer, the more bodies that pile up... It messes with your head, feeds your insecurities. I wish I'd protected Ronnie better."

"Your partner?"

"Yes. I was in the same building but they still got to her."

"You tried to protect her, so did I. Your partner is very stubborn."

Jonah laughed. "You have no idea how so, but after this..." He quickly sobered, remembering the fear she'd shown. "Hell, I think the damage done to her was far more than physical. I wouldn't be surprised if she turns in her badge after this."

"What did happen? Why did I see beasts eating her?"

"Because that's exactly what they would have done," he said, shivering as he watched Deja run up the steps to the slide. If he hadn't had those silver-coated bullets in his gun... He didn't even want to think about the carnage he would have found if he'd not made it to Ronnie in time. "It can't happen again, Malaika. We have to find out why you're having the visions and what they mean. I have to stop whoever is doing this before anyone else loses a life."

"You said you killed two men who attacked your partner. Were there more?"

"Not there. That doesn't mean there aren't more where they came from though." Jonah sighed, running a hand down his face. "You saw a woman leading men to their death and my gut instinct suggested something similar. That's at least one suspect we know of. I'm going to hunt her down, whoever she is, and I'm going to end this."

Malaika's hand covered his as she whispered. "You're a good man, Jonah Porter."

He looked down at where their hands met and barely caught a glimpse before she retreated, once more appearing stiff and untouchable, her arms folded across her chest. She wouldn't meet his gaze, instead she stared fiercely at her daughter, being far more protective than necessary.

"What is it, Malaika?"

She closed her eyes and shrugged, her lips thinning. Obviously something was going on inside her mind and she didn't want him to know.

Wonderful, he thought as he brought the coffee cup to his mouth, sipping down the much needed caffeine.

"I'm going to have sex with you."

The coffee burned its way through his nose as it came back out. Fortunately he was too busy trying not to choke on the hot liquid to worry about how bad his reaction looked.

Hell. She was going to kill the man. Malaika ran to the small vendor nearby and grabbed some napkins, returning to blot the liquid from Jonah's jacket as he struggled to breathe.

"Are you choking?" she asked as she patted his back hard. "Jonah?"

He let out a strangled noise and sucked in air. "I'm fine," he said, waving her hands away and grabbing some napkins from her in the process. He chuckled as he wiped coffee from his nose. "Man, am I smooth or what?" He laughed again, the sound coming out slightly embarrassed as he wiped at the coffee running down the side of his Styrofoam cup. "Sorry about that," he said after regaining his composure. "As much as it hurts my ego to admit, I'm not used to women announcing their intentions with me so bluntly and out of the blue."

As heat rose to her face, Malaika silently cursed herself for blurting out such a stupid statement. "I d-didn't mean it like that," she said, fighting not to stammer.

"Oh?" He wiped at the wet spot on his jacket while glancing around, most likely hoping the embarrassing incident wasn't being heavily reviewed. Fortunately, no one seemed overly interested in them. "How did you mean it?"

"I didn't...I..." Malaika threw her hands up in the air and groaned. "I had a vision."

"Another one?" His head jerked up, his eyes wide. "Did you see the killer?"

"No, no," she said, realizing he wasn't following her. "I had a vision last night, of us."

"Oh." He crumpled the napkins in his hand. Then he stilled as his eyes heated, understanding now. "Oh."

"Yeah, oh."

"Last night?"

"Yes."

"Are you sure it wasn't just a dream?"

"I did not have a sex dream about you!" she growled, indignant. "What do you think I am, some sex-starved loser who dreams of doing every guy she meets?"

His cheeks reddened and if she didn't know better she'd say he was embarrassed but she didn't have time to figure out what was going on in his mind. She needed to get things straight right away, before that vision had a chance of happening.

"I just told you so you know it can't happen."

He cocked his head, gazing at her curiously. "I thought visions were future events."

"Visions are warnings of future events. Nothing is set in stone. Which you proved yourself by saving your partner."

"OK," he said, still looking at her curiously. "So why tell me about the vision? Why not just make sure it doesn't happen yourself?"

"Because I'm an idiot who doesn't know how to keep her mouth shut," she muttered, scratching her head. "Look, there's obviously a mutual attraction between us or the vision would have never happened. I just want you to know that under no condition am I sleeping with you or even entertaining the idea of any romantic notions with you whatsoever. You got that?"

His hazel eyes darkened, leaving little green showing. "The last time I checked I hadn't said or done anything inappropriate toward you."

"Really? Quit acting like you're such a great guy then. I know how it works. You think you can befriend my little girl, use her to work your way into my bed—"

"I wouldn't have to use your daughter to get into your bed," he said, his voice low and barely controlled, "and you had the vision to prove it. And I don't work like that. I'm hunting down a murderer and thus far you're the closest thing I have to a lead. That, Ms. Jordan, is why I came by your apartment last night. I stayed on your couch per *your* request and I fixed your daughter cereal because she asked me to. I picked her up because she was tired and if I've been nice to her it's because I'm a decent man, obviously unlike the previous men you've known or you wouldn't have just said something so stupid."

Malaika opened her mouth, then snapped it shut, repeating the process a few times before finally regaining the ability to form a sentence. "I'm sorry, Detective. I didn't mean to offend you, I'm just—"

"Full of yourself?"

"Hardly." She folded her arms before her chest as anger resurged through her. "What I am is a single mother who has to constantly be on alert. I know how men think."

"So I take it Deja's father left you for another woman and now every male you have contact with has to pay for his mistake?"

Malaika gasped, outraged by his assumption. "Oh here we go. I suppose this is the part where you inform me I'm just a bitter, dejected black woman with too much attitude to maintain a relationship with my saintly white—"

"And I suppose I'm the white bastard that's just slumming in the ghetto trying to get a little *flavor*."

"I know you did not just call me ghetto!"

"Hey, you're the one who brought up stereotypes."

Malaika opened her mouth, ready to continue their battle of words but the spirit of her grandmother hovering at Jonah's back, shaking her head from side to side, made her snap it shut. She'd first appeared while they'd been sitting on the bench, smiling in approval at the detective and that combined with her own attraction to the man had scared her into the verbal sparring match.

"Look, it doesn't take a genius to look at your daughter and see her father was white. Obviously, he didn't treat you the way he should have but you can't go jumping down the throat of every other white man you meet who might happen to show an attraction to you. We're not all bad guys."

"I know that," she conceded, looking away as her grandmother's spirit nodded her head in agreement with the detective. Shame crept into her chest as she realized she'd been allowing her mother's prejudiced ideas to influence her thoughts. "I apologize. Deja's father did... He wasn't a bad guy but he could have been a lot better in the way he treated us and when I had the vision..."

"It scared you," the detective said softly, the light of understanding in his eyes.

"Yes, so I pushed you away."

"No, you didn't," he commented with a smug grin. "You just made an ass out of yourself. Now, if you don't mind I have a job to do and I need to check on a few things. Would you kindly go get your daughter? I'd hate to be accused of using a small child in order to seduce her mother."

He chuckled softly, managing to do so without the slightest trace of a smile, and abruptly walked away, crossing the street to walk toward his car.

"So foolish," a soft, aged voice said from her side.

Malaika turned to find her deceased grandmother shaking her head at her, disappointment clear in her eyes.

"Grandma Mahdi? I've tried to call you before. Why are you here now?"

"I am here to guide you. You must think clearly."

"What are you talking about?"

"Craig is alive."

"He survived the attack?" Malaika noticed a passerby glance at her oddly and quickly lowered her voice, turning her face so her moving lips couldn't be seen. "Where is he? Why hasn't he returned home?"

"Your home is no longer his," her grandmother responded sadly. "You must stop him."

"Stop him?" A cold chill raced along Malaika's spine. "Stop him from what?"

"You must stop him... before he destroys the person sent to save you." The older woman's gaze shot across the street to rest on Jonah as he sat in the driver's seat of his unmarked Crown Victoria, waiting for them.

THREE

"**Y**ou're shitting me, right?"

Jonah turned away from the window, where he'd been watching Malaika as she described the fisherman to a sketch artist, and faced the police chief. The balding man, not exceptionally tall, but powerfully built, sat behind his desk staring at Jonah as though he'd sprouted a second head.

"I mean, a psychic? Surely, you're joking."

"She's been at more than one crime scene."

"There are other ways to explain that." Chief Granger narrowed his gray-green eyes and redirected his gaze so that he could see Malaika through his office window. "Have you checked her background?"

"It was the first thing I did." Jonah barely contained his anger, unsure whether the sudden rise in his temper was due to the chief questioning his common sense, or the fact the man was looking at Malaika as though she were guilty. Hell, it'd been an assumption he'd made right off the bat too, but now that he'd met her, his gut told him she was no killer. He didn't like the chief looking at her as though she were. "Her background check came back spotless, not so much as a parking ticket or overdue library book. She's a website designer, not a murderer."

"Then why is she hanging around the crime scenes?"

"I told you." Jonah shot one more glance toward his desk to make sure Malaika was all right, and then sat in one of the chairs opposite the chief.

"Yeah, I know. She's psychic." Granger rubbed a hand over his smooth head and let out a sigh. "Look, son. I know you've been through some shit lately—"

"You know there have been cases where psychics have been brought in," Jonah interrupted, tired of having his sanity questioned. "It may seem weird as hell, and not logically explainable, but there are psychics. Remember that

41

little girl who went missing last year, and a psychic led the police right to the abductor's home?"

"Yeah, I'll give you that one, but I'm not so sure this woman is a psychic. Why can't she tell us who the killer is? Uh-uh. Not buying it." Granger sat back in his chair and shook his head. "And I'm not buying you being perfectly fine either. Something is going on with you, Porter."

"I've passed the mental exams."

"Yeah, well, that don't always mean shit." Granger sniffed and his mustache twitched. "I talked to a buddy of mine with the feds. He was with the team that went down to Hicksville after Curtis Dunn."

"And?" Jonah prompted after Granger affixed a hard stare on him and went silent.

"Do you know what they found?"

"No." Jake hadn't divulged much during the one brief contact he'd had with him during that time.

"A bloody massacre. The majority of that town is gone. There was this one house... It looked like a battle had been fought inside, with a whole damn army. The carpet was soaked through with blood."

"You make it sound as if an entire town was killed off."

"It was."

Jonah gulped. Jake had been there. If it was that bad and he hadn't answered his cell in all this time...

"We talked to the Sheriff there. Peewee Porter. Your cousin."

"So he's alright?" Like Jake, Peewee also hadn't returned his calls.

"I wouldn't say that. Whatever happened there messed up the man's wiring. He's convinced vampires took out his whole town and would have killed him too if not for a little help from the family. I'm betting you know who he was referring to."

"Where's Jake now?" Jonah ignored the suspicious glare he received from the chief, more concerned with his younger brother's safety.

"Hell if I know, but I'd sure like to find out. What the hell was he doing there, Porter?"

"He's a detective too."

"A private detective, or so he says." Granger leaned forward. "I find it highly suspicious he wound up in the same county Curtis Dunn was suspected of being in."

"He has the right to search for the man too." Jonah clenched his jaw, barely restraining his temper. "And we have family there. He's allowed to visit our family."

"I hope your brother isn't looking to serve a little vigilante justice for what was done to you." Granger narrowed his eyes, and lowered his voice to a threatening tone. "And I hope to hell you aren't supplying him with information regarding a case I ordered you off of."

"I haven't heard from my brother in quite a while, close to a year, actually. He tends to disappear for periods of time. I haven't given him any information regarding Curtis Dunn or that case," Jonah lied through his teeth. "Jake's a smart man, and a good detective. If he knows anything about Curtis Dunn's whereabouts, he figured it out on his own, and I can't stop him from looking for the guy."

"He's your little brother."

"In case you haven't noticed, my little brother is a grown man with an aversion to authority."

Granger let out a frustrated sigh and sat back in his chair. "If he screws with my investigation, I'm bringing him in, in cuffs."

"Won't be the first time he's spent the night in a cell," Jonah responded, careful to keep his tone neutral. He was already on the chief's shit list, and he'd just killed two cops. What he really needed to do was grovel and kiss major ass, but that just wasn't in his genetic makeup.

Granger let out a mirthless chuckle, and scratched his head. "Give me your gun and your badge, Porter."

"What?" Jonah brought his hands down on the edge of Granger's desk with a loud thump.

The police chief widened his eyes in surprise. "You killed two cops, Porter. You know there's going to be an investigation."

"Yeah, but, I, but—" Jonah sputtered, anger wiping out his ability to think straight. Yes, he knew there would be an investigation, but to take his badge? When he'd saved his partner's life?

"Porter, you know it's protocol."

"Fuck protocol!" Jonah rose out of his seat lightning fast. "I saved Ronnie's life. If I hadn't pulled the trigger when I did, she wouldn't be in the hospital, she'd be in the morgue, and you damn well know it!"

Granger stood, rested his fists on the desk. "I'm going to remind you who I am, son."

"You know this is bullshit." Jonah stared his boss in the eye, too mad to give a damn about repercussions for his immediate actions.

Granger looked away, the slight blush of red in his cheeks giving away the truth. He did know it was bullshit. "I'm sorry, Porter. My hands are tied."

Jonah clenched his fists tight as Granger held out his hand.

"Give me your gun and your badge. Don't make me have to take them from you."

He was tempted to do just that. But he loved his job, lived to serve. Jonah took a deep breath and pulled out his badge. He rubbed his thumb over it reverently before handing it to the chief. The gun was easier. He had another one in his car, and several more at home. "This is fucked up, Chief."

"Off the record?" Granger lay the gun and badge on his desk, and looked Jonah square in the eye. "You're a good detective, Porter. If it were my choice, I wouldn't have done this. You saved your partner's life, but the details surrounding the situation..." Granger shook his head and frowned. "Why in the hell were your bullets silver-coated?"

Jonah's heart slammed into his throat. He'd totally forgotten about the bullets. He opened his mouth while struggling to think of a good reason which wouldn't sound like a pathetic excuse, and snapped it shut when he failed to come up with anything halfway decent.

"Ah, save it," Granger said with a wave of his hand. "Whatever you think up to say isn't going to sound sane to me. You've been hung on a damn wall by some devil-worshiping psycho, found in the same building with charred remains of a serial killer, and now you're walking around with silver-coated bullets, killing cops-gone-bad with them. There's not a thing you can say to make sense of all that, Porter. Therein lies the problem."

Granger plopped back down into his seat with a heavy sigh. "Go on home, Porter. Watch ESPN, get drunk, and get laid. Take the damn vacation you're being given until I can find a way to convince the higher-ups that you're not a walking disaster area."

Jonah nodded his head, unable to say anything to change the outcome of the situation, and turned for the door.

"And stay the hell away from Malaika Jordan. You're to go nowhere near this case."

"What?" Jonah whipped around to face the chief. Desperation clawed through his belly. He didn't know why, but his gut insisted he stick to Malaika. "You have my badge and my gun. Isn't that enough?"

Granger's eyes widened as Jonah loomed over him. "Porter—"

"I know I'm off the case in official capacity, but why—"

"You're off the case in any and all capacity," Granger said, rising from his seat. "Dammit, Joe, I'm trying to help you keep your damn job. Stay away from this case. All of it!"

"She'll talk to me. I've built a rapport with her."

"Another detective can do the same."

"Another detective probably won't even believe her!"

"Lower your voice, son." The chief's order came out between clenched teeth. "We'll question the woman, and if there's anything—"

The door to the office flung open and Malaika stormed in, hands firmly planted on her gently rounded hips. "I'm not talking to anybody except this man right here," she announced, pointing at Jonah.

"Now, wait a minute—"

"No, you wait a minute," Malaika snapped, cutting Granger off. "I've dealt with people like you all my life. You don't believe in anything unless it's right in front of your face. I can help with this case, but I need to work with someone who believes me, someone I can trust."

Jonah's chest swelled with warmth, touched by Malaika's declaration of trust, even though he'd only just met her. He turned his gaze back to the chief to take in the man's flabbergasted expression, and couldn't suppress the grin tugging at his lips.

Granger quelled his amused expression with a lethal glare before turning back to Malaika. "Miss Jordan, I'm going to have to ask you to step back out of my office while I—"

"And I'm going to have to tell your wife where you really were last Tuesday night when you claimed to be stuck here working."

Granger's jaw dropped open, the older man's face reddened the color of ripe strawberries. All the while, Malaika stood her ground with hands on hips and a satisfied grin.

"I work with Jonah, or I go to your wife."

Granger finally closed his mouth, swallowing hard. "How could you possibly know?"

"I'm psychic, which you'd already know if you'd bothered to listen to Jonah. I saw everything, and I saw it weeks ago. I just didn't know why until a few minutes ago when I got a mental flash of what was going on in here."

Granger looked away sheepishly. "It wasn't anything, just a momentary weakness."

"Please." Malaika held up her hand, palm out, to ward off any further explanation. "I saw it all, honey, and believe me, some of it—no—make that most of it, I wish I hadn't seen." She shivered visibly and made a small sound of disgust. "We have a deal here, or not?"

Granger sighed heavily in defeat, looked between Malaika and Jonah, and let his shoulders sag as he returned to his seat. "Go on, but dammit, Porter, be discreet if you want to keep your job."

Malaika directed a smug grin his way, and Jonah let out the chuckle he'd been holding since the moment she'd stormed into the office like a bat out of hell. He nodded toward the door and allowed her to precede him out.

"Porter!"

He stopped in the doorway and turned back toward the chief.

"Not. A. Word. Of. This. To. Anyone."

Jonah laughed at the desperate expression on Granger's face and closed the door behind him. "I think you may have made my boss piss himself," he whispered softly to Malaika as they walked over to his desk, where Deja was doodling on his desk planner.

"Deja, stop that!" Malaika admonished.

"She's alright." Jonah noticed the little girl's bottom lip tremble and lightly caressed her plump little cheek, bringing out a smile, before she turned back to her drawing.

He picked up the image on his desk that the sketch artist and Malaika had worked on and studied the old, withered face of Malaika's mysterious fisherman. The man had several wrinkles, thin lips, and a prominent hook-shaped nose. His lower face was covered with thin, white hair, and his eyes were hidden due to the shadow from the hood of his raincoat. "You didn't get a good look at his eyes?"

"No." Malaika frowned. "I'm sorry. I should have looked harder." She shrugged and looked away. Jonah had already seen the failure in her eyes.

He gripped her chin and turned her face back toward his. Her breath hitched in her throat, revealed by the little gasp she emitted, and only the sound of a throat being cleared pulled him back before he dipped his head to kiss that frown off her pretty face.

He directed a look of annoyance toward the cop who'd issued the intruding sound and was now looking at them with curious humor sparkling in his gaze, and dropped his hand. "I can't even begin to understand what it's like to be psychic, Malaika. I'm sure you saw all you could, and you're a tremendous help."

Her eyes brightened a little before closing on a nod. "I just wish I could see the actual killer. Then I'd feel helpful."

"I know, but your gift works however it works. We'll find the killer." Jonah rolled the sketch up and inserted it into the inner pocket of his leather jacket. "I think it's lunchtime."

"Lunch!" Deja's head bobbed up from where it'd been hovering over her drawing. "I want fries!"

"Deja Serene Jordan." Malaika used a stern tone, but failed to hide the twinkle in her eye as she fixed her gaze on her daughter's pushed-out bottom lip. "Mr. Porter is a busy man and doesn't have time to take you for fries. We'll go home and—"

"Fries sound great to me," Jonah said, scooping up the little girl who gave him an earful of happy giggles as they made their way toward the exit. "You coming?" he asked as he looked back over his shoulder to where Malaika stood with her arms crossed.

"You're spoiling her," she said tersely as she reached them, and passed them by.

"It's one of my many skills," Jonah replied with a laugh as he watched the sway of her hips while she led them out of the precinct.

"So, what exactly did you see Granger do?" Jonah asked as he eased his Crown Vic out of the parking lot, onto the busy street.

Malaika shuddered in disgust at the horrid image. "I'd rather not say. It's one thing to accidentally intrude upon someone's personal business, but to blab about it is far worse. I can't help what I do with my mind, but I have control over my mouth."

Jonah looked at her thoughtfully and nodded before redirecting his gaze to the road before him. "That's kind of you. I imagine some people with your gift wouldn't be so considerate."

Malaika shrugged. It wasn't as if she'd ever met anyone with her gifts. Her grandmother had supposedly been psychic, too, though the family had treated her as though she were crazy. "I can say this much. Some men should not wear boxer briefs."

Jonah barked out a hearty laugh. "Well, it's a good thing you saw whatever it was. It came in handy."

"Not handy enough. You still had to hand over your badge." Guilt filled her chest. Why hadn't she seen something to prevent that? "I'm sorry."

"Don't be. It wasn't your fault."

"Maybe if I'd told *you* not to go into the building—"

"My partner would be dead." He pulled the car to a stop along the curb and looked at her pointedly. "You saved her life. You have nothing to feel sorry for."

Yeah, except withholding the whole truth. Craig is wrapped up in this mess somehow and according to my deceased grandmother, he's still around. Panic set in. How could Craig be alive? She'd been inside him in the vision, had felt the white-hot pain as he'd been attacked. She'd felt the life seep out of him.

"Let's go get some fries." Jonah opened his door and got out of the car, quickly opening the back door to retrieve Deja.

Malaika's feet felt like two blocks of cement as they hit the sidewalk. Why hadn't Craig come home if he survived the attack? Was he in a hospital somewhere? She hadn't bothered to call, so certain he'd been killed. She hadn't filed a missing persons report either, too scared to face the truth. The vision was one thing, but to have an actual verification of his death... There'd be no way she couldn't tell Deja then, and she didn't want to do that. She was too young to deal with death. Surely, thinking her daddy was out there somewhere was better than knowing he was dead.

But he wasn't dead. He *was* out there somewhere. What if he returned home now? Why had her grandmother said their home wasn't his anymore? Was the guilt over what he'd done keeping him away?

"Malaika?"

She looked up to see Jonah standing at the entrance of a small cafe with Deja firmly held by one masculine arm, waiting for her.

Serves him right if he's too guilty to come back. He can stay gone. Malaika closed the distance between Jonah and herself, unable to hold back a smile as she saw how her daughter looked adoringly at the man holding her. The man who looked perfectly natural holding her. A cold chill ran through her as she recalled her grandmother's final words.

"You must stop him... before he destroys the person sent to save you."

Oh, no. Nuh-uh. Craig had done his dirt and he could stew in it. It was time to leave his cheating ass behind and move on. And if he laid one finger on Jonah Porter, he'd wish he was dead.

"You are spoiling my child." Malaika tried to sound stern and disapproving, but couldn't quite get the tone right as Jonah paid for the bright pink stuffed unicorn Deja had spotted at the gift stand near the park.

"I told you, it's one of my skills." He grinned at her as he handed the unicorn to Deja and patted her head as she jumped up and down in glee.

"Momma, can I go slide?"

"Be careful," Malaika cautioned, but Deja was already running toward the slide. "Are you sure you don't have things to do?" she asked Jonah as they found a bench to sit on facing the playground. Jonah had bought lunch for her and Deja and then suggested walking to the park. He was being awfully nice for a detective who'd just lost his badge because of her.

"I'm supposed to be on vacation," he answered with a wry chuckle. "I've got plenty of time to spare, and it's the first warm day we've had in a while. Might as well enjoy it."

"I'm sorry."

Jonah turned his head to look at her and frowned. "For what?"

"Your badge. Everything."

"I already told you none of this is your fault."

True. It didn't take away her guilt.

"What is it, Malaika?"

My dead grandmother told me we're in danger, and I should tell you the full truth about the vision I had of Craig, but it's too crazy to believe. "Nothing."

"Do you always look so upset over nothing?"

"I've got things on my mind."

"There's an understatement." He stretched his long legs out before him, getting comfortable. "I'll go back down to the harbor in the morning and look for the fisherman. Since I have the sketch artist's rendering, you won't need to go with me."

"Good," Malaika said before catching herself, but the relief swamping over her caused her to blurt out her thought, despite how ungrateful it made her sound. "I'm sorry. It's not that I minded going with you. I know it's important to find the fisherman if the case is to be solved."

"But you don't like the water."

She jerked her head toward Jonah to find him watching her, knowingly. "That obvious?"

"You turned a little green when we got to the harbor. I thought maybe you just didn't feel well, but you got better after we left. So what happened?"

"Huh?"

"What happened to make you dislike the water? Almost drown? Have a bratty cousin hold you under in the pool?"

"No, nothing like that." She'd never given anyone the chance to hold her under water. "Large bodies of water just freak me out. They always have. From the time I was born, I've had this irrational fear of water. I even avoid being in the rain if at all possible."

"Really? You were just born scared of it?"

"I told you it was irrational." She shrugged, ready to change the subject. "So what are you going to do now that you've been ordered off the case?"

"I'm going to make sure nobody catches me working it," he answered with a sly grin and a devilish gleam in his eyes.

"How are you going to do that?" Unease skittered through Malaika's body. She didn't want Jonah in any further trouble with the department.

"I have you. You see the murders happen."

"But I'm always too late."

"I can still use your gift." He leaned toward her. "Everything you see, I will use until I track down whatever is killing these people."

She gulped. "But you'll always be a step behind. My visions don't—"

"Malaika." He touched the side of her face, and she realized she'd been shaking her head back and forth. "Believe a little bit more in yourself. You have this gift for a reason. You're seeing these murders *for a reason*. I seriously doubt the visions are in your head just to tease you."

"But—"

He halted her reply with a finger pressed to her lips. He looked down at where his finger rested, and replaced it with his thumb, smoothing it over her bottom lip before pulling his hand away and shifting uncomfortably in his seat.

"Have you ever been properly trained in using your gifts?" he asked while staring out at where Deja frolicked.

"Properly trained?" Malaika laughed. "What, like a psychic academy?"

The look Jonah spared her with held no hint of humor. He'd been serious. "There might be people who could help you learn how to hone your skills."

"Yeah, sure. Well, I can tell you this. They're not in the Yellow Pages."

"They wouldn't be." He opened his mouth to say more, then snapped it shut.

Malaika studied him while he watched her daughter play, and noticed the tight set of his jaw, the way he rubbed his thumb along the backs of his fingers. It was a nervous gesture. A strange thought popped into her head. Surely, he didn't...

"Jonah, am I the only psychic you've met?"

He sighed heavily, grinned a little uncertainly before facing her. "Not really."

Surprised excitement caused her to intake a sharp breath. Another psychic? Someone like her?

"A real psychic? Not one of these two-dollar-a-minute-phonecall-fake-psychics?"

"I've known some... people... who can see things before they happen, talk without speaking, that sort of thing." He looked away again, and ran a tan hand through his short, brown hair.

"What is it? Is there something you're not telling me?" Unease crept inside her again, replacing the momentary excitement she'd felt.

Jonah chuckled. "Sweetheart, there's a ton I'm not telling you. Hell, if I did, you'd think I was a nutcase." He scratched his head. "Just trust me when I say you are not the only person with these particular skills, and I think there is a way you can be trained to use them more efficiently."

"Trained by who?"

He chuckled again, no humor to the sound. "Tell you what. Let me run an idea by my brother, and if he gives me the all clear, I'll let you know."

His brother. She recalled the mental flash she'd received at the police department while Jonah was arguing with his boss. "Jonah, I saw what was going on inside the police chief's office. I heard your discussion."

He leaned forward to rest his elbows on his knees, and lowered his head until it was supported by his fists. "How much?"

"Enough to know something bad happened to you. You were... hung on a wall?" Her chest tightened. "Your brother is some sort of reckless detective, and your cousin thinks... *vampires* killed off most of his town?"

"That about sums it up." He didn't look up.

"No, not really. What happened to you?"

"You heard it. I was on a case and the bad guy got me before I got him."

"Jo—"

"I survived." He raised his head to face her full-on. "It's no big deal."

His tone said entirely different. Malaika squared her shoulders and pressed on. Something was gnawing at her, something was being held from her, and she intended to find out what.

"Explain why the police chief hates your brother, and why your cousin thinks vampires raided his town."

"How am I supposed to know what goes on in my cousin's head?"

"You know something. The chief knows it, too. That's why the department is treating you the way they are. Something strange is going on around you."

"Drop it, Malaika." He closed his eyes, and let out a deep breath. "Sorry. I'm not trying to snap at you. I appreciate your concern, but some things... People just don't understand certain things until they see them for themselves."

She laughed out loud. "Are you serious? I'm psychic. My whole life has been spent either trying to convince people to believe in something they can't see, or just hiding what I do in order to feel a little less like a freak. Jonah..." She placed her hand on his, "You can tell me anything. You'll find I'm not that close-minded. I can't be."

He stared at where their hands met for a moment then cleared his throat. "Fine. I was the lead detective on the serial killer case from last spring."

"The man who was dumping bodies in parks?"

"Yes." He took in another deep breath, let it out slowly. "He wasn't just a man. He was a monster."

""I'll bet," Malaika said softly. Had he been hung on a wall by that man? It was a miracle he'd not been killed and left in a park, too, but if she recalled correctly, the serial killer only murdered women.

"No, Malaika. Not that kind of monster. He was *really* a monster."

She frowned as he looked at her intently, tried to figure out where he was going. "He was an evil, horrible being. I get it."

"He was worse than that. He was a demon."

She nodded her head in agreement, but Jonah shook his in return. "A real demon, Malaika. He'd died and gone to hell. From there he'd made a pact with the devil to reincarnate through his own family line. The man who murdered those women had a real, live demon possessing his body."

Ohhhh-kay. Maybe he did need a break from his job. Though Malaika knew what it felt like to feel something so strongly inside your own body, a source of power that threatened to overwhelm... Demons possessing people?

"You don't believe me." He laughed, mirthlessly. "I knew it."

"Jonah, I..." She what? Knew what it felt like to feel something alive inside you, but couldn't put a name to? Now, who sounded crazy? "I know that sometimes things can seem—"

"Carter Dunn, the man who killed women all over Baltimore, was a demon, Malaika. Plain and simple, cut and dry. Do you remember what happened to him?"

She thought back to the article she'd read in the paper last spring. "He was found burned to death in his home. The detective found at the scene—" She gasped, recalling how badly beaten the detective—the detective she now knew was Jonah—had been reported to have been. "You were unconscious, and didn't know what had happened to him."

"I lied."

Dread filled her stomach. "You lied about what really happened?"

"I had to. If I'd told them the truth, I would have been put in an insane asylum, for sure."

"What happened? How'd that man wind up burned to death?"

He looked at her, met her gaze with steel determination. "My brother and a small group of vampires saved me, a woman who was being drained of blood, and another vampire. One of those vampires, a vampire who runs his own church right here in Baltimore, said a prayer and that bastard went up in flames. You have to believe me, Malaika."

She shook her head from side to side. "That's too—"

"Crazy? Insane? All the things you've undoubtedly been called?"

"That's not fair."

"No, what's not fair is that I'm sitting here talking to a woman who sees murders before they happen and talks to dead people, but she doesn't believe me."

She looked down in shame. She knew what it felt like to see things no one else could, to know some little part of truth everyone else failed to believe. "I want to believe you, Jonah. I really do. But vampires? Demons?"

"You've seen strange, unexplainable things, too."

She bit her lip. "I know, but being psychic is a mind thing. It has nothing to do with fangs and... the devil."

"What specifically did you see when you had the vision about my partner being attacked?"

"I told you."

"Tell me again." His tone broke no room for refusal. "Tell me exactly what you saw."

Malaika licked her lips, suddenly wary. "I saw her being attacked by beasts."

"What kind of beasts?"

"Dogs," she replied.

"Dogs?"

Letting out a sigh of frustration, she checked to make sure Deja was still on the swing she'd recently perched on, and conceded. "Not normal dogs, no. Some weird, huge... dog-like creatures with sharp teeth and glowing eyes."

"And that's normal?"

"I told you I don't always see things exactly as they are. Visions are a weird science. They don't always make sense."

"What if I told you your vision was spot-on?"

She blinked at him, confused. "You killed two cops in there. Two men attacked her. Not beasts."

He shook his head. "No. What attacked my partner were not men. They had sharp teeth and muzzles. A silver-coated bullet, which I fortunately had in my gun, is the only thing that stopped them. They changed back to look like humans after I killed them."

Now she knew he was crazy. "What are you saying?"

"Simply put, I think I killed two werewolves yesterday."

She could feel her mouth drop open, but couldn't close it. She was numb, completely and utterly stupefied. The man she'd grown to trust, the man she'd envisioned being as intimate as one possibly could be with, was a stark-raving lunatic.

"Well?" he prodded. "You saw it correctly. What do you say to that?"

"You must have lost your damn mind!"

FOUR

Unbelievable. Un-friggin' believable. The psychic who spoke to the dead didn't believe him. Jonah fumed in silence as he navigated down the streets of Baltimore, passing the street that would take them to Malaika's neighborhood.

"I live that way."

"I know, I've been there," he replied curtly, steadily driving away from the area.

"Where are you taking us?"

He glanced toward Malaika to see her looking at him with wide eyes. They matched the hint of fear he'd picked up in her voice.

"Relax. I'm not taking you to my evil lair." He glanced in the rear-view mirror to check on Deja and saw the little girl had fallen asleep.

"Jonah, I'd like to go home."

"Why? Scared of me now that you think I'm a psycho?" He didn't bother looking at her, not overly eager to see her looking at him as if he were Charles Manson and the freakish clown from Stephen King's *It* all rolled into one.

"I don't think you're a psycho. I just think you're tired, confused." Her voice softened. "You've been working hard and in your line of work, I can only imagine how high the level of stress—"

"Just stop it." He turned left, his hands gripped tight around the steering wheel. "I'm tired of people acting like I've lost my mind. I can expect it from most, but you? You of all people, I thought would understand."

He heard her sigh. It was a soft, sad little sound, but it did nothing to tamp down his anger. He'd trusted her enough to tell her about the worst thing that had ever happened to him, and she'd scoffed at him. Actually asked him if he'd lost his mind.

"I'm sorry if I offended you, Jonah."

"I'm sorry, too, sorry I actually thought I could confide in you without being laughed at."

"I did not laugh at you." Anger laced her tone.

"It was close enough, but it doesn't matter. You're going to believe me soon enough."

He pulled his car into the small parking lot of the Blood Of Life Non-Denominational Church and cut the engine. "Come on."

He'd already exited the car and picked up a still-sleeping Deja from the backseat before Malaika got out, her eyes full of wary hesitance.

"Why did you bring us here?"

"To make you believe. My gut never steers me wrong and right now, my gut is telling me you need to believe there are things in this world that aren't quite human."

She gulped heavily, but followed him to the church.

"You mentioned a vampire who ran a church. This church?"

"Yes," he answered as he opened the wooden door.

"Well, at least it's still daylight." She entered the building, walking slowly and doing her best to look in all directions at once. Jonah couldn't help but chuckle.

"Why, Malaika, one would think you actually believe in vampires." He closed the door and turned toward the interior of the church. He'd barely made it three steps before his breath caught in his throat.

A long aisle with rows of pews on either side stretched before them, leading to the pulpit. And in front of the pulpit stood a pregnant woman, the vampire who'd destroyed Carter Dunn, and Jake Porter.

Before Jonah could open his mouth to ask what his brother was doing there and why he hadn't returned any of his calls, Jake pulled a gun from the back of his waistband and aimed.

"Get the hell away from my brother!"

Jonah jerked his head toward Malaika, his brother's target, and saw her freeze in wide-eyed fear.

"What the hell are you doing, Jake?" Jonah stepped in front of Malaika as his brother slowly advanced toward them, and looked at Christian for help. The vampire stepped before the pregnant woman to shield her from possible danger, and watched Jake advance.

"Move away from her, bro, unless you want that kid shot."

Jonah glanced down at the small girl whose sleeping head rested on his shoulder and shook his head. "No way, Jake. Put that damn gun away. What the hell are you even doing here?"

Jake had stopped advancing, but still held his finger on the trigger, ready to shoot. The expression on his face was deadly, and even Jonah trembled a little despite knowing his brother would never put a bullet in him.

"Better question. What the hell are you doing with *that*?"

Jonah blinked, confused. "What the hell are you talking about?"

"She's a witch. Get away from her."

Alarm slammed into Jonah's chest and he quickly stepped away from Malaika, holding onto Deja more securely. "What?"

Malaika looked between him and his brother, and swallowed hard. "Both of you are crazy!" Her voice was panicked, her body frozen still. Jonah felt the urge to hug her to his chest, but Jake knew his stuff. "First, vampires, now witches? You're out of your damn minds!"

"Oh really?" Jake chuckled, the sound bordering on menacing. "What if I dipped you into the lake?"

Malaika inhaled a sharp gasp of air and tightened her fists.

"How about I put chains around your ankles and throw you into the ocean? Watch while the water sucks you under so it can fill your lungs?"

Malaika shook her head from side to side as tears streamed down her face. "How do you know about my phobia?"

Jake's brow furrowed for a moment, but he pressed on. "I know what you are. What I don't know is why you're hanging around my brother."

"I'm not a witch, you crazy freak!" Malaika started shaking, and her mouth set in a firm line. "I'm warning you to back down."

Something was happening. Her voice was determined, not scared, and the air around her seemed to spark with static.

"She's about to blow, stand back!"

Jonah started to step back, but faltered when Deja's sleeping body flew out of his arms and into Malaika's. With one arm, she gripped her child tight to her body, and with the other she raised her hand palm-out toward Jake. Jonah's jaw dropped in shock as he watched a ball of green fire form in her hand.

"Get your brother away from me, Jonah. I don't want to hurt anyone." A tear trickled down her face, but she didn't stand down.

Jonah couldn't say anything. He'd trusted her, felt sorry for her. Hell, he'd wanted her. She was a witch, not even human! The conniving little... *witch*.

Jake reached inside his jacket with his free hand, and the green fireball flew directly at him. He jerked out of the way as Jonah watched in stunned horror. The fireball flew toward the pulpit, and Christian quickly spun out of the way, the pregnant woman in his arms. The ball hit the podium Christian stood before while delivering his sermons, and left a burning hole.

Another ball of green fire started to form in Malaika's hand, but Jake pulled his hand out of his jacket and flung something at her. Jonah watched as silver dust flew around her and she froze. The fireball fizzled out.

"Get the girl," Jake ordered as he advanced on Malaika.

Jonah grabbed Deja out of Malaika's frozen hands and watched as the dust formed a web-like material. Jake tied it tight around Malaika, binding her arms to the sides of her body. All the while, she stared at Jonah in horror. "I'm not a witch. I'm not!" She choked on a sob. "I didn't want to hurt anyone."

"Save it, sweetheart," Jake growled through clenched teeth. "Nyla, baby, you alright?"

Nyla? Jonah wrestled his gaze away from Malaika, determined not to fall for her act. She'd just thrown a frigging fireball at his brother. So what if she looked traumatized? She'd pulled the wool over his eyes once and he wasn't going to allow her a second time to perform the same trick.

His gaze landed on the pregnant woman, a beautiful violet-eyed vision in black, with long, black hair to match.

"I'm fine," she answered, running a hand over her round belly.

Jonah's gaze lowered to follow the movement. Jake hadn't answered his calls for nine months. Nine months since he'd told him about a female hunter named Nyla joining up with him on the Dunn case. Nine months since he'd undoubtedly impregnated her. "Jake?"

"Yeah, we need to talk," Jake responded as he pushed a crying Malaika toward the back of the church. "I'll tell you all about my honeymoon in a little bit, but witch's net only lasts so long."

Jonah blinked back his shock as Jake passed him by. His womanizing brother who hadn't bothered calling him in nine months was married with a child on the way, the woman he'd started falling for was a witch who could make green fire in her hands, and he'd killed two werewolves. The week couldn't get any crazier.

"Care to explain?"

"I could ask you the same question, Family Guy."

They'd convened in a small room in the back of the church and all sat around a table while Deja slept on a cot in the corner. Malaika was at the foot of the table, Christian at the head, and Jonah sat across from his brother and the sister-in-law he'd not been aware of having for nearly a year.

Jake dealt him a hard look before squeezing his wife's hand and resting his elbows on the table to lean forward. "I've been busy for the past nine months."

"I can see that. I find it hard to believe you couldn't find one spare minute to answer at least one of the dozens of voice mails I left for you."

Jake squirmed in his seat, a move so slight Jonah barely caught it, and exchanged a look with his wife. A look that said they weren't telling him something.

"What is it? What happened in Hicksville?"

Nyla looked down into her lap, and Jake closed his eyes. "Let's deal with the life and death stuff first, shall we?" The look he gave when he reopened his eyes suggested it didn't matter if Jonah agreed or not. He wasn't going to discuss Hicksville yet. "Where'd you pick up the witch?"

"I'm not a damn hooker one *picks up*," Malaika interrupted. "Don't speak of me as if I am."

"No, you're worse," Jake responded with a sneer. "Most hookers can't fry people."

"I didn't mean to do that." Remorse flashed through her eyes before she lowered her gaze to the table. "When I'm threatened, things happen. It doesn't make me a witch. There's no such thing."

Jake frowned and exchanged an odd look with Christian. "Where'd you meet her, Joe?"

Jonah took a deep breath and willed himself not to cuss out his brother. "If you'd bothered to check the messages I left you, you'd already know. I was working a case and Ronnie and I noticed she'd been standing outside a few of the crime scenes."

"Well, that bodes well."

"I had nothing to do with the murders," Malaika interjected.

"She warned Ronnie not to go in the building where a body had been found. She said she'd had a vision of Ronnie being killed."

Jake flicked a curious look toward Malaika and leaned forward more. "What happened?"

"Ronnie didn't believe her. She went in the building and was attacked by two... I think they were werewolves."

"Werewolves?"

"Yeah, werewolves."

Jake sat back and scratched his chin. "Are you positive they were werewolves?"

"They were half-human, half-beast, with sharp teeth and muzzles. A silver-coated bullet was the only thing that stopped them."

"Silver-coated bullet?"

Jonah shrugged. "I got some after the Carter Dunn incident. Yesterday morning... I don't know, I just had the feeling I should load my gun with them."

Jake's brow furrowed. "You get these feelings often?"

"I'm a cop. You tend to develop a good gut instinct after a few years."

"If you say so. So, what happened to Ronnie?"

"She's in the hospital. She was jacked up pretty bad."

"Was she bitten?"

"No." Panic squeezed Jonah's chest. "She was just clawed. Why? You always said a bite from a shifter couldn't turn a person into one."

"I said a bite from a Were couldn't. A bite from a Lycanthrope can infect a human with the disease, and if you killed something that looked half-human, half-beast, it was a Lycanthrope. Weres can't partially shift." He let out a crude curse and shifted his gaze back to Malaika, who was staring at him as if he'd been speaking in tongues. "So... you decided to bring the witch here because...?"

Malaika rolled her eyes, but didn't say anything, apparently figuring it didn't matter if she did.

"Because I may not have known she was a witch, but I did realize she was psychic. I figured she was the best lead I had for the case."

"And the case is this one you've left messages about? Wild dogs chewing on murder victims?"

"The bites came from a human jaw."

"With canine teeth."

"Yup."

Jake grinned from ear to ear. "So did they take your badge for killing the cops?"

"Yeah, they did."

"Dude, you have got to break out of the mold and go private eye." Jake laughed, but only for a moment before he looked toward Malaika and sobered. "So... how exactly is she helpful?"

"I see the murders," Malaika snapped. "I've been trying to help Jonah with this case. I haven't hurt anyone and—"

"Yeah, because we ducked the powerballs."

"That wouldn't have happened if you hadn't threatened me and my child."

"The child you've put a spell on to sleep through all this?"

Jonah jerked around in his seat to look at the child sleeping peacefully on the cot. Now that he thought about it, it was strange that she'd managed to sleep through all the excitement. "You put a spell on Deja?"

"I didn't put a spell on my daughter," Malaika protested. "I just... I made a mental suggestion that she sleep. I did it for her well-being!"

Jonah's mouth dropped open as he looked at his brother to find him looking back at him with a "Man, you can sure pick them" smirk. He cringed inside, knowing he was going to be seriously ribbed for this one, but instead of starting in with the ribbing, Jake turned toward the vampire who'd been silently observing their conversation.

"Christian, I need you to get Seta here. This woman's a witch, but honestly, I don't think she's aware of it."

"All of you are crazy," Malaika scoffed. "A vampire who is awake in daylight. Werewolves killed by silver bullets. Me, a wit—"

A dark-headed, petite tan woman appeared at Christian's side as if conjured out of thin air. Jake and Jonah both reached a hand toward the Glocks in their waistbands as Malaika let out a frightened gasp, but the brothers paused as they recognized the beautiful, voluptuous woman.

The vampiress-slash-witch glanced down at Jake and Nyla and sighed. "Jacob Porter, I see Nyla has not tired of you yet."

She leaned down to touch a hand to Nyla's extended belly. "They'll be coming along soon."

They'll? Twins? Jake was going to have two babies? Jonah bit back a chuckle, imagining how out of his element Jake was going to be with two tiny tots on his hands.

"Why did you summon me, Christian?" Seta turned and looked down at the other vampire. Annoyance lit her eyes. "And who is this witch?"

Malaika gulped as Seta's gaze fell upon her.

"She's not aware of what she is, and nearly fried us," Jake answered for the boyish-looking vampire. "You know an untrained witch is a highly dangerous one."

"So she's my responsibility?" Seta arched an eyebrow.

"Can you train her?" Jonah asked, recalling his reason for coming to the church. Granted, he'd only thought Malaika to be psychic, but still... She had visions, and he could use them to solve the case. If she could be trusted. And nobody would know that better than Seta. From what Jake had told him, Seta was an extremely powerful witch, one you did not attempt to screw with.

Seta glanced toward him and frowned. A smile tugged at the corner of her mouth as recognition sparked in her gaze. "Jonah Porter, Jacob's brother. I must say you look much better than the last time I saw you. Attractive, even."

"Thanks," he replied, unsure how to respond to a compliment by a vampire-witch. "Can you help her?"

"And why is it of importance that I train this witch?"

"Other than the fact an untrained witch is like a walking bomb," Jake interjected sarcastically. The statement earned him a lethal glare from Seta.

"She's valuable to a murder case I'm working."

"Really?" The vampire-witch's head swiveled back toward Jonah. "How so?"

"She's shown up at the crime scenes, says she sees the murders before they happen."

"Interesting." Seta looked at Malaika. "Since she's untrained, I'm assuming her visions aren't as clear as they could be."

"No. Werewolves attacked my partner, but she saw beasts."

"Werewolves?"

"Yeah. Two cops at the crime scene my partner and I were checking out turned out to be werewolves. They attacked her."

Seta frowned. "You saw them with your own eyes?"

"Yes."

"I need that image."

Before Jonah could part his lips to ask what she meant, Seta was at his side with her palm against his temple. Heat seemed to burn into his skin under her hand. He saw Ronnie being attacked again, and then the image was quickly sucked away.

"Were-hyenas," Seta announced.

"Oh, hell," Jake groaned. "Not those nasty bastards."

"Unfortunately, I do not lie." Seta wiped her palm on her jean-clad thigh. "And you know wherever you find a cackle of were-hyenas..."

"You find their evil leader."

They both turned their heads to leer at Malaika, who squirmed in her seat. Jake let out a deep breath and pushed away from the table. "That witch's net isn't going to hold much longer. Christian, take Nyla where it's secure. Joe, come with me, and Seta—"

"Drain her of information and find out which side she's really on," the vampire-witch said in a menacing tone with a sparkle in her eye. Her mouth curved upward into a ruthless smile.

Jonah had risen from his seat with the others, but paused in walking toward the door to look at Malaika. Her eyes pleaded with him as Seta stalked toward her.

"Come on, Joe. Let Seta find out what she's really about."

Jonah gulped past the knot that had formed in his throat and looked at his brother who was standing by the door, waiting for him to leave the two witches alone. Jake jerked his head toward the door and careful not to glance back at the woman who still managed to spark his protective instincts, Jonah forced his feet to move him out of the room.

"Will she hurt her?" he asked once they'd cleared the door.

"If she's innocent, Seta won't touch a hair on her head." Jake took the lead, guiding them down the narrow hall leading to the main doors of the church. "The little girl will be fine. Seta would never harm a child."

"What if Malaika isn't innocent?"

"Seta will rip her head off and use it for spell ingredients." Jake chuckled, but sobered when he realized Jonah wasn't laughing with him. "Here you go again," he muttered, pushing open the door to lead them outside where the sun was descending.

"What does that mean?"

"You always want the ones you can't have." Jake sat on the steps and glanced up, cocking an eyebrow.

Jonah reluctantly sat next to him. "I don't know what you're talking about."

"Kathy Sabato from seventh grade, Tia Lawson from sophomore year, Angie Jackson, Jennifer Santiago, Aria Michaels."

"Aria Michaels?" The image of the woman bound to a metal table, hooked up to a machine that drained her blood, flashed through Jonah's mind.

"Well, her last name's different now, but yes." Jake looked at him and chuckled. "Dude, you wanted her like a fat kid wants a Ho-Ho."

Jonah grunted, choosing to ignore the ribbing, and the ache in his chest at the reminder that the beautiful woman he'd instantly fallen for while investigating the case of the murdered women being left in Baltimore parks had been changed over into a vampire by her vampire lover, and now husband.

"Whatever, Jake. Malaika is a lead, nothing more." Even if she did have a vision of them having sex, a vision he'd wanted to become real not that long ago. Before he knew what she really was. He glanced down at the ring on his brother's left hand and shook his head. "So what happened? Condom break?"

"No condom," Jake replied, staring out past the parking lot for a brief moment before turning his head to meet Jonah's gaze with sincere eyes. "And I would have married her without her being pregnant."

Jonah blinked, replayed Jake's response in his head. "Who the hell are you and what have you done with my horn-dog brother?"

Jake barked out a laugh. "I'm reformed. What can I say? I found a beautiful woman with a killer body who can behead a flying vampire in mid-air. I don't need to look anywhere else." He looked sternly into Jonah's eyes. "And I don't care what you say. I know you, Joe. You got a thing for that woman in there."

"I told you—"

"I know what you said, and I know what I witnessed. Even after knowing what she was, you still looked at her with compassion. Right now you're worrying about what Seta's doing to her."

Jonah sighed in frustration. He should have known his brother would see right through him. The younger man had an uncanny knack for reading people.

"For what it's worth, I think she's alright. She truly doesn't seem to know what she is."

"How did you?" Jonah searched his memory for any tell-tale signs and came up short. Even knowing she was afraid of water, he'd had no idea it meant she was a witch. "And what was with the whole taunting her with water thing?"

"I took a shot. A lot of witches are terrified of water. It's due to their past life, when they were drowned during the Salem Witch Trials. Unless they were burned alive, then their fear is fire."

Jonah sat speechless. Malaika had been drowned during the Salem Witch Trials? A shiver tickled its way up his spine. The paranormal stuff was starting to creep him out. "How'd you know she was a witch?"

Jake chewed on his bottom lip a while before letting out a deep breath. "I'm a slayer."

"Yeah, I know. You kill vampires."

"No, I don't mean I'm a slayer as in I happen to have killed some vampires." Jake glanced his way and just as quickly glanced down at the ground. "I'm a slayer in the same way Christian is a vampire and Malaika is a witch. It's not what I choose to do. It's what I am."

Jonah stared at his brother, taking in the tight set of his mouth, the shadow of shame crossing over his eyes. "I don't understand."

"I have a supernatural gift. I can sense witches, vampires, shifters—you name it—and I'm drawn to kill them. Whether they're evil or not."

Jonah stared at his brother, unsure of what to say. He'd always been told supernatural creatures were evil. Then Seta, Rialto, and Christian had helped Jake free him from Carter Dunn's lab. Jake hadn't killed them, had even developed a friendship with them. "You haven't killed Christian or Seta."

"Thanks to Nyla."

"What did she do?"

"Nyla has an empathic ability. She drains the darkness out of me and keeps me from spinning into a bloodthirsty rage." Jake looked him square in the eye. "She's what keeps me from losing control."

Jonah swallowed hard. "You make it sound like you're a cold-blooded killer."

"I am."

The two brothers stared at each other for a long moment before Jake looked away. Jonah took a breath and scratched his head, wishing the awkward moment would pass. What did one say when their brother confessed to being nothing more than a murderer?

"It's just vamps and shifters, right? I mean, you've never killed a human."

Jake angled his head back around to look at him, then glanced back down at his feet. "I've killed vampires before with no regard to whether they were good or evil. I've killed witches... who are basically humans with powers, and shifters—"

"But never a regular human being?"

"No. I'm drawn to protect humankind, but if the need to shed blood ever got too intense, or if one got in my way..."

Jonah shook his head emphatically. "You wouldn't do it, Jake. You're a good person. Hell, back in school you wouldn't even fight a kid if he was smaller than you."

Jake grinned as if recalling such an incident and shrugged his shoulders, seeming to shake off the intensity of their conversation. "Enough share-time, cake boy. Tell me about these were-hyenas."

Jonah grinned at the ribbing, glad for the change of subject. "Bodies have been popping up in abandoned buildings with strange bites. There's a lot of blood drainage, but none around the bodies."

"Sounds like a vamp."

"The bodies have been mauled by what appears to be a mix of dogs and ... a dog with a human jaw."

"The were-hyenas." Jake shuddered. "I hate those fugly bastards."

"Could they chew up a body and not leave a bloody mess all over the floor?"

"No." Jake pursed his lips in thought. "Were-hyenas are messy. They feast on bodies with no regard to neatness. I'm guessing organs were eaten?"

Jonah nodded. "The last vic's heart was munched on."

"Vampires don't eat organs, but they can siphon enough blood out of a body to keep it from spilling all over the place while the body is being chewed on."

"So you think a vampire is involved?"

"Definitely." Jake stretched his long legs out in front of him. "Were-hyenas are powerful, but not the brightest creatures on the planet. They need a leader, someone to order them around."

"A vampire?"

"In this case, yes."

Jonah frowned. "Wouldn't they just have, like, an alpha hyena or something? It seems like they'd want a leader who was one of their own kind."

"These are were-hyenas, Joe, not anything you'd see on the Discovery Channel. They can shift shape to look like a hyena, and since these ones are lycanthropes, not pure Weres, they retain a great deal of hyena traits, but they're basically stupid."

"How so?"

"All they care about is feeding. Their main concerns are filling their stomachs and rutting their brains out."

"Um, Jake, that actually sounds a lot like you."

"Funny." Jake speared him with a glare. "The point is they need someone to lead them or else the stupid things would never survive. They'd expose themselves to the general population and people would learn of their existence and snuff them out. This would lead to humans realizing there are supernatural beings out there and there would be more hunters."

"So other, smarter, supernatural beings step in and lead them to prevent their own exposure."

"That, and just to keep them as pets. They make good attack dogs."

"Yeah, I know." Jonah rubbed his shoulder, where the were-hyena had sank claws into him.

"You sure you weren't bitten?" Jake eyed him suspiciously.

"Absolutely. I just got clawed." He recalled the attack and something niggled at him. "These were-hyenas, the ones I killed, were men I'd worked with before. One was a regular cop and the other was the crime scene photographer. Could they have been lycanthropes for a long time?"

Jake frowned and shook his head. "I don't know. I've never heard of any lycanthrope activity here in Baltimore, and these guys travel in cackles. They were probably newly made. Which makes sense, considering you managed to kill them with bullets that were only *coated* in silver. "

Guilt filled Jonah's chest. "They had families, loved ones, and I killed them."

"You had to." Jake's hand clamped onto his shoulder. "And trust me, they would have either infected their family members or ate them." He nodded firmly to press his point and removed his hand. "What I'm wondering is why two cops were conveniently turned into were-hyenas."

Unease prickled across Jonah's skin. "You don't think it was a coincidence."

"No, I don't. You said the woman sees the murders before they happen?"

"Yeah."

"And she goes to the crime scenes?"

"Yes." Cold sweat trickled down Jonah's spine.

"You know, some vampires can sense when someone is aware of them, especially if that someone is a witch or other supernatural being."

"And you think the vampire committing these murders has sensed Malaika at the scenes?"

"It's a definite possibility."

Irrational alarm slammed into Jonah's chest. The woman was a witch, and had nearly torched his brother, but still, he worried for her safety. And the fact that he knew he probably couldn't do shit against a vampire scared him even more. He was a cop, dammit. He wasn't used to feeling helpless.

"Are you going to protect her?"

Jake looked at him, his face devoid of expression. "I'm going to use her as bait."

FIVE

No. None of it could be true. Malaika studied her young daughter, watched the steady rise and fall of her chest, and hoped her influence continued to work until she figured out a way to get them out of here. If she woke and heard this madness...

"Answer me."

Malaika redirected her gaze to the powerful woman standing to her left. Her arms were folded under her ample chest and what looked like a mixture of curiosity, suspicion, and amusement glittered in her dark eyes. The question was *How well do or did you know your grandmother?*

Malaika frowned. What did her grandmother have to do with anything? She'd been kept from her since she was just a young girl. Her mother had always been so scared of the harmful influence she claimed Grandma Mahdi had.

"If you do not answer, you will soon discover how much I loathe to wait."

Malaika cringed under the threatening tone the proclaimed witch used. *Proclaimed, my ass. Girlfriend poofed up in here out of the damn air.* Malaika shook her head. No. She had a psychic gift and maybe this woman had some special gift, too, but witches weren't real.

"My mother quit letting me see my grandmother when I was just a little girl."

"Before she could train you."

"Train me for what?" Malaika let the annoyance slip through her voice. These people were on her last nerve. Especially Jonah, just leaving her in here with this crazy woman. Seta. The witch.

The dark-haired beauty rolled her eyes and turned to pace the room. "True witches are born every other generation. We come into our powers as we hit adolescence, and usually it is our grandmother who trains us." She frowned, her body coming to a stand-still. "Alas, sometimes they don't," she said after a moment of silence, "and sometimes they can't, like in your case." She studied Malaika and the barest hint of a smile swept past her lips. "I was once like you."

Malaika squirmed under the woman's stare. "What do you mean?"

"I was an untrained witch, completely unaware why strange things happened to—or around—me... until I was changed into a vampire."

Again with the vampire stuff. "Look, lady. I'm not a witch and you're not a vamp—"

Seta growled and brought her face down before Malaika's.

Malaika gasped as the woman's lips pulled back to show her canines elongate into deadly fangs. There was no faking those.

Seta's fangs receded and she backed away. "Believe in vampires and witches now?"

Malaika shook her head and fought the urge to scream. She tried to wake up, but couldn't. If it wasn't a dream... *No.* "Fine. Maybe you are a witch and even a vampire, but not me. I'm not—"

"Maybe this will help." Seta clapped her hands together, spoke a few strange words and placed her fingertips to Malaika's temples.

Scorching heat seared Malaika's head before everything went black.

"Grandma Mahdi!" Malaika ran inside the small house without bothering to knock, impatient to see her grandmother. She'd just turned four and knew Grandma Mahdi would have a gift for her. She sped past the small living room into the kitchen, where she found Grandma Mahdi sitting at an oak table, cracking almonds out of their shells and depositing them into a cobalt blue bowl.

"There's my baby," she said with a warm smile as Malaika eased her small body into a chair next to her. The smile wavered as Malaika's mother stepped into the kitchen.

"Malaika! You are supposed to knock before—"

"My grandbaby can enter my home anytime she feels the need," Grandma Mahdi said sternly, cutting off her daughter's reprimand.

Helen Jordan squared her shoulders, clearly unhappy with having been cut off. "She is still my daughter, Mother, and I will raise her to act appropriately."

"She is acting appropriately," Grandma Mahdi said with a kind laugh as she winked at Malaika, "for a four-year old."

Helen rolled her eyes and straightened a barrette clamped at the bottom of one of Malaika's many braids. "I'll be back to get her as soon as my shift ends." She walked back out of the kitchen, pausing at the door to issue a command over her shoulder. "Don't be filling her head with all that hoo-hoo nonsense."

Malaika frowned as she picked up the angry tone in her mother's voice and stayed silent until she heard the front door close. "Why is Mama so mean?"

Grandma Mahdi chuckled and gave a dismissive wave of her wrinkled, brown hand. "Your mother is full of anger, child. She'll be that way until the day she dies if she doesn't learn to accept."

"To accept what?" Malaika crinkled her brow in confusion, and looked at her grandmother expectantly.

Grandma Mahdi sighed as she cracked the last almond shell and dropped the nut into the bowl. "Everything, sweetheart, everything. She must learn that the world does not always work as we want it to, and that not everyone you love is going to love you. And not everything in this world makes sense." Grandma Mahdi glanced in her direction and smiled. "Don't you worry about your mama, baby. She can't keep you from your callin'."

"What is my calling?" Malaika scrunched up her face, even more confused. Her grandma was always talking about her calling, or her special gifts she would receive when the time was right. That was usually when her mother picked her up and took her home, telling her not to listen to one word her grandmother spoke. But her mother wasn't here now to pick her up and take her away. "Tell me."

Grandma Mahdi placed a warm hand against her small cheek and shook her head. "Not yet, angel. If I tell you too much and you tell your mother, she'll never let me watch you again." Sadness entered the older woman's brown eyes and was met with a matching frown.

"I can keep a secret!" Malaika bobbed her head up and down enthusiastically, eager to chase away the sadness on her grandmother's face.

"Very good, child. You'll need to." Grandma Mahdi smacked her hands together to brush off the fragments of almond shells left on them, and twisted her frown into a smile. *"Are you ready for your favorite treat?"*

Malaika looked at the bowl of nuts and remembered the tasty treat she'd been given during her last visit. *"Yes!"*

"And you remember our rule?"

"Don't tell Mama the recipe!"

"Correct." Grandma Mahdi's eyes lost their sparkle for a moment, that same sadness washing over her again, but it didn't last very long. She reached out, palm up, and Malaika placed her small hand into hers. Excitement burst through her as they placed their joined hands over the bowl of almonds. *"Remember the recipe?"*

Malaika nodded, and was rewarded with a loving smile.

"Then say it with me."

Together, she and Grandma Mahdi said the rhyming words, and the funny words that didn't sound English at all, and Grandma Mahdi released her hand as heat grew from her palm. Malaika watched as a ray of white light shot from Grandma Mahdi's palm, into the bowl. More funny words were spoken and Grandma Mahdi flicked her wrist. When she was done, she scooted the bowl toward her.

Malaika licked her lips as she reached into the bowl and pulled out a few warm, cinnamon-covered almonds. *"You make the best roasted almonds, Grandma Mahdi."*

"And someday you can," her grandmother said softly as she looked at her adoringly, *"and so much more than that."*

Malaika blinked the room into focus as the memory fled. She wasn't four years old, sitting in her grandmother's kitchen. She was twenty-five and sitting in the back room of a church, being interrogated.

"What did you remember?" Seta stood before her. A knowing smile adorned her beautiful face.

Malaika blinked again to clear her mind, but the memory was still there, so clear it could have happened yesterday. "My grandmother. She..."

"Yes?"

"She could roast almonds just by saying a few words and holding her hand over a bowl of them."

Seta frowned. "Well, I guess there are worse ways one could waste her power."

"I was four years old and they were my favorite snack," Malaika rushed to defend her grandmother as the enormity of what had just happened hit her. "How did she do that? And what did you just do to me?" She rubbed her temples. They didn't feel warm, but her head still felt... violated.

"Your grandmother was a witch, as are you. We have the ability to harness properties of the elements."

Malaika soaked that information in. She'd never understood why she could form the fire balls when she felt threatened. She'd just figured it was another part of her being psychic, another thing she had to hide. "And what about the second thing I asked you?"

Seta shrugged. "I didn't do much to you. I attempted to pull a memory from you, but as a witch, you have a natural armor against such intrusions. All I could do was stir up a memory in your own mind."

"You can't see in my mind?" Relief flooded Malaika's chest. If she could, she would see that she'd been following Craig's presence to the murder scenes. She'd know what Craig had done, and then Jonah would know that her man had left her for some nasty skank that... *Jonah*. He'd just left her in here, not knowing what this woman could do to her. That slimy little—

"Why are you concerned?" Seta's eyes narrowed as she sat on the edge of the table. "Do you have something to hide?"

"No," Malaika snapped quickly. "I'm just trying to understand all this. Maybe my grandmother was a witch. Now that I remember, she did seem to have some sort of magical ability. It's why my mother kept me from her. But if I'm a witch, and what you're saying is true, I should have come into my power at adolescence, correct?"

Seta nodded.

"Then why didn't I? I have visions. That's part of being psychic. I don't have any witchy powers."

"You hurled power balls at Jacob Porter, and you've managed to work a strong sleeping spell on your daughter. You have power. You just haven't been taught how to use it. "

Malaika glanced over to where Deja lay sleeping. "I didn't put a spell on my daughter. I just ..."

"You just what, dear?"

Malaika struggled to find the right words to explain how she'd convinced her daughter to sleep through everything. "I just kind of sent a thought to her, I *hoped* she would sleep through everything until I got her to safety."

"An influence spell."

"But I never said any spell! I don't even know any spells." Malaika shook her head in emphasis and flung an arm out, surprised to find she could move her arms again.

"The witch's net has worn off, which brings us back to Jacob Porter. Why did you attack him?"

"I did not—"

Seta raised a hand, palm out, to cut her off. "You tried to fry him with power balls. Whether you meant to or not, you attacked him. Why? What made you think you had to go to that extreme?"

Malaika took in a breath, thinking back to the moment she'd entered the church. She'd been scared, but not because Jonah had told her a vampire ran the church. She hadn't believed him. She'd sensed something... and seconds before Jacob Porter had aimed his gun on her, she'd felt a chill run the length of her spine. She'd instinctively known he was a danger to her. Of course, she'd sensed darkness in people before, but this... This was so much stronger. She looked up to see Seta smiling knowingly at her.

"You sensed what he was, and that he was a danger to you."

Malaika shook her head, confused. "I sensed danger, yes, but I don't understand what you're referring to. What is he besides a man with a gun?"

"A slayer."

Goosebumps prickled along Malaika's flesh as warning bells sounded in her mind. The word sent a shiver of fear through her body and sparked anger inside her chest. Her palms tingled, aching to form mounds of protective power. "He's a murderer."

"He's a slayer," Seta clarified. "He can sense witches, vampires, demons, and every other kind of not-purely-human. And, yes, he kills them. It's in his genetic makeup to seek us and destroy us."

"Then why do you help him?"

"Because unlike every other slayer, he has a conscience. If he didn't, you would have been dead before you ever got the chance to throw a single ball of power his way."

Malaika felt her eyes go wide in surprise. "But I was holding my daughter. He—"

"Never do that again when you are faced with a slayer," Seta snapped, and her eyes darkened with anger. "A slayer will kill the offspring of their prey without a second thought. You're damned lucky Jacob Porter was the first one you came across."

Malaika gasped as tears filled her eyes. She tried to speak, but her throat was clogged. Deja could have been shot because of her! She looked at her child, so small and defenseless, and a tremor wracked her body.

"Now you realize why you must be trained. Whether you are fully willing to embrace it or not, you are a witch, and even if you don't want to accept it, there are others out there who will accept it. Unfortunately, their version of accepting it means they'll also accept their impulse to kill you."

"But why?" Tears fell down Malaika's face as she hitched in a shaky breath. "Even if I am a witch, I haven't done anything to deserve being hunted like an animal."

"But you could, and you could do it easily." Seta fixed a hard stare on her. "Some of our kind abuse their power. They use it to hurt humankind instead of to help. They are the ones who blacken our name and bring hunters down upon us. Not just slayers. Those are born to hunt us. These evil beings do so much blatant evil, they cause regular humans to hunt us down. Like in the Salem Witch Trials."

Malaika cringed as an image of sinking under water flashed through her mind. For the first time in her life, she made the connection. "That has something to do with my fear of water, doesn't it?"

Seta's eyes widened briefly before she nodded her dark head. "Quite a few modern day witches fear water. It's due to drowning during the trials in a previous life."

"Do you fear water, too?"

"No." Seta shook her head slowly, her dark eyes narrowed. "I have no phobias."

Malaika swallowed hard, suddenly uneasy. There was something threatening in the vampire-witch's tone. "So you weren't drowned during the trials?"

"No." Seta shrugged. "But not all witches were drowned in past lives. And not all witches lived in the places those sort of things happened. During this life I came from Spain, and I believe I may have in my past lives as well."

"So I was just lucky, I guess."

"Yes, you were lucky. You could have been burned alive or worse." Seta stood straight and placed her hands on her hips, ignoring Malaika's sharp intake of air. "We've established that you can do influence spells and detect slayers. Both will serve you well, as will the visions, once we fine tune your ability."

"You can do that?"

"*We* can do that. You must open your mind fully and embrace the entirety of what you are." She narrowed her eyes. "If I am to be your teacher, there can be no secrets between us. I need to know everything, starting with these visions you've had of the were-hyenas."

Malaika wiped a sweaty palm against her jeans-clad leg, remembering the discussion Jonah had earlier with the vampires and his brother. "Were you guys serious about that?"

Seta grinned slightly, just a barely visible upturn of her lips. "If witches and vampires exist, why can't shape-shifters?"

Malaika's stomach rolled, and she bent forward, suddenly light-headed. If she was sensing Craig at the crime scenes and shape-shifters were there... What had Craig gotten himself into? And could whatever he was messing around with find her and Deja through him?"

"What is it, Malaika?"

She glanced up at the woman standing before her, the vampire-witch who oozed power. The woman who looked at her through accusing eyes and despite her power, could not hide her suspicion. She recalled how Seta had promised to drain her of information and report back to Jacob Porter, the slayer. She would allow this woman to teach her how to use her abilities, but she wouldn't trust her. She couldn't. And she couldn't trust the man who'd left her and her child alone with a vampire-witch either. The man who'd jumped out of the way to allow his brother a clear shot at her.

With anger coursing through her veins, she met the vampire-witch's eyes. "Nothing. I'm just overwhelmed by all this stuff I'd always believed was fairytale nonsense."

Seta peered at her, seeming to study her over before shrugging her shoulders dismissively. "It helps to not pay attention to anything you may have seen in a movie or television show, or might have read in a book. You'll find that real paranormal beings are different in various ways."

"So I've realized. I always thought witches had green skin and warts."

"Only the ugly ones," Seta quipped with a smile that didn't reach her suspicious eyes. "I'm concerned about your visions."

Malaika tried not to squirm in her seat. "Why is that?"

"You haven't been trained, and until today, were not aware of what you are. You should only be having visions of matters pertaining to you or someone you know." The vampire-witch crossed her arms and tilted her head to the side. "Who is killing these people?"

Malaika tried to swallow but found her mouth had went bone dry. "I don't know. I can't see any faces." And that was the truth, despite her sensing Craig's presence. And no matter what Craig's faults, he was not responsible for killing anyone. He'd been killed himself... No. According to Grandma Mahdi's spirit, Craig had survived his attack.

Unease clawed at Malaika's gut. Why hadn't he come home? Shame could have kept him away. She didn't know what happened after the end of her vision. He might have stayed with the woman who lured him to that building. Maybe she belonged to some weird cult and had sucked him in. Maybe the murders were part of some sick ritual. It would explain his presence there, but Craig wouldn't be a part of anything that involved murder. He was a bastard. A liar, and a cheat, definitely. But a killer? No.

But why would he have not visited Deja? He could leave her without a problem, but his own daughter? No. Despite his faults, Craig would not just abandon his child like that. There had to be something—or someone—preventing him from seeing her.

"Are you sure there isn't anything you're not telling us about these visions?"

Malaika looked into Seta's eyes and shook her head. Her newly-found witchy sense warned her that the woman before her was dangerous, the type who exacted justice on her own terms. Her witchy sense was also telling her Craig was directly tied in with all that had been happening, and until she knew just how, she was better off keeping it a secret. Or else Deja's daddy would be dead for sure, and a portion of his blood would be on her hands. She might want the jerk castrated, but not killed. "I don't know why I'm having the visions. I don't know any of the victims, and I can't see the killer."

Seta studied her silently for a long moment, then sighed. "I need to see what you're seeing."

"How can you do that? You said you can't extract another witch's memory."

"Seta gave her the same grin she imagined a cat would give a trapped mouse. "You can share it with me."

"H-how?"

Seta closed her eyes briefly and snapped her fingers. Malaika's chair turned sideways and the chair Jonah had been sitting in earlier vanished, instantly reappearing in front of hers. Seta stepped over to the vacant chair and sat, facing Malaika. "Let me in."

The vampire-witch held out her right hand, palm up, and waited.

Malaika took a deep breath and glanced behind her, where her daughter lay. She looked peaceful and unbothered, her small chest rising and falling in a steady rhythm.

"Your daughter is fine, Malaika."

Yeah, until she finds out her daddy is... What? The thought niggled at her, grinding away at her exposed nerves. Something dark was going on with Craig. She knew it. And if she let this powerful witch inside her head, she'd know it too. She and her friends would kill Craig. They'd kill Deja's father. And she'd be the one who led them to him. How could she do that to her baby girl?

"Do you wish to hide something from me?"

"No!" Malaika responded too quickly as she whipped her head back around to face the witch in front of her, and Seta's eyes narrowed. "I ... I'm just not sure I can do whatever it is you expect me to be able to do. This is all new to me."

Seta's frown wavered for a moment before she straightened in her seat and held her hand out firmer. "This is part of your training, and you need to be trained if you want to make sure you never kill an innocent by accident."

Malaika blinked, ran Seta's words back through her head. Could she possibly do such a thing? Seta nodded as if reading her mind and made a *come here* gesture with her hand before straightening it again.

Malaika took a breath, cleared her mind the best she could and slowly, cautiously, placed her hand on Seta's, palm to palm. The sensation of warmth coming from Seta's hand surprised her, and she struggled to keep from running. She could feel the witch drawing something out of her, and the sense grew stronger as the fingertips of the witch's left hand were pressed against her temple.

"With your free hand, touch your fingertips to my temple," Seta instructed.

Reluctantly, Malaika did as she was told. Heat enveloped her body, an electric currant pulsated between the points where she connected to Seta. As heat filtered into her body, images rolled through her mind. She could feel them being pulled away, and transferred into Seta's mind. Her information was being shared, much like the way information could be shared on a computer.

Malaika held Seta's gaze, determined not to let the witch see her unease. The vampire-witch filtered through her memories, much like sifting through files, and located her visions. Malaika could no longer see Seta as images from her visions flashed through her mind, seemingly right before her eyes. The vampire-witch was draining her of every vision she'd ever had, even silly little pointless ones that made no sense. It was a complete invasion.

Malaika tried to pull away, but couldn't move her body. She was frozen in place by the currant streaming through her body. But she recalled Seta's earlier statement. A witch could not invade another witch's mind. If she chose what to show and what to conceal ...

Malaika envisioned a wall of strong, silver bricks in her mind. Each brick was laced with protective power, completely impenetrable. Behind that wall, she forced every vision and sensation she'd had of Craig. The witch draining her of information could find him in her memory bank, and could feel her emotions for him, but she was not tapping into any vision concerning him. The only information she'd get involving the murders would be the vision of Jonah's partner being attacked. She gave that one freely.

What seemed like hours passed as Seta drained her of every inch of information she could. Malaika felt the other witch searching inside her head, seeking out something in every crook and cranny, but she couldn't penetrate the wall, couldn't even seem to see it. Her limbs started to shake uncontrollably and cold dampness clung to her back. She felt Seta start to withdraw, and then she felt nothing at all.

SIX

Jonah sprang forward as Malaika's eyes rolled back in her head and she slumped sideways out of the chair. He'd barely managed to slide under her before she hit the floor. "What the hell?"

Seta shook her head as if coming out of a trance and stood from her seat to kneel at their side. Jonah cradled Malaika on his lap while Seta ran her hand over the witch's forehead, her eyes closed. "What are you all doing in here?"

"We wondered what the hell was taking so long," Jake answered for the small group assembled in the room. "It's been hours."

Seta's eyes opened as a frown marred her beautiful face. "She was supposed to be sharing her visions with me, but I could tell there was something hidden in her mind. I didn't realize I spent so much time searching for it."

"What did you do to her?" Jonah couldn't bite back the anger in his tone, despite knowing Seta was a volatile vampire-witch with a hair-trigger temper. When she pierced him with a lethal glare, he held her gaze steadily. "If you hurt her—"

"Jacob, you might want to educate your brother on how to respect his elders," the vampiress, who didn't look a day over eighteen, snarled.

"Joe, cool it, dude," Jake said softly, but his hand was already reaching toward his lower back where a gun specially equipped for killing vampires rested. "Seta, I think you do need to tell us what's going on here."

"She's just drained," Seta answered, giving Jonah a narrow-eyed glare as she rose to a stand and turned toward Jake. "Are you going to shoot me, Jacob?"

Nyla rested her hand on Jake's shoulder, and he dropped his hand back down to his side. "Not unless you give me reason to. Don't ever threaten my brother."

"You know I don't threaten, Jacob, and if I wanted him hurt, he'd already be bleeding. Same for the witch. She's just not strong enough yet to take a long psychic drain."

The two stared each other down for a long, tense moment, and though he couldn't see Seta's face from where he was positioned behind her, Jonah knew Jake never blinked an eye. Until his gaze changed direction to rest on Deja. "Why hasn't she woken up yet?"

Every head in the room, with the exception of the still-unconscious Malaika, turned toward Deja. The little girl was resting soundly on the cot. Though she was breathing, it was apparent something was wrong. Full night had fallen and she'd been asleep since daylight without moving a muscle.

"Malaika isn't conscious. The hold over her daughter shouldn't be this strong," Seta said as she walked with Jake and Christian to the side of the room, to hover over the cot.

Unease crept through Jonah's gut, and he twisted to take off his jacket one-handed while keeping a hold on Malaika's lifeless body. Nyla bent over him and helped to remove his jacket, then balled it up into a makeshift pillow.

"Thanks," he said softly as he lowered Malaika to the floor, his jacket cushioning her head, then rose to join the others.

Seta sat on the cot, at Deja's side, running her hands over her body. They slowed as she reached the little girl's neck and inched over her small face. "An influence spell shouldn't have put the girl in this deep of a sleep," she murmured. "Her energy level is unusually low for a child her age. I wonder how many spells her mother has worked on her."

Anger surged through Jonah's blood and he stepped toward the witch, but was blocked by Jake's arm. "Calm down, bro."

"Your brother is becoming a nuisance," Seta stated. Her jaw set hard before turning her attention back to Deja. "This girl is much too weak for my liking."

"Malaika didn't do a damn thing to harm her."

"Joe, you've only known the woman how long?"

WITCH'S NET

Jonah stared at his brother in disbelief, his blood growing hotter. "How long did you know her"—he jerked his head in Nyla's direction—"before you *married* her? You're one to talk."

Jake's eyes widened in offense, his mouth twisted into a sneer. "I've known Nyla a whole hell of a lot longer than you think, definitely a hell of a lot longer than you've known that witch." Nyla put a hand on his shoulder and he seemed to calm. With a conferring look at his wife, he put his arm down, no longer blocking Jonah. "Nobody's accused her of anything yet. Just chill your ass out."

Jonah stared between his brother and Nyla, knowing there was something Jake was hiding from him. He didn't know Nyla before she'd met up with him while searching for Curtis Dunn. He knew it because Jake had called him and asked for him to dig up everything he could find on Nyla Katt. The woman was a ghost on paper. He hadn't found a single scrap of evidence she existed while running the search. And thinking of Curtis Dunn, he still didn't know what came of their search or what really happened in Hicksville. As soon as he knew Deja was alright, he intended to get some answers.

"I can infuse her with some of my power and see if that helps," Seta suggested, breaking into his thoughts.

"What will that do to her?"

Seta met his gaze. "Don't worry, Mr. Porter, being a witch is not a disease one catches. Not that being a witch is a sin," she muttered angrily as she turned her attention back to Deja, and rested her hands over the young girl's chest.

Jonah looked at his brother for reassurance, and the younger Porter nodded his head, indicating Deja would be fine. Jake's reassurance did a little to ease his mind as he saw the yellow glow of power grow from Seta's palms, but not enough to keep a trickle of sweat from sliding down his back. He balled his hands into fists to keep from fidgeting nervously and offered up a silent prayer for Deja's well-being.

The light from Seta's hands spread over Deja's small body, flickered, then disappeared. Deja gasped and opened her eyes. The sight of three strangers standing over her induced a small cry from her throat and she quickly jerked into a sitting position. Before Jonah could take a step, her big green eyes fixed on him and she jumped from the cot, launching herself at him. "Who are they? Where am I? Where's Ma—"

Jonah rubbed a hand on the little girl's head as she loosened her arms from around his thighs and glanced at where her mother lay resting on the floor. "Your mom is going to be fine, Deja, and these are friends." He glared at Seta, not giving a damn if she could break him in two with a simple snap of her fingers. The witch had better not harm one hair on the child's body. He'd kill her himself, even if he had to come back from the dead to do it. "No one here will hurt you."

Deja looked around, studying each one of the strangers before turning her gaze back to Jonah. With the pink stuffed unicorn he'd bought her fisted tightly in one little hand, she raised her arms up. Jonah scooped her up effortlessly and held her tight. "You hungry, sweetheart?"

"I want fries."

Jonah chuckled, a little tension easing from his shoulders. "Of course you do. Let's get you and your mom back home, if that's alright with our friends."

"Actually, I'll need to talk to Malaika first," Jake cut in.

"Interrogate her, you mean."

"Do you want to keep finding chewed up—" Jake glanced at Deja and didn't finish his sentence. "She's the one with the answers right now."

"Didn't your little commando witch over there get enough information when she mind-raped her?"

"I did no such thing!" Seta exclaimed. "She gave me every drop of information I gleaned, willingly."

"See, I'd believe that if she had been able to pull away from your hold when it got too intense."

Seta looked away and he knew he was right. He shifted Deja's weight in his arms and glanced at his brother over her head. Jake looked away, too, and the action stung. If he couldn't fully trust his own brother to ensure the safety of the hu—But Malaika wasn't a full human, he reminded himself. Not like himself, or Deja. He glanced back down at Deja. Hell. Was she a witch, too? Dammit. What had he done to get in this mess? Why couldn't he be ignorant to the supernatural like millions of other clueless people? Life had seemed a lot easier before he'd learned his brother knew what he was talking about when it came to vampires, shifters, and all that crazy stuff.

And why did he have to feel something for these two? A witch and her adorable, possibly also a witch, daughter. "Does Malaika have to rest or can you do something to wake her? Deja's hungry."

"Seta." Jake deferred to the vampire-witch, and she kneeled at Malaika's side, her eyes closed and brow knit in concentration.

"There's safety in numbers," Christian said softly. The vampire who'd only observed up until then looked at Jake pointedly. There was something going on there, some reason why Jake had come to Christian's church instead of to his own brother, and Jonah sucked in a long, deep breath, barely controlling his anger. Dammit. He would find out what was going on, even if he had to beat it out of his brother. "I'll get the little girl some food."

"Maybe Christian could take Deja with him."

Deja wrapped her arms tighter around Jonah's neck and he shook his head at his brother. "She stays with me."

"It's best she does," Christian said as Jake opened his mouth to speak. "There are more here to protect her in case..." His words trailed off and he stuffed his hands into the pockets of his black pants. "What would you like with your fries, little one?"

Deja rose her head from Jonah's shoulder to peek out at the boyish-looking vampire and a shy smile formed on her little face. "Nuggets."

"Nuggets?"

"Chicken nuggets," Jonah clarified. "You can get them at a McDonald's or Wendy's."

The vampire nodded and left. Jonah turned his attention back to Jake while Seta let her hands hover over Malaika's chest. The witch started to stir.

"You have a lot to explain," Jonah stated firmly. "I want to know what happened in Hicksville and why you're suddenly buddy-buddy with these people."

"These people helped save your life."

"Did they need to? I thought you were some almighty slayer. You couldn't save me yourself?"

The two brothers stared each other down, neither budging until Seta cleared her throat, snagging their attention.

"The junior witch has awakened," she announced as Malaika sat up and rubbed her temples.

"What happened?" Malaika asked. "I feel hungover. I think. I've never actually been hungover before."

Malaika's skin was full of color, her eyes bright and clear. She looked fine. Relief swelled inside Jonah's chest, quickly causing his nearly-smiling mouth to twist into a frown. The woman was a witch. He couldn't forget that despite his gut instinct telling him she was a good person.

"What do you think?"

Seta sighed and took in the scene. They'd moved out of the cramped room and into the sanctuary. Malaika sat in a front pew with Deja close at her side, watching over the girl as she ate the food Christian had brought back from a fast food restaurant. Jonah Porter sat across the aisle, watching the two as a variety of emotions played across his face.

Nyla rested a few rows behind them, stretched out along one of the pews. Christian was near the altar, talking in low tones with a young pregnant woman who had come into the church seeking his guidance.

That left Jacob Porter, who sat next to her in the back row. Never in a million years would she have guessed there'd be a day a vampire-witch and a slayer could sit side by side in a church, of all places, and have a conversation not filled with death threats. It troubled her with its easiness, for it was surely a sign the impending war between good and evil forces drew closer.

"I think this is all a big mess," she finally answered.

"Understatement." Jacob snorted before raising his booted feet to rest on the back of the pew before him. There were shadows under his eyes and his body lacked its usual abundance of raw energy.

"You're spreading yourself too thin, Porter."

"Why do you think I came here for Christian's help?"

"You'd trust a vampire to help protect your child?" Seta's mouth turned up at the corners and she tried to ignore the warmth surrounding her heart. Warm and fuzzy emotions served her no purpose.

"Who better to protect my son than his own people?"

"You think he will be part vampire?"

"Possibly."

Seta pondered the thought. She knew her own grandchild, due any day now as well, would be part vampire, but as for Jake and Nyla's child... There was no telling what traits that child would inherit. Maybe he'd inherit them all. What an amazing warrior he would be for the side of good. If the child could control his own darkness.

"When do you plan on telling your brother about his nephew, and more importantly, about yourself?"

Jacob rested his head along the back of the pew and closed his eyes, his throat bared to her attack. Seta's eyes widened, acknowledging how deeply the man who lived and breathed to battle her kind had grown to trust her. Never before learning the truth about Nyla would he have made himself such an easy target.

"He knows I'm a slayer."

"That's the easy part," Seta said softly, almost a whisper. "What about the rest?"

"It's not easy, Seta." He opened one greenish-brown eye and peered at her. "Jonah is the only member of my family who never wrote me off as a stark-raving freak. If he knew what Curtis did to me—"

"He will love you anyway. He's your own blood."

"So are my parents, and they don't give a flying fuck if I live or die."

Seta closed her eyes and swallowed hard, the tortured pain seeming to come straight up from Jacob's soul and through to his voice tore at her heart. She'd given her life—literally—to protect her son, and could never in a million centuries understand how any mother couldn't love her own child. "Even if by chance he couldn't accept it, you know you'll always have Nyla. And your... friends."

Jacob met her gaze and an awkward moment of silence passed between them. Seta nearly laughed at her own stupidity. She was like Cain telling Abel to just forget about the whole murder thing. They could still be buddy-buddy no matter what.

"Enough touchy-feely counseling time," Jake muttered, straightening in the pew. "Let's get back on track. Were-hyenas. In Baltimore. Dead bodies piling up, and my brother is smack-dab in the middle of it and just happened to pick up a witch and her kid along the way."

"A witch and child he is growing attached to," Seta added as she followed his troubled gaze to where it roamed back and forth between the three.

"I don't like it."

"Because you genuinely sense a threat from her, or is your opinion bigoted?" Seta couldn't help but let the irritation she felt slip through her tone.

"What did you see when you broke into her mind?" Jacob asked, ignoring her question.

"I did not force my way into—"

"I'm not complaining, Seta. It's exactly what I wanted you to do."

Seta growled a little, easing some of her frustration. She may have been manipulative, but she'd been given the information she filtered freely, even if she held Malaika in the psychic link a little longer than the younger witch had wanted.

Jacob turned his face toward her, his eyebrows raised in expectation.

Seta recalled the snatches of information she'd received from the psychic drain and told him what she knew. "Her mother and grandmother didn't get along well, so she wasn't allowed enough time with her grandmother to properly learn about who she was or what she would become. The grandmother seemed to have no ill intent, not an evil bone in her body. Malaika led a pretty normal life with her mother and father. Good student, athletic, creative, but she didn't use her powers to gain anything."

"What has she used her powers for?"

"From what I could gather, she's pretty much only tapped into her magic by accident. Influence spells, which are spells invoked through concentrated thought, have been used. You already know about the sleeping spell. She's used a healing influence spell a few times when her child has been sick. Other than that, the only magical abilities she's used have been her raw, untrained psychic powers, and a few times she has defended herself with the power balls."

"I understand her using the power balls with me," Jacob commented. "I'm a slayer and she's a witch. It's natural. When else has she used them?"

"She had a boyfriend who tried to beat her," Seta answered and Jacob balled up his fist with a sneer of disgust that she was sure matched her own. "And once during a very heated argument with her mother, she felt the power starting to come to life. She broke away and locked herself in another room so she could control it."

"So she doesn't enjoy using her powers for dark purposes," Jacob surmised.

"You're forgetting that she's went through life thus far unaware of the havoc she could wreak. Who knows how she would have used her powers if she understood the depth of them."

"I'm not forgetting," Jacob replied, looking at his brother. "I'm just hoping. That fool down there is sprung on her."

"I noticed. Her and the little girl. Your brother appears to be a very decent, caring young man."

"Yeah, but unfortunately, when he falls, he falls fast. And hard. Very, very hard. I don't want this... *woman*... ripping his heart out. Figuratively or literally."

They sat in silence for a moment before Jake yawned and moved his neck side to side, loosening a kink. "Did you tap into her visions of the murders?"

"Yes. She saw the victims entering the places they were killed, and she saw the were-hyenas chewing on the bodies after they'd been killed."

"She didn't actually see the murders?"

"No, and she didn't look through her own eyes." A cold chill careened down Seta's spine as she met Jake's wide-eyed gaze. "She's viewing these scenes through someone else's eyes."

"Whose?"

"I couldn't tell, and believe me, I searched. Do you know what a silver wall is?"

Jacob blinked slowly. "No."

"A witch, even an untrained witch, has the ability to build defenses, to shield herself in different ways."

"I take it a silver wall is a wall of defense?"

"Pretty much." Seta narrowed her eyes on the witch sitting in the front pew, stroking her child's hair. "It's a wall that witches and talented psychics can build inside their mind to block out intrusion. It's an ideal place to keep your darkest secrets. Being a slayer, you were born with one surrounding your entire mind."

Jacob's eyes widened in surprise, then narrowed again as he zeroed in on the witch they were discussing.

"Malaika had a silver wall in her mind?"

"I think so." She met Jacob's now confused gaze. "I couldn't see it, of course, but I'm powerful enough to sense when there's something there out of my reach. Any other witch probably wouldn't have suspected a thing. She did a very good job of erecting it."

"Does this silver wall have anything to do with her passing out?"

"I was determined to find what she was hiding. She was determined not to let that happen."

"She used every last drop of her power to keep that wall up, until she pretty much shorted out and you had access to nothing."

"Correct." Seta held Jacob's narrowed-eyed gaze for a long moment, then they turned their heads in unison to study the witch at the front of the church.

"What the hell was she hiding?"

SEVEN

Adrenaline spiked as the man's lust turned into fear. It was dawning on the man that he wouldn't be experiencing pleasure with the woman who'd led him there. What he'd be experiencing was far from that...

Malaika shot out of the pew, jerking to a stand. Out of the corner of her eye, she saw the others quickly rise, reacting to her sudden movement. Deja was tugging at her and, saying something. She tuned her out, focusing on the snatch of thought that had invaded her mind, tried to snatch onto it again, but it faded fast and the sense of death took its place. And the knowledge that Craig was out there somewhere. She felt the tug so strongly she took an involuntary step forward before being halted by the sharp bark of Jacob Porter's voice.

"You see something?"

She took a deep breath, tamped down the overpowering sense Craig was in trouble, and blinked her eyes to bring her surroundings back into focus. Jacob, Jonah, and Seta stood before her, their brows crinkled, eyes wary, suspicious. She expected those types of looks from two of them. Not Jonah. Then she remembered how he'd left her alone to be interrogated by the witch, and had easily, quickly, stepped away from her to allow his brother a better shot. She almost laughed, disgusted by her foolishness.

"I asked you a question, witch."

Maybe it was from being mentally exhausted, or the hunger clawing at her belly. Maybe it was the way he said the word *witch*, making it sound like a racial slur, but she'd had enough. With no thought to repercussions, Malaika balled up her fist and rammed it straight into Jacob Porter's face.

"How's that for an answer?" she snapped as Jacob's head jerked back. Pain ricocheted through her hand and she wrung it out while bracing the rest of her body for the blow she knew was coming.

Jacob Porter righted himself, touched his cheek and checked for blood. She thought she heard Seta laugh, but didn't dare take her eyes off the man she'd just popped. Jacob looked at his blood-free hand, then raised his eyes to her. When they narrowed, she instinctively shoved Deja behind her.

Jacob lunged, but didn't make it very far. Jonah stepped in front of her and blocked his brother with his arm. "You had that coming, Jake."

"What?" The slayer's eyes widened in disbelief. "You're taking up fo—"

"Give her a little respect."

"That's rich coming from the man who led me to my own interrogation," Malaika snapped. She ignored the look of surprise on Jonah's face. What? Did he actually expect her to be grateful he was defending her now? Not a chance in hell. She'd had enough of men walking all over her and not expecting her to bite their hand when they deemed to treat her nicely for one hot minute. Screw that. She was over it.

The urge to locate Craig tugged at her again, stronger than before. She looked at the three people standing before her. A slayer, a vampire-witch, and a homicide detective. It would be stupid to refuse their help. People were dying and if she had any information that could help end the murders, she'd be evil for withholding it. "I've sensed another..." She glanced at Deja, then back at the trio before her. "I feel the urge to go. I can lead you to the scene."

Seta cocked her head to the side. Jonah's eyes widened. Jacob's narrowed. "Already dead?" he asked.

"Probably. I never seem to make it in time." And standing here isn't helping, she thought, and did her best to send the message with her eyes.

Judging by the irritation in Jacob Porter's gaze, he got the message loud and clear. "Let's go."

Malaika watched as he walked over to the corner of the sanctuary where his wife was sitting with the vampire who ran the church. He kissed her goodbye and spoke sternly to the vampire. He was a slayer, and according to Seta, designed to kill supernatural beings. Yet, he was leaving his very pregnant wife with a vampire and from the looks of it, instructing that vampire to guard her. From what? And why would he entrust someone he obviously cared about to a vampire?

When he turned away, his gaze met hers, and was filled with so much contempt, Malaika's palms sweat. As he neared, his gaze shifted to Deja. "Your daughter can stay here with Christian and Nyla. She'll be safe."

"No damn way," she responded as Deja wrapped her thin arms around her hips. "My daughter stays with me."

He looked between Deja and her, and let out a very frustrated sigh before turning toward the exit door. "Fine. But no sleeping spells."

"What— "

Jonah's hand came down on her arm, halting her. "Trust him on this. Her energy level... You don't want to accidentally do any damage to her," he said softly so Deja couldn't hear.

Malaika looked at Seta and was met with a warning look before the powerful witch turned and followed Jacob toward the door.

"What about her energy level?" She shook Jonah's hand off her arm, ignoring the tingle of awareness it caused.

"Just... no more spells." He turned toward the door. "Come on."

Malaika hoisted Deja onto her hip and followed, unease gnawing at her gut. The look on his face was one of concern. For her daughter. She glanced down at Deja, studying the little girl, and wondered what she wasn't being told.

The worry still lingered with her as Jonah pulled his car over in the dark alley two blocks away from the building she sensed Craig in. It had been Jacob's idea that she and Deja ride with Jonah, and that he and Seta follow behind them in his Malibu. The ride had been tense, the only talking coming in the form of her giving Jonah directions.

Jacob pulled his car to a stop behind them and got out, followed by Seta. He came up to them along her side of the car and opened the door.

"You, out." He barked the command tersely.

She looked from Jonah to his brother, and folded her arms. "I don't jump at your commands," she informed the younger Porter.

She'd barely managed to finish the statement before Jacob's hand clamped onto her upper arm and she was tugged free of the car.

"Hey!" Jonah quickly stepped out of his side of the car and slammed his door shut before rounding the hood. "Take it easy, Jake."

"I will just as soon as your girlfriend here cans the attitude."

"You don't have to be so rough."

"Can I talk to you for a minute?" Not waiting for an answer, Jacob released her arm to grab hold of his brother's and led him away from the car. Malaika rubbed her arm and watched as the two brothers spoke closely. She couldn't hear their words, but judging by their expressions and harsh tones, the two were clearly arguing.

She heard a soft tsk and glanced over at Seta to see the vampire-witch shaking her head, her arms folded below her ample breasts. "And to think for hundreds of years, men ran everything." She clapped her hands loudly. "Boys! We are working within a short window of time here!"

Both Porters swiveled their heads toward Seta, gave each other one last glare, and walked back toward the car. "You remember what I said, little brother!"

"Yeah, yeah, yeah," Jacob griped as he grabbed Malaika's arm and led her away. She looked back toward the car, concern for her child bursting through her chest.

"Your little girl will be fine," Seta said as she followed them toward the direction of the building. "Jonah will guard her with his life."

"I thought you couldn't read my mind."

"I don't have to. I am a mother, too. I know the constant worry."

Malaika's feet came to an abrupt stop, frozen by shock. There was a sharp tug on her arm and she was moving forward again. Jacob Porter was not a patient man. "How does a vampire have a child?" she asked as she was pulled along.

"I wasn't born a vampire," Seta responded in an amused tone.

Meaning she'd had a child before she was turned into one. Chills crept along Malaika's spine as she wondered how long ago that was. And how many other vampires and beasts like the ones she'd seen in her visions prowled the streets.

Her breath caught in her throat as they neared the back of the building. Craig was inside. She felt it with every fiber of her being. She also felt impending doom. Fear slithered through her body, squeezing tightly around her heart. Whatever Craig was doing in that building, it wasn't good. It couldn't be, because in that building dwelled death.

Jacob came to a stop behind the building and cocked his head to the side. During that short period of time, the sense of Craig being inside evaporated. It was as if he'd simply disappeared.

Jacob frowned and turned a questioning gaze toward Seta. "Well?"

Seta shook her head. "Nothing. You?"

"Something was here, and not that long ago. Like, a second ago, actually." He narrowed his eyes as he turned them on Malaika. "Ready?"

Malaika swallowed, or tried to. Her throat was bone dry. Jacob Porter couldn't possibly have detected Craig there. He only had the power to suspect supernatural beings. And why would Craig be hanging around with... those dog things? Were-hyenas?

"Malaika?"

"Imagine that, you know my name," she said, fighting the waver in her voice. "And all this time I thought you'd assumed my name was Witch."

His facial expression didn't change, apparently stuck in annoyed mode. "You ready?"

"For what?" Then it dawned on her. "Wait. You expect me to go in there?"

"Why else would we be here?"

"But it's a crime scene!"

"Not until the police arrive, it isn't." With that remark, he kicked down the back door and swept his arm out, indicating for her to precede him inside.

Malaika held her breath, waiting for alarms to split the calm night air. They didn't. "Well, that was certainly discreet. Thank goodness there was no alarm."

"If the doors were armed, there'd probably be motion sensors inside, too. If there were motion sensors inside, it'd make it awfully damn hard for somebody to be killed inside without tripping them." He swept his arm out again, his eyes lit with impatience.

Malaika turned toward Seta, and could tell from the woman's stone-like expression, she'd get no help from her. She took a deep breath and stepped inside the building. It was pitch black inside and for that she was thankful. If the stench filling the space was any indication, she didn't want to see what was inside the building. Especially not when she knew a dead person lay in there somewhere. She'd seen enough in her visions to know the sight would be gruesome.

"Why do I have to come in here with you? I'm not a detective."

"No, but you're connected with this somehow," Jacob answered as he and Seta stepped in behind her.

Alarm slammed into her gut at his choice of words, but before she could question his intent, energy pulsated in the air. She turned just in time to see the broken door magically rise and reconnect to the door frame.

"How did you do that?"

"Be a good student, little witch, and you will learn in due time," Seta said with a hint of boredom, "and as for you, Jacob, kicking down the door really was unnecessary when you have two witches with you."

Jacob shrugged. "I suppose it'd be too much to ask you to use some of your witch skills to find the damn light switch."

"Well, since you asked so nicely…" The room suddenly flooded with light. Enough light to show Malaika the dead body lying six feet ahead of her on the concrete floor.

A large hand covered her mouth to muffle the scream that erupted from her throat as she took in the man's body. More notably, the bloody and mutilated cavity where his chest should have been.

She continued to scream and Jacob continued to muffle the sound, occasionally tossing in a soothing word or two. The realization of his concern broke through the moment of horror, surprising Malaika out of the fit of hysteria. Why would the slayer who'd shown nothing but distaste for her be so… nice?

"You good now?" he asked as her screams died.

She nodded once, and his hand moved away from her mouth. She breathed in deep, instantly regretting it as the foul odor of decay assaulted her. With a cry of disgust she bent forward, fighting back down the bile threatening to rise. It may have been her first time actually stepping inside a crime scene, but even she knew leaving her vomit behind for the police to find would be a bad move.

"Whoa." Jacob grabbed her, and helped her to straighten. "Breathe through your mouth, Malaika. You don't want to throw up at the scene of a murder, or for that matter, leave any other kind of DNA."

"Yeah, I figured that," she managed to say into his shoulder. As much as she despised the slayer, leaning into him was better than looking at the dead man on the floor. "I want out of here."

"Not yet. Seta." He nodded toward the witch, a silent command, and once again the pulse of energy filled the air. Stronger than before.

"What is she doing?"

"Reading the body."

"Reading the what?" Malaika turned toward the body and saw Seta kneeling at the dead man's side, her hands resting on his pants, just above the knees. She gagged and quickly turned away. "What can she get off a dead body?" she asked after getting her stomach back under control.

"Last memories," he answered, and gave her a little prod in the direction of the body. "I need to know exactly what you saw down to every minute detail."

Malaika took in a shaky breath, careful to only let air in through her mouth. "I can do that outside."

"Yeah, but I can't get the full picture outside." He looked toward the body. "Tell me how that man died. Tell me who his killer is."

"I don't know who the killer is."

"Then feel around, dammit! You're a witch. You have psychic abilities. Use them."

"I don't know—"

"Put your hands on the body."

"Are you out of your damn mind?" Malaika looked at the body, then back at Jacob Porter's face. The slayer didn't blink an eye. Clearly, he didn't realize how crazy his suggestion was. "I am not touching a dead man!"

"So you'll just let his killer walk?"

"How am I supposed to stop his killer? I see visions, just snatches of the killings."

"And why is that? Why do you see the murders? Not Seta? Not a stronger witch, but you. Why in the hell do you suppose that is?"

"I don't know!" Malaika raised her voice to match Jacob's tone and volume. Unlike him, tears formed in her eyes. Why was he pushing her so hard?

"Come on, sweetheart. You know damn well why you're the one seeing these images."

"I don't—"

He crowded into her personal space, his threatening nearness cut off her protest. "There's only one way an untrained witch would keep seeing these images without purposely casting a spell to do so. What's your connection?"

Malaika gulped. Or tried to. It felt like a large stone was lodged in her throat. She took in Jacob Porter's face as she struggled to think of a response. The eyes slit so narrow she could barely see the color, the mouth set in a tight straight line, the jaw clenched harder than a vise. Looking at that face did nothing to help her think of an answer. All it served to do was scare her to near death. This was the face of a warrior, a killer hell-bent on taking her out if she dared say one wrong word.

Something rustled behind her, and Jacob's gaze left her face to focus over her shoulder. "Well?"

Malaika turned her head to follow his gaze, and saw Seta standing over the dead man's body, brushing her hands together. She carefully avoided the body on the floor, maintaining her focus on the vampire-witch instead. The woman's face was pale, her eyes tired looking. "I could only pull emotions, and a few surface thoughts lingering behind."

"And?" Jacob's tone reeked of impatience. He was not a man who liked to wait.

"The man was overwhelmed with lust, sexual excitement. I believe he followed a woman here, anxious to have sex with her. Then his lust turned into terrible fear." Seta glanced down at the man's body, her full lips turning down into a sad frown. "He experienced tremendous pain, and guilt."

"Well, that goes along with what Jonah told me of Malaika's visions."

Malaika turned to find Jacob's dark stare boring into her once more.

"A beautiful woman no man could deny. Correct?"

Malaika nodded, her stomach queasy as she recalled the vision of Craig leaving her for the Hispanic woman with the weird singing voice.

"We're probably dealing with a damn siren," he announced, taking a moment to rake one large hand through his short brown hair, leaving it in tousled disarray. "A siren, a pack of were-hyenas, and probably some vampires."

"None I know," Seta said shortly.

"Teach your student here how to help us find out which vampires are involved." He jerked his head toward Malaika. "And what the hell it is they're after."

"Come here, Malaika."

"No way." Malaika grit her teeth together, clamping her mouth shut against the threat of vomit as she looked down at the dead man's body. They could torture her until she screamed, but she wasn't touching that damn body.

"I could show you the faces of this man's children."

Malaika's breath stilled on a gasp. A punch in the stomach wouldn't have been as hard of a blow. "You wouldn't."

"I would, and will."

Malaika glanced over at Jacob, received an empty expression back. The slayer jerked his head in Seta's direction, silently ordering her to do as told.

With a shaky breath, and far shakier legs, she gave in and walked the distance to the body. The smell of blood, rich and coppery, overwhelmed her, as did the fuzzy feeling inside her head as she neared.

"Block out the smell," Seta said softly as she neared. "Don't let the sense of death mask the undercurrents."

"What the hell are you talking about?" Malaika's question came out a growl. She stopped beside the body and closed her eyes, no desire to see inside the cavities in the man's chest.

"Kneel down. Touch his leg, or anywhere you're comfortable—"

"That's a joke, right? How could anyone be comfortable touching a corpse?"

"Don't think of it that way. The body is just a shell, a casing for one's spirit. Someone stole this man's life, stole his spirit. There is nothing more valuable than that. Touch the casing of that spirit, draw from it the last remnants of his memory, the last pictures taken with his eyes, delve into his thoughts. Find his killer."

Malaika shook her head, her fingers trembling at the thought of putting them on the man's body. Even if jeans separated her from his decaying flesh, she knew she would still be touching a dead man. "How can I find anything more than you if you're a more powerful witch?"

"You're the one drawn to these murders. You're the one the dead are seeking."

Malaika's eyes snapped open, locking onto Seta's. "They're drawing me to the scenes?" No, they couldn't be. It was Craig drawing her.

Seta shrugged. "It doesn't matter who is drawing you here, it only matters that you are being drawn. The dead will share their secrets with you. Shall I show you the faces of this man's small children?" she asked after Malaika didn't respond.

"No. Don't do that," Malaika said on a defeated sigh. "This is bad enough without those images."

With one last deep inhale—through the mouth, not the nose where the smells would surely upset her stomach—Malaika knelt beside the man's body and slowly placed her trembling hand on his jean-clad thigh.

Melanie's going to kill me. I can't go through with this. Fuck it. I have to. When in my lifetime am I ever going to have the opportunity to get a piece of that?

He looked at the woman before him. Long, silky blonde hair fell between her shoulder blades, dipping low enough to touch her full, round ass. He could see a tribal tattoo on the back of her waist, etched into the flesh exposed between the space where her black studded bra ended and her black leather skirt began. A skirt not even long enough to cover her.

His shaft thickened, painfully hard. *Melanie will never know. I'll buy her something nice. Diamonds. Well, cubic zirconium. She'll be clueless.*

The woman turned, her lush, plump red lips turning up into a seductive smile. Her icy blue eyes were almost sinister. The look in them—the look of a woman who would eat him flesh, bone and all—shocked him for a moment, but the feeling of unease quickly faded away as his gaze lowered to the DD's spilling out of the black lace barely covering her. *She can do whatever she wants to me, even kill me, as long as I die with a mouth full of those.*

"Your wish is my command," she said in that sexy sing-song voice of hers, and licked her lips.

Fear slammed into his stomach, stole his breath. He took in his surroundings. He was in some building, vacant by the look of it, with empty shelves lined along the walls, clutter and debris strewn over the floor. Something was behind him. Something... not quite human. Little Johnny and Norene's faces popped into his mind. They were crying, cuddled close to Melanie... crying over his grave. He glanced back at the woman who'd drawn him to the building. She was perfect, the exact image of what he pretended Melanie looked like when they had their twice-a-month five minutes of sex... and he closed his eyes, holding her image there while liquid fire blazed into his neck, ripping a scream from his body before he thought no more.

Malaika gasped as she felt herself being ripped out of the dead man's mind. Jacob Porter's hand clamped over her mouth and held her close, her back pressed firmly into his chest, and backed her away from the body.

Adrenaline soaked the air. Jacob's heart raced, the quickened tattoo beat against her upper back, matching her own. A quick cursory glance found Seta tucked into a narrow space between a bookshelf and the far wall, her eyes narrow, fists clenched. Something not right had entered the building, its strangeness heightening her senses. The smell of unwashed beast grew strong as the sense of danger closed in.

"Stay here," Jacob whispered into her ear as he released his hold on her to retrieve a gun from the back of his waistband, the same gun he'd pulled on her earlier. He checked the chamber, revealing bullets which looked to be made of pure silver, slid on a silencer he withdrew from an inner jacket pocket, then bent down and pulled up a pant leg to retrieve a small but deadly silver blade sheathed there.

Malaika pressed her back against the side of the bookshelf he'd placed her next to, and did her best to cover herself in shadow. Across the room, a staircase stretched upward. Something dark and twisted was on the second floor and headed down.

"What is it?"

Jacob took his gaze off the staircase to look at her, but for only a second before posturing himself for battle. He raised the gun with both hands, despite still holding the blade in one, and aimed it for the opening to the second floor. "It's were-hyenas," he answered in a low voice, with his back to her. "Hungry, filthy were-hyenas."

Malaika looked back over at the body. For the first time since entering the building, she actually paid attention to the cavity in the man's chest, recalling what she'd seen while standing over it. It had been ripped open, but none of the organs had been chewed. Someone—a vampire?—had killed the man and left his body behind for the were-hyenas. The poor bastard had been left as a feast for them.

Poor bastard, whatever. He walked right into his own death, led by his nasty, greedy dick. Malaika closed her eyes and tried to dispel the images of the man's wife and children from her mind. Those poor people. No, she'd feel no sadness over the man's death, but she would help stop the killings if she could. Not for the ones who'd died, but for the families they were leaving behind.

A board creaked and she opened her eyes, swiveling her head in the direction of the sound to see a man's foot on the top of the stairs. He was followed by more. Men of different sizes and ethnicities crept down the stairs, unaware of Jacob's gun trained on their leader. Some wore jeans and sneakers, others wore suits and dress shoes. All wore the eyes of a starving man as they rested their gazes upon the inviting body on the floor.

By the time the leader, a tall and lanky blond man with a torn muscle shirt, reached the bottom of the stairs, there were nine men behind him. The leader licked his lips and started to smile. Jacob blew his face off before he could finish the task.

The men behind him snarled as his body went down and surged forward. Jacob and Seta pounced from their hiding places and struck. Malaika watched in something akin to awe as they weaved in and out of the group of were-hyenas, avoiding blows and dealing their own. Jacob used his gun and blade. Seta formed fire in her hands and burned her opponents, but they quickly regenerated, their facial features changing from human to animal. Malaika gasped as she saw noses and mouths elongate into muzzles with snapping jaws, and hands morph into claws.

The were-hyenas were fast and strong, but Jacob and Seta held their own. Blood flew as Jacob expertly carved his blade into the beasts' bodies, shooting others while he cut.

Malaika

Malaika stilled, her body frozen cold. *Craig?*

Malaika

He was there with them. In the building. But where? She closed her eyes and reached out with her senses. She couldn't smell anything past blood and filthy beast, but deep in her heart, she sensed his presence. He was above her, on the second floor. Her eyes flew open. Before her, the fight still raged. Jacob had ordered her to stay put, and she knew it was for her own safety. She could form fireballs, but didn't want to take a chance on battling the were-hyenas. There was no way she could make it to the staircase without the beasts seeing her. Or distracting Jacob and Seta, potentially throwing them off their focus to the point they could be harmed. Or killed.

She glanced behind her, saw a small path she could take between rows of metal bookshelves. Slowly, keeping her eyes on the battle to make sure none of the beasts caught sight of her and broke away to catch her, she backed away. It seemed to take forever, with her heart pounding, threatening to explode, but in a matter of minutes, she was at the other end of the large room, and to her left was another staircase.

Quickly, she ran up the stairs, Craig's essence calling to her. He was there! She'd strangle him once she got her hands around his lying, cheating throat. Then she'd deliver him to Jacob for questioning. Maybe let the slayer slap him around a little bit. It would serve him right.

She emerged into a long, empty hallway, and felt with her senses, discerning his location. There. Three rooms to her left. She walked quickly, knowing Jacob and Seta would find her missing soon. Jacob would be furious she hadn't followed his command. Grinning, she realized she was acting like a grade school child, afraid of the big, bad principal. Hell, big bad principals didn't have anything on the blade-wielding slayer.

She closed her hand around the door knob, pushed, and froze. A dark figure stood before an open window, head down, back toward her. He was encased in pale moonlight, but from that angle she couldn't be sure ... "Craig?"

He jumped, escaping the building through the window. "Craig!"

Malaika ran two steps before she was halted. Two strong arms enclosed her, a cold, clammy hand covered her mouth to hold in her scream.

"Where is the child?"

Her heart seized in her chest as the man's question registered. Deja? This man wanted Deja? Deja, who was right outside the building, within his reach? "Wh-what child?" she asked as his hand loosened enough to allow her an answer.

"The child sent to kill us."

Huh? Malaika stilled, pondering the question. Deja was supposed to kill ... What? Vampires? Were-hyenas? She turned her head to see who she was dealing with, but found herself pushed to the hardwood floor.

"Where are they hiding the child?" The man picked her up by her throat, and held her before him. He was tall and thin, with midnight hair and eyes of deep cobalt. He snarled and she saw the tips of two pearly white fangs slip past his thin lips. He actually wasn't a bad looking man, except for the pure evil swimming in the depths of his gaze.

"Who the hell is *they*?" she managed to ask through the grip he had on her neck.

The man growled and flung her from him. She hit the floor hard and what little breath she held escaped her lungs. Pain reverberated through her body, bringing tears to her eyes.

"Don't toy with me, witch. You will find the child and bring it to me."

The hell I will. Malaika narrowed her eyes, the thought of turning an innocent child over to such a beast boiled her very blood. She rose to her knees, her entire body aching with the effort, and faced the man, whom she was now pretty sure was a vampire. "Even if I knew what child you were speaking of, I'd never turn it over to you."

The vampire smiled, a dark and eerie sight. "Would you still protect the child if you knew doing so would earn you a slow, painful death?"

An image flashed into Malaika's mind. It was a dream she'd had when she was younger. Delivering a baby. A beautiful, gorgeous little baby girl. She did not know the parents. One was a tall, golden-skinned man with long, dark hair, and the woman... She was gorgeous, with mocha-colored skin, wavy brown hair, and green eyes that shone with the brilliance of emeralds.

"Where is the child?"

Not born yet, bastard. Malaika let out a breath, realizing that somehow this vampire knew she was to deliver a child... a child he obviously wanted. But how?

He stepped closer. "I will peel your flesh from your bones, if you do not tell me the location of the child."

Malaika rose to a stand and spread her arms wide. She said a silent prayer that God would protect Deja, her heart already aching at the thought of her growing up without parents, but no way in hell was she leading this creature to an innocent child.

"Then I hope you like dark meat, jackass. I'm not leading you to any baby."

The vampire froze, his mouth dropped open. Obviously, he wasn't used to being denied. "You smart-mouthed little witch." He lunged forward.

Something boomed and blinding blue-white light filled the room. Malaika stepped back, covering her eyes as cold wind swept past her. The vampire fled the room. Before she could let out a sigh of relief, she found herself lifted off her feet, captured in a set of muscular arms.

"No!" She beat at her abductor's chest as tears streamed down her face. Realizing she was beating on the equivalent of a steel wall, she closed her eyes and reached deep inside with all her strength. She'd fry the mother—

"Don't, Malaika."

"Jacob?"

"The name's Jake. I'm getting you out of here, sweetheart."

She sagged in relief and allowed Jacob to carry her out of the room. Once they emerged past the light, her eyes refocused. He carried her down the stairs and into the room where they'd found the dead man's body. The room now littered with even more corpses. Seta was on her knees beside one of the were-hyenas, reading his deceased body.

Alarm slammed into Malaika's chest the exact moment Jake's body stilled. The slayer set her down and cocked his head, his hand going for something inside his jacket.

A flash of pain swept through Malaika, and she saw Jonah's face mottled with it. Craig stood over him, his hands wrapped around his neck. "Jonah!"

Jake swept a gun out of his inner jacket, a different one than he'd used earlier, and ran out of the building. Malaika ran on his heels, but froze as she hit the alley and saw two dark figures fighting by the front of Jonah's car. One of the figures—Craig—looked up as Jake neared. He glanced her way, let go of Jonah's throat and vanished with a speed that defied nature as a bullet from Jake's gun zipped through the air, missing purchase.

Jake covered the ground between he and his brother and checked Jonah's vitals.

Malaika reached the car, jerked open the back door, and pulled Deja into her arms. "Deja!" She was weak, her eyes heavy-lidded and drowsy. "Deja, baby! Look at Mommy."

"Mommy?"

"Oh, baby." Malaika held her daughter close, glancing up to see the Porter brothers looking down at her. Jonah rubbed his throat with a hand, his fingers caressing thick red marks left there by his attacker. Jake let out an angry huff of breath.

"She alright?" he asked, his voice gruff.

"Yes. I think so."

"Who the fuck was that, Malaika?"

She glanced down at Deja and let a tear fall free from her eye before kissing the top of her little girl's head. "That was Deja's daddy," she admitted on a whisper, seeing no way she could hide the truth any longer. "But he... he..." She shook her head, trying to grasp what she'd seen. Craig had led her to the building, lured her to the room with the vampire... and jumped out of a second-story window to attack Jonah, and what had he done to Deja? There were no marks on her neck, but she was weak, dazed. "What happened to him?"

"He's a fucking vampire."

EIGHT

"Stay behind me."

Yes, sir. Malaika crossed her arms, warding off the bitter cold clinging to her body. Not that it did any good when she was chilled from the inside. They'd left the building full of death, and split ways. Jonah had taken Seta and Deja back to the church.

Jake had brought her home, and now they slowly crept up the stairwell to her apartment. She'd never been so afraid to go home in her life.

Craig was a vampire. A *pranic* vampire. He sucked the energy out of his victims, and had apparently been doing so to Deja while she slept at night. How could she not have known? Deja had mentioned seeing Daddy in her sleep, but she'd thought it was just in dreams. Why hadn't she sensed him? Why had she been stupid enough to get involved with the creep at all? She couldn't think like that. That creep had given her the most beautiful gift in the world. He'd given her a child, a gorgeous, sweet, innocent child. A child she prayed for as she climbed the last few steps to the third floor, doing her best to ignore the pain in her side. That damned vampire had beat her ass good.

She'd never left her child with anyone outside of her own family before. But she could trust Jonah to care for her. She might have had her misgivings about his intentions earlier in the—geez, had it only been a day since she'd met him?—but she knew he would not harm her daughter. He'd proven that when he moved Deja out of the line of fire at the church. Granted, he hadn't given *her* that much consideration, but he definitely was the type of man who would do all in his power to protect a child from harm.

"Feels clear," Jake announced, and moved aside so she could fit her key into the lock of her apartment door.

He entered first, his gaze sweeping the room while his hands gripped his gun before him. "Get only what you need. We need to get back to the church."

Malaika nodded and stepped inside, checking the wall clock first. It was going on five in the morning. No wonder she was so tired. "Tell me more about pranic vampires," she requested as she walked the narrow hallway to her room, Jake right behind her.

"The term, energy-sucking leeches, pretty much sums it up," he responded, standing against the wall as she rifled through her closet for clothes. "They're greedy bastards, overwhelmed with the urge to satisfy themselves no matter the cost. They're arrogant, and incredibly narcissistic. I'm guessing Craig tended to take more than he gave?"

Malaika glanced up from the duffel she was packing, and caught sight of Jake's raised eyebrows. Was he asking her if Craig took more than he gave sexually, or just in general? Did it matter? The answer to both was a resounding Yes.

"You're not married?"

"No." She tossed a few shirts into the duffel. "Are you here to judge me or help protect my ass until you catch the animals killing these people?" *Until you catch Craig.*

Jake laughed, the sound deep and throaty. "Sugar, I wouldn't dare judge you when it comes to something like that. I'm probably more of a sinner than ... hell, everybody."

She looked into his eyes, gauged his sincerity. There was no condemnation there. "Craig never asked me to marry him, and I didn't push." She tossed the duffel onto the foot of her bed and opened a dresser drawer. "You realize you're kind of being nice to me."

"Is that a bad thing?"

"You weren't nice to me when we first met."

"I saw a witch walk into a building with my brother. My instinct was to kill first, ask questions later."

She turned from the dresser. "You can't ask questions of the dead."

He opened his mouth to speak, looked down at the lace panties in her hand, and turned his head away. "Seta can. And so can you. Speaking of which ..." He turned toward her again, careful to keep his gaze on her face—Malaika held back a grin, amused by the big, bad slayer's obvious discomfort of seeing her undergarments—and cocked his head to the side as if studying her. "What did you read off the dead man's body?"

Malaika shuddered and dumped the panties into her duffel, turning back for her bras and a few pairs of socks. "Seta could have shown me the faces of his children. I saw them anyway."

"I'm sorry."

She stilled, curious as to what caused his change of heart toward her, but shook it off. She needed to hurry up and get back to her baby girl. "The man was a pig. He married, had a few kids, and then basically despised his wife for gaining weight. He saw some blonde hoochie with inflatable breasts and followed her to the building." She opened another drawer and pulled out some jeans. "He actually realized he was going to die and his children's faces flashed through his mind. But you know what his very last thought was?"

"That he hoped he could go out fucking the woman of his dreams?"

Malaika's gaze snapped up to meet his. Disgust churned in her stomach. "What? Is that a common way men want to die or something?"

Jake frowned for a moment, studying her again, then slowly grinned. "I can think of worse ways to die than making love to my beautiful wife, but I can't say it's a dream I long for. What you just described was a siren snaring."

"Sirens? As in, women who sing and draw pirates into the sea and drown them?"

"Sirens are female nymphs, a form of succubi. They have the ability to morph their features, projecting themselves as their intended victim's ultimate fantasy. They make it damned hard to refuse them, even if the victim knows they're walking into a death trap."

So Craig's fantasy woman was some Hispanic bitch, not her, the mother of his child. Malaika slammed a pair of jeans into the duffel, harder than necessary. The action pulled at her sore muscles and she bit back a curse, not wanting the slayer to see how bad she felt. She hated showing weakness.

"I take it Craig didn't see you when you had the vision of him getting snared by the siren?"

Malaika stilled. "How did you know?"

"Not that hard to figure out." Jake shrugged his shoulders. "You told Jonah he'd walked out the door and never came back, and tonight he was there at a murder scene where a siren had lured another man to his death. It explains why you're the one having these visions. It all started with his death, didn't it?"

Malaika nodded, and brushed away an errant tear. "But he's not really dead, is he? He left me and his beautiful daughter for that nasty bitch. How the hell do I tell my daughter that?"

"You don't." Jake crossed his arms and rested the back of his head against the wall, his gaze traveling the length of her. "And you don't pay a second thought to him leaving you for the siren. You're a gorgeous woman, Miss Jordan. If I hadn't already found my own dream woman, my brother and I would probably be arm wrestling for you right now."

She laughed, caught off guard by the unexpected, and bold, compliment. Yet, there had been nothing sexual in his tone or even his gaze. The same gaze he'd averted when she was handling her underthings. Out of respect for his wife, maybe? Maybe there were some decent men left in the world, after all. "You're doing it again."

"Doing what?"

"Being nice to me. Why the change?"

He swallowed, his jaw setting. "I heard your conversation with the vamp before I tossed the UV-bomb. I heard the honesty in your voice. You would die before handing over an innocent."

"Damn straight." She released a yawn she didn't have the strength to hold back. "So now I have your seal of approval?"

"Possibly."

Possibly as in No. The big, bad slayer wasn't going to go all buddy-buddy on her overnight. But at least he no longer glared at her with that cold, calculating look in his eyes, the one which suggested he was thinking of the bloodiest way to destroy her. It was progress.

"You'd better hurry and pack up some clothes for your daughter. You look like you're about to fall asleep standing up."

Pack up some clothes for her daughter, the daughter who'd been attacked by a vampire almost every night for the last several weeks. And she'd been right there across the hall, oblivious. "I can't believe I slept all these nights while Deja was..." She allowed her voice to trail off, unable to speak through the sob pressing to be set free.

"Pranic vampires are shifty little suckers, no pun intended. And this one knew you well enough to know how to mask his presence."

Malaika shook her head, still struggling to comprehend it all. "How did Craig become such a thing? I thought vampires just drank people's blood. But stealing their energy? How?"

"Pranic vampires are actually quite rare. They have to have some trace of psychic ability in them before being turned. And even then, it has to be a pretty psychically powerful vampire who turns them." Jake scratched his chin. "Jonah told me about your vision. It sounds like the siren is drawing people to abandoned buildings, where this psychic vampire is waiting. The vamp kills the victim, then leaves the body behind for were-hyenas to munch on."

"So why didn't this vampire just kill Craig?"

"Because he sensed Craig's psychic ability."

"Why the hell didn't I?" Malaika let out a sigh. "All those years I kept my abilities a secret from him, but he was psychic too? Why didn't he sense his own death approaching?"

"That's a lot of questions coming from a woman so in need of sleep." He jerked his head toward the door. "Finish up. I'll take you to the church to get a little rest, and we'll try to answer those questions in the morn... well, afternoon I guess."

"Alright." She noticed the frown on his face as she passed him to get to Deja's room, but didn't inquire what had brought it on. Like he said, she needed rest. She'd get her answers after she had refreshed her mind with a few hours sleep. "Are you positive Craig can't get to us in the church?"

"The good thing about pranic vampires," Jake said, following her into Deja's small room, "is that unlike regular blood-sucking vamps, they have to be invited inside private residences."

"So because Craig already lived here, he had easy access."

"No. Because Deja lived here, and he intruded upon her mind while she slept and asked for an invitation, he was able to come inside."

Malaika sucked in a breath, her hand hovering just out of reach of Deja's dresser. "What's to stop the same thing from happening at the church?"

"Deja is staying there. She does not truly live there. The invitation must be from someone who lives in the residence."

"But a church is not a private residence. It's a public building. He can walk right in."

"You'll see."

She glanced up from the shirt she was packing into the duffel and caught site of the hardness in his hazel eyes. "You're going to kill him, aren't you?"

"It's what I do," he said unapologetically. "I'm assuming that's why you kept it a secret that it was him drawing you to those buildings."

Caught, Malaika nodded. "He's the father of my child."

"He's a beast."

"You think I don't know that now?" Malaika snapped, tossing a few more clothes inside the duffel bag. "He repeatedly came into this house and fed off his own daughter, his precious little—" Her voice caught on a gasp of despair, and Jake was behind her, his hands on her shoulders.

"You're a good mother. We've all seen that."

"You don't understand." She shrugged his hands off and stepped across the room, in need of space, before turning to face him. "He must die, I know that, but I've failed to protect her from him, and all that's left is to protect her from the knowledge of what he is. How am I supposed to do that?"

"You don't want her to know her father is a monster." Understanding dawned in his brownish-green eyes.

Malaika gave a weak nod.

"To think she is a monster for coming from such a person."

"Exactly." Fresh tears fell down her cheeks. "I'm her mother, and I'm a, a *witch*? Her father is a pranic vampire who fed off her energy while she slept. While I slept right across the hall. How can any child deal with that and not go insane?"

Jake ran a hand through his short, light brown hair and huffed out a breath. "Let her believe her father is just some bastard that ran off with another woman and was never heard from again. I promise I..." He grimaced. "I won't kill the son of a bitch in front of her, not unless a life depends on it. There's no reason she has to know what he became that night the siren snared him."

Malaika nodded, forcing a small, empty smile. "Thank you for that. But what about me? What about when she finds out Mommy doesn't happen to just sense things sometimes? What about when she learns Mommy is a witch?"

"It won't matter as long as Mommy doesn't abuse her power." There was a dark undercurrent to his tone, a warning.

Malaika swallowed hard. "You still don't fully trust me."

He stared at her, holding her gaze evenly for a tense moment before speaking. Even then, there was no inflection to his tone, no way of truly knowing what he thought. "I know you love your child, and I know you protected mine. But you're still a witch and there have been many who couldn't resist the dark side of power."

Malaika blinked, the vision she'd had back at the abandoned building replaying through her mind. "Your child?"

"The child the vampire sought." He frowned. "The child whose location you wouldn't give. I'm still puzzled how you know about him."

"And I'm puzzled about what it is you're talking about. The baby I saw in my vision was a girl, and you and your wife aren't the parents."

Jonah shifted in the chair, finding it difficult to sleep, but knowing it was necessary. A well-rested guardian was better than one so damn tired he couldn't think straight. And he certainly had a lot to digest.

Deja's father was a vampire. Some sort of freakish, energy-sucking vampire at that. He'd barely managed to fight the bastard off. If Jake hadn't come running when he had...

He cracked open an eyelid, checking on the little girl with the screwed-up family. She was too cute a little girl to have to deal with the things she'd have to deal with. A vampire daddy and a witch mother. A beautiful witch mother. Hell, he still wanted the damn woman, despite knowing what she was. Despite his suspicion she'd known all along why she was having the visions of the murders. She was following that bastard. *Craig.* Filthy son of a bitch. What he wouldn't have given to have had a stake in his hand when the bastard attacked. It probably wouldn't have killed him despite the lore so heavily circulated through books and movies, he knew that, but it would have hurt like hell. A grin worked at the corners of his mouth. *Next time, bastard. Next time.*

And there would be a next time. The thought sobered him. Could he protect them? He'd barely managed to fight off the vampire the first time. His hands curled into fists just thinking about it.

"Come on guys, what's taking so long?" Jonah muttered while glancing at the time displayed on his car stereo and yawned. He'd been awake for far too long, and had dealt with too much shit for one day.

"Jonah?"

"Yeah, baby?" He turned his head to look at the little girl in the backseat. The little girl with the oh-so-hot but oh-so-wrong mother.

"What's my mom doing?"

He sighed, taking a moment to think of a good answer. Telling a young child her mother was checking out a murder scene probably wasn't the way to go. Not unless he wanted to give the cute little girl nightmares. "She's helping my brother find someone." There, that wasn't a total lie.

Deja's brow creased, her mouth turned down into a frown. "He's a meanie to my mommy."

"He's having a bad day," Jonah replied, guilt gnawing at him. He should have stood up for Malaika more than he had. She may be a witch, but so was Seta, and Jake didn't treat Seta so harsh. Of course, though he'd never admit it, Jonah suspected Jake was more than a little intimidated by the vampire-witch. The woman was dynamite wrapped in a Playboy centerfold's body. You never knew when she'd go off and blow your ass to bits. "Tell you what, if he's not nicer to her, I'll punch him right in the nose for you."

Deja smiled, emitting the cutest little chuckle he'd ever heard. "You'd hit your brother?"

"Jake needs a few punches in the nose every now and then," he answered.

"My mommy hit him hard." She giggled again.

Jonah smiled, remembering the look on Jake's face. Served the little jerk right. "That she did, and she did a good job, too."

All traces of humor left Deja's angelic little face. "Will he hurt her?"

"*Absolutely not,*" Jonah said quickly, without a second's need to think. "*I would never let him.*" He wouldn't, he realized. Even if Malaika turned out to be a dark magic-loving witch from hell. He knew how Jake took care of such matters, and there was no way Jake was doing those things to Malaika. Even if it meant he, himself, would be the one to kill her just to make sure she didn't suffer unnecessarily. He closed his eyes and wished with his entire heart Malaika was one of the good guys.

"*Do you promise you'll keep my mommy safe?*"

"*I promise, angel. I'll keep both of you safe.*"

That's when his detective's gut alerted him to danger. His eyes snapped open and locked onto Deja. Her gaze passed him, focusing on a point past his shoulder, her mouth parted open, starting to turn upward into a smile. Despite the smile, he knew something was wrong. Something in the air shifted unnaturally, and the fine hairs along the back of his neck stood on end.

"*Daddy!*" Deja squealed, and Jonah swallowed hard. Daddy? Why the hell was her missing daddy so close to the place a man had been murdered?

Jonah reached for his gun the same time he whipped his head around. Before he could finish either task, his car door was yanked open and a hand clamped around his throat.

He was ripped from the car and slammed against the hood. His attacker was tall, lean, and strong. His hair was a dark brown, similar to his own color, and his eyes... an unnatural shade of blackish brown. As he looked at him, the color in the man's irises actually appeared to swirl. He wasn't a bad looking guy, Jonah had to admit grudgingly, but he was a bit of a pretty boy. The knowledge Malaika had once been intimate with the man pissed him off nearly as much as the fact he'd yet to release his grip.

"*Daddy, stop! Don't hurt him!*" Deja's voice cut through the night, snapping Jonah out of his thoughts of jealousy. Dammit, this bastard was Deja's father, and he was supposed to protect her. He knew deep in his gut, the man would snatch Deja if he didn't fight him off.

"*All will be fine, sweetheart,*" the man said to Deja, his deep voice softening to a gentle, calming tone. "*Stay in the car.*" When he whipped his head back to lock gazes with Jonah, his face was mottled in rage. "*Why are you watching over my daughter? How dare you think to take what is mine?*"

Jonah couldn't respond, not when his breath was being choked out of him. He raised his arm and brought it down hard on the man's wrist, dislodging his hand. Before his attacker could make another move, he rammed his other fist into the pretty boy's face, knocking him backward, but the man didn't go down. He went up—literally—levitating two feet off the ground.

"What the fuck?" was all Jonah managed to croak out before he found himself once again thrown over the hood of his car, the man's hand clamped around his throat.

"Stupid mortal," his attacker growled. "I will suck you dry."

Oh, screw my ass with a sledgehammer, Jonah thought, I've just provoked a fucking vampire, a levitating vampire. He tried the same move to break the vampire's hold, but didn't have the strength this time. He grabbed the gun resting at the small of his back, but it was knocked out of his hand before he squeezed out a single bullet. His lungs fought for air, burning in his chest as his hands worked at prying off the vampire's grasp. All the while, the vamp's face darkened into a mask of fury. "Why can't I drain you?"

Uh, maybe because you're not biting me, Jonah thought, but didn't bother mentioning, not that he could.

"Open for me!" The vampire lowered his face closer to Jonah's, his dark irises swirled like two small tornadoes. "Open!"

Open what? His mouth? The dude wanted to kiss him? Oh, hell no! Jonah mustered up his strength and shoved forward, ramming his head into the vampire's. The monster backed away as stars danced before Jonah's eyes. He'd nearly knocked his own self out.

"Deja, I need strength!"

Alarm bells rang out in Jonah's mind. Blocking out the pain he still suffered from the near-concussion he'd given himself, he jolted upright and twisted. Deja's father had opened the back door of his car and held Deja's tiny face in his large hand. His dark eyes swirled, and a stream of golden-hued smoke misted out of Deja's nose and into his. He was sucking out her—what? Her soul? Her life essence? Whatever it was, it didn't matter. He'd just had his last taste of it.

With a battle cry of rage, Jonah surged forward, gripped the vampire by the shoulders and tore him away from the little girl. As her body fell backward onto the seat, Jonah spun, his grip still firm on the vampire, and propelled the beast

*away from the car. The vampire tripped, fell, and immediately regained ground.
Dammit.*

*Before Jonah could blink, he found himself once more bent back over the
hood of his car, the vampire's grip squeezing against his throat. Tired of the
repeated choking, he decided to give the vamp a taste of his own medicine, and
reached out with both hands, wrapping them around the evil bastard's throat.*

*The vampire's eyes widened, clearly surprised, and satisfaction flared, but
the sensation was all too brief as darkness started to creep in. Jonah fought
against it, squeezing his hands tighter, but no matter how hard he squeezed, he
couldn't weaken the vampire to the point of letting him go. He'd nearly blacked
out completely before Jake intervened, coming to his rescue again.*

Someone stepped into the room and Jonah bolted out of the chair,
instantly bracing himself in a fighting stance. Malaika gasped and backed
away, smacking into Jake's chest. He grunted and gripped her shoulders,
steadying her. "Easy, darlin'. Calm those reflexes, tiger," he added for Jonah.

"Shit. I'm sorry," Jonah apologized, guilt assaulting him as he took in the
wary set of Malaika's face. "I was half asleep and ... I don't know. I thought
you were—"

"Please don't say his name," Malaika whispered a plea, moving past him
to reach her daughter's bedside. She leaned down and swept back an errant
lock of hair from her daughter's forehead, and let out a sigh that sounded as
if it'd been pent up forever. "How is she?"

"She'll be fine," Jonah reassured her. "Seta infused her with some energy,
replenishing what was stolen—" He barely kept from growling the last
word—"and wiped her memory clean of what happened tonight."

Malaika let out a small cry of relief, nodding with her face in her hands.
Jonah was behind her immediately, his hands at her shoulders.

"I'll leave you guys alone," Jake said from the door, then backed out to
give them their privacy. Jonah was a little surprised, knowing how his brother
felt about Malaika. But then again, he'd been the one to offer words of
comfort to Malaika in the alley while he'd been too busy trying to breathe.
Something major had happened in that building, something his brother had
yet to divulge. Whatever it was could wait. Jonah had a more pressing matter.

"Deja will be fine, sweetheart. You need to rest." So did he, but he didn't look nearly as frail as Malaika at the moment. At least he hoped he didn't. It wouldn't exactly fit the macho image he tried to project.

"Oh, Jonah." She turned and wrapped her arms around his waist, her head tucked gently against his chest, right under his chin. "What if you hadn't been there? What would he have done to her?"

What if Jake hadn't showed up in time to save us both? Swallowing hard, fighting back the tide of bitter jealousy he knew he shouldn't be feeling, Jonah gently rubbed Malaika's back. "Don't dwell on it. You're both safe now. You have some of the most powerful people I can think of protecting you now." He couldn't help feeling a twinge of envy, wishing he'd been the one to scare the vampire off. No, the vampire had enjoyed playing with him. One look at Jake, though, and he'd vanished.

"Yes, well, I thank you for protecting Deja." She broke away, stepping back so no part of them touched, then walked to the other side of the room. "But it's hard to feel safe when you're underground with people who've threatened to kill you."

Jonah glanced around at the room, taking in its lack of homey décor. Christian's home was under the church, literally. A hidden trap door beneath the pulpit hid the staircase down. The vampire had carved a series of tunnels and bigger openings, serving as rooms, in the ground beneath his church. He'd been pretty awe-struck by it, himself, but could understand how Malaika might find it intimidating to be, in a sense, trapped underground with the slayer who'd pulled a gun on her.

"Jake told me about the slayer thing, and from what I've gathered, witches and slayers don't mix."

"You're saying you had no idea he was a slayer?" Her voice was hard, accusing. It chafed. A minute ago she'd wrapped her arms around him, leaned on him. Now she was cold and aloof. Or at least trying to be.

"I knew he killed vampires and ghosts, and other... beings. I didn't know he was some sort of supernatural super-warrior."

She made a sound of disgust in her throat and looked away. Jonah took a deep breath, let it out on an angry rush. "Dammit, Malaika, my intention when I brought you here, was to help—"

"Help me straight to my grave."

WITCH'S NET

"No."

"I can't just forget it, Jonah." She looked him square in the eye, her own eyes glistening with unshed tears. Tears of anger, he was sure. "You protected Deja, and I will always appreciate that, but I can't forget how you just served me up on a platter to your brother."

Jonah blinked, opened his mouth, but had to close it again. The thoughts in his head jumbled together, muddled further by his emotions. Guilt, anger, and confusion twisted and churned inside him. "Malaika," he said her name slowly, an effort to calm himself so he wouldn't raise his voice and disturb Deja's sleep. "I thought you were just a psychic, and you needed a little help honing your gift to see your visions more clearly. I brought you here because I knew Christian could get in touch with Seta, who I knew was also psychic. My only intention was to find someone who could help you sharpen your visions."

She shook her head, rolling her eyes in disbelief.

Anger burned through Jonah's blood. "You know, if you'd been truthful about what you saw in those visions, a lot of this might have been avoided."

Her eyes sparked with outrage. "If *I* had been truthful?"

"I didn't even know my brother was here, and yes, when he told me you were a witch, I stepped the hell away," Jonah growled, darting his gaze to the bed Deja rested on. Finding her still deep in slumber, he continued, making sure to keep his voice low despite the growl that had worked its way in. "Are you forgetting I was hung on a fucking wall by a demon? I hear someone's got some sort of supernatural power, I go on high alert. It was a reflex. Sue me."

Malaika's face flushed with color, and she had the decency to look away. Good. She should feel bad, Jonah thought. He, on the other hand, shouldn't be turned on by the cute way she pursed her lips in anger. But he was. Disgust with himself fueled him on. "You say you didn't know you were a witch. Fine, I'll take your word for that, but we both know well that your pretty-boy boyfriend was the star of your visions, and that you were following him all this time. Why not tell us? Maybe if I'd known about him, I'd been more prepared for his attack."

"I had no idea what he'd turned into," Malaika stated vehemently. "How was I supposed to know what would happen?"

"Why'd you protect him?" Jonah voiced the question that had been haunting him since the attack, and moved closer, stopping right in front of Malaika. "Why were you so hell-bent on protecting his name?"

"Why does it matter?" Her voice was a low growl. "It sounds to me like you're just jealous."

"Jealous?" Jonah laughed at the idea, despite the twist in his gut indicating her words were true. The thought of that bastard putting his hands on her, being inside her... He balled his hands into fists, but kept his cool. A grin tugged at the corners of his mouth, remembering the conversation he'd had with Malaika that morning. "Why should I be jealous when you've already confessed to having wicked fantasies about me?"

Her eyes grew wide as she scoffed, a small gasp of sound escaping her parted lips. Full, smooth lips, perfect for sucking. "I did not. A vision is not the same thing as a fantasy. And besides, how do you know if I enjoyed the vision? You might not have been any good." She grinned smugly.

"I know you enjoyed it, honey, because—" He inched his face closer until their lips were a breath apart— "there hasn't been a word invented yet to describe just how *good* I am. And when I do get you into bed, and we both know I will, you'll forget pretty-boy ever existed."

She gasped, their lips so close, she sucked a little of his breath out. Anger contorted her face, but she couldn't hold it. Her eyelids lowered to half-mast, and slowly, she moved forward...

Jonah stepped back. "But seeing as how I'm such a bad, untrustworthy person, I understand how it will take time until you feel comfortable enough to explore that vision."

Malaika blinked, her jaw clenched as realization dawned in her eyes. It was all Jonah could do not to laugh. "You dirty little..."

"Sweetheart, you have no idea how dirty I can be."

Her mouth fell open, the anger at his trickery gave way to desire, if the hunger in her eyes was any indication. Jonah nearly said to hell with teaching her a lesson and closed the distance between them, but he knew one touch, not even one kiss would be enough. He'd fling her on the nearest surface and ravish her if he gave in to the pull to taste her right then. And at the moment, the nearest surface was the bed where a small child slept.

"Get some rest, Malaika. You've had a long day." On a sigh of regret, he stepped toward the open door.

"Jonah."

He stopped in the doorway and turned to face the pretty witch who'd somehow managed to bewitch *him*.

"I'm sorry you were... hurt by the demon... and that I didn't believe you."

Jonah nodded. "And I'm sorry my reflex was to get away from you when I found out you were a witch. I promise if anyone ever pulls a gun on you again, they'll have to shoot through me first."

With that, he stepped out of the room. "And I'm sorry I'm stuck with this damn hard-on," he grumbled as he made his way down the narrow tunnel-like hall to find a place to sleep, somewhere Malaika's arousing scent wouldn't follow and keep him awake.

NINE

"Hey, gorgeous," Jake whispered, sliding into the bed next to his wife. Her eyelids fluttered open, revealing violet orbs perfectly capable of taking his breath away. Her long black hair fanned over the white pillow beneath her head. Even with her face slightly chubby from her pregnancy, she was the most beautiful creature he'd ever laid eyes on.

"Hey," she responded, her voice soft and sleepy. With a little groan of discomfort, she shifted in the bed to snuggle in to his side, and Jake wrapped his arm around her, holding her close. "I tried to wait up for you."

"You need your rest. Pretty soon, neither of us will be able to sleep through a night."

"Like we ever did before, between all the hunting and the... after the hunting."

Jake's groin tightened at the thought. He'd always thought he'd had a healthy sexual appetite. Nyla was damn near insatiable. Or had been, before her belly had gotten so big. Now she was too uncomfortable for sex.

"Seta told me there's a siren involved in the murders your brother was investigating."

"That's what it looks like." He ran his hand down Nyla's arm, let out a yawn as his eyes grew weary.

"Sirens are very powerful. I imagine even powerful enough to seduce a slay—"

Jake placed his index finger over Nyla's lips the second he realized where she was going, and chuckled. "Same old jealous kitty-cat."

"Bite me."

"I'd love to, just as soon as you're back in the mood. Then I'll lick the sting away."

With a grunt of—anger? frustration?— Nyla hefted herself into a sitting position and swung her legs over the side of the bed. She sat there with her shoulders slumped, her back toward him. Jake didn't have to see her eyes to know they were wet with unshed tears.

"Dammit, Nyla, what now?" He sat up and scooted to her side. She turned her face away as if doing so would prevent him from knowing what was in her eyes. He took a deep breath, gearing up for whatever came next. The woman's hormones were all messed up, her emotions all over the map. Personally, he didn't know which he'd celebrate more the moment his son was born: The birth of his son, or the fact that Nyla would go back to being her normal self. "If you don't tell me what's wrong, it's just going to stew inside you and make you feel really lousy. You're tired, sweetheart. Let's get this over with and get some rest."

"Now I'm your sweetheart?" Her voice was broken, fragile, and held the slightest trace of anger.

Jake sighed, his eyes aching to close, his head aching to rest on a pillow. He was too damn tired for this. "You're always my sweetheart. My wife, my partner. My best friend. The only woman I want. You know that."

"I'm fat."

Here we go again. "You are not fat. You're pregnant. There's a big difference between the two."

"*You* think I'm fat."

"No, I do not think you're fat. I may think you're crazy right now, but never have I thought you were fat."

"If you go after that siren and she—"

Oh, for crying out loud. "Woman, what am I?"

"What?" She turned her face toward him, wet tracks sparkling on her cheeks, where silent tears had fallen. The sight made Jake's stomach clench. She'd only cried in front of him once before she was pregnant, and he'd felt helpless, out of control. What the hell was a man supposed to do with tears? He hadn't gotten any more used to the damned things in the last few months despite her releasing them so freely. "What am I?" he asked again, softer this time.

"A slayer."

"Exactly." He reached out and hooked a lock of obsidian hair behind her ear, amazed as always by the beauty of her flawless face. Even pink from crying and a little bloated from pregnancy, no other woman on the planet could compare. "Because I'm a slayer, I have quickness to aid me in battling with vampires, an impenetrable mind to protect me against any psychic attackers, and I'm immune to lycanthropy. Wouldn't it make sense that I have a little something in my system to protect me from a siren?"

She furrowed her brow in thought, and her nose scrunched a little. It was so cute, he wanted to kiss it, but didn't dare kiss her anywhere until he knew he was in the clear. The way her moods had been swinging the past few months, an innocent little kiss might just get him a punch in the face. Her moods were that damn erratic.

"I guess so. So what ability do you have to protect you from sirens?"

"I don't know." He shrugged. "Maybe I can see them."

She blinked, confused, then her eyes darkened to deep amethyst. "So can every other man. That's why they follow them and get their horny asses killed."

"I mean maybe I can see the real thing, Nyla, not the image they project. Or maybe this psychic shield I have will keep out the bitch's allure. There's gotta be something."

"And if there isn't?"

"Then I'll see the most amazingly sexy woman I've ever seen in my life, and she'll try to lure me to my death." He grinned at the way her teeth ground together. The poor woman was going to break a tooth. "She'll have long, midnight black hair and beautiful violet eyes that look like two dark amethysts when she's pissed, and her belly—" he lay his hand gently on Nyla's stomach—"will be round with my child. I won't be able to catch my breath, she'll be so beautiful... but then she'll try to seduce me and I'll know it's not you because you haven't given me any in over a month."

Jake grinned, waiting for Nyla to laugh. Then he remembered this wasn't the old Nyla. This was the woman whose hormones were berserk, the woman who needed to hurry up and pop out his baby before they both went crazy trying to deal with each other. And if looks could maim, he'd be looking at her through the eyes of his disembodied head. "Just like amethysts," he muttered. "There was a time you would have thought that was funny."

"There was a time when..." She bit her lip, turned her face away, and released a sigh so soft Jake barely heard it. "Because they'd melded their minds earlier, Seta was able to tap into Malaika's thoughts and see part of her vision when she was reading the dead man's body. She saw how that man was so easily seduced by the siren because he and his wife were barely having sex."

"I'm not that man," Jake snapped, finally getting angry. He could put up with her insane ideas that she was fat or somehow unattractive, her mood swings, and even her tears. But he wouldn't tolerate her thinking he'd cheat on her, not after everything they'd been through. "And as you said, Seta saw a snatch of what Malaika saw. She told me exactly what that man was thinking when he followed the siren. He and his wife were having sex, twice a month. He simply no longer desired her because he was a fucking pig who obviously never even loved the woman. Do you remember what I did to save you from Demarcus?" His blood grew hot when referencing the vampire's name, remembering the bastard who'd killed his childhood friend, and tried to kill Nyla.

"Yes." She nodded, and a trio of tears slid down her face.

"Well, trust me. The pig who died in that building wouldn't have done that for his wife, and I sure as hell wouldn't have done it for you if I wasn't so damn deep in love with you that the thought of losing you or seeing you hurt in any way was my ultimate nightmare." He realized he'd come close to shouting and softened his voice. "I'd die for you, baby, over and over again. You know that."

"Exactly." The tears started streaming now. "You don't get it. I'm not just jealous, Jake. I know what sirens can do, and you're weak because of me."

"What?"

"Because of me, you haven't had sex in so long... and if you go after that siren she'll snare you and you won't be able to fight off whoever is helping her."

"Honey, I've went longer than a few months without sex before," he said. "I'm not weak just because we haven't done anything. I'm strong, because I love you. That has nothing to do with sex. You of all people should know that."

"Don't remind me," she ground out, her tears ceasing as her eyes warmed with anger. "That part of me is dead."

"I know, and I'm sorry. You know I don't ever want you to think of that." He didn't want to think of that, of the things she'd been forced to do before they got together. Risking her hostility, he wrapped an arm around her shoulders and pulled her close so her head rested under his chin.

"We could... try..."

"No." He barely got the word out, had to force it out before he sucked it back in. He grew hard just thinking about being inside Nyla again, but he was determined to not be a greedy bastard. "The last time we did, you hurt."

"It was just... uncomfortable. I can handle it."

"You hurt, Nyla, and I won't do anything that causes you pain. Ever." He gripped her chin in his hand and made her look him in the eyes. "Like you said, that part of your life is over. You will never have to service a man again, especially not your husband. When you have the baby, and have had time to heal, we'll get back to normal. I can wait."

"Are you sure?"

He ran his thumb over her jaw before releasing her face. "I wouldn't enjoy it if you didn't, too. It should never be a chore."

"There's nothing I can say to keep you away from this, is there?"

"No." He leaned in and planted a kiss on her forehead, hated the look of defeat in her eyes. "I need to find out why sirens, vampires, and were-hyenas are working together, and what their ultimate goal is. One of them is luring that witch to every crime scene, and my brother is involved. He won't give up on this case. You know him well enough to know that."

"I never knew Jonah like I know you." She ran a hand over her belly. "And I guess I'll never really know him."

Jake frowned, wondered where she was going with the statement. She didn't seem angry now, just... sad. "What do you mean by that?"

She laughed lightly, but the sound was hollow. "Are you ever going to tell him about me? About the baby?"

"He knows we're married, and obviously, he knows we're having a baby."

"You know what I mean, Jacob."

Ouch. She never called him Jacob unless she was mad. Really mad. "It's not like I've had a lot of time."

"You've had plenty of time. You're ashamed."

"Of what?" The question snapped out of Jake like a whip.

128

"Me. Your son. Us."

"Nyla—"

"No!" She stood from the bed and stepped across the small underground room Christian had offered them for the night. "You're too ashamed of us to tell your brother what I am, and what your son will be."

"We don't know what he'll be," Jake snapped, standing. "And I've already told you I don't care."

"That would be easier to believe if not for the fact your initial reaction when you first found out what I was, was to kill me."

"Oh, here we go again." Jake threw his arms up in the air. She'd reminded him of that moment at least ten times in the last month. "I didn't, Nyla. I didn't even cut you. I couldn't. Damn, do I keep throwing it in your face that you once came within an inch of cutting my balls off?"

Her eyes widened as she whipped around. The long, black T-shirt she wore to sleep in swished with her. "Are you really comparing something as simple as a castration to *killing me*?"

"Well, it might not seem a big deal to you, but I'm rather fond of my balls."

Nyla's lips trembled perilously, then her entire face crumpled into a mask of despair before she hid it behind her hands. The sobs forced from her body tore at Jake's heart. He was in front of her in an instant, wrapping her in his arms. "I'll go wake up Jonah and tell him now, okay?"

"No." She shook her head against his chest, wetting his skin in the process. "I'm being unreasonable, and I'm sorry," she apologized between sobs. "I hate being like this. So bitchy... *sob*... nervous... *sob*... worried all the... *sob*... time..."

"And scared?" Jake rubbed his hand in circles over her back, and tilted her chin up to see her red, puffy face, everything suddenly so clear. Nyla was a warrior, but her people couldn't shift form when pregnant, so for months she'd felt lost, out of control. Weak. She'd had to deal with her feelings the worst way possible: She'd actually had to do nothing but *think* about them. "Why can't you just admit you're scared to have this baby?"

She heaved out another sob, and wiped her eyes with the back of her hand. "Whenever I've been scared before, I could just fight and push my fears to the back of my mind. I could inflict pain on others and not have to deal with my own."

"I know." He wiped away an errant tear with the pad of his thumb. "And since you can't fight physically for now, you're just lashing out at me any way you can to help yourself cope with all that's happening."

A fresh sob tore from her throat as she pressed her face against his chest, burrowing into him. "I'm sorry. You don't deserve all the grief I give you."

"Ah, I probably do," he said softly, kissing the top of her head before resting his chin on the same spot. "Like you said, there was a fraction of a moment I'd considered killing you. I should always suffer for that."

"I know you would have never killed me."

"Good."

"And I would have never cut off your balls," she added. "I'm rather fond of them, myself."

Jake chuckled, the tension in his shoulders easing up. "What's really going on in that crazy head of yours, Nyla? What's got you so worked up tonight?"

There was a long pause, but just when Jake was about to ask the question again, she answered softly. "Back when I was with the Pantherians, before I met you... I'd been around long enough to witness the births."

"Yes?" Jake prodded, after another lull.

"The way those women screamed, Jake... I can't describe to you the pain."

Jake started rubbing her back again, and planted another reassuring kiss on her head. "I brought you back here so Seta can help with the delivery. She's a powerful witch, and I'm sure she'll whip up some magic to ease the pain." He prayed she could. If Nyla were a normal, mortal, human they could just go to a hospital and get her an epidural when the time came. But she wasn't. They couldn't take the chance of the doctors learning what she was, and there was a chance the epidural wouldn't even work in her system. Far scarier than that, was the thought of the doctors inadvertently doing something to damage—or kill—their child.

"What if she can't? And what if I go through all that pain just to have this child alone because you've been killed by a vampire while snared by a siren?" She trembled. "And if you're not here, who'll help me make sure nobody gets their hands on our son? You know how he'll be hunted." She choked on a sob. "I can't do it without you. I can't."

Jake took a deep breath, tried to soothe the knot in his chest. "Nyla, you know I will not die."

"You can't be sure."

"I. Will. Not. Die." He held her face in both hands, and looked her in the eyes, protectiveness churning fiercely in his gut. "And if any evil bastard so much as touches a hair on my son's head, or even thinks about hurting you, they'll learn quick and fast I'm not the slayer to fuck with."

Malaika cracked open her eyelids, reached over to snuggle her baby girl... and found the bed empty. Alarm slammed into her chest, stealing the breath from her lungs. Deja was gone. She glanced around the small room, a not-quite-square room carved out of the ground, and her anxiety level rose. The chair Jonah had rested in when she'd arrived earlier that night—morning?—was abandoned, and the door open. She'd closed it before sliding into the bed next to Deja and allowing herself to rest.

Had Craig found a way in? Had he taken her? A cry spilled from her mouth as she slid off the bed to search Christian's underground home. She didn't make it one step. Instead, she snagged her foot on something and fell to her hands and knees with a loud thud, barely managing to keep her face from slamming into the wooden plank-covered floor.

"Malaika?" A drowsy male voice said from behind her, and she turned her head to see Jonah sitting up, rubbing his eyes. Her feet were still in his lap. Looking down, then over at her, realization chased the drowsiness from his eyes. "Oh, damn. I'm sorry. The air is best in here, and I couldn't sleep in any of the other rooms so I thought I'd just lay here on the floor and get some rest. Are you okay?"

Just a little bit mortified, Malaiaka thought as she rubbed her sore palms together. She could almost feel the bruises forming on her knees. Jonah reached out and took her hands in his, rubbing his thumbs over her stinging palms. A jolt of electricity arched from Malaika's palms and through her arms, from the slight touch. "Good. You're not bleeding."

He stood up and pulled her to a stand. Malaika saw the bed behind him and remembered why she'd been too preoccupied to notice the tall man sleeping on the floor. "Deja!" Alarm sparked fresh, and she ran from the room.

She ran into the narrow tunnel-like hall and came to a stand-still, causing Jonah to ram into her back, as the sound of Deja's laughter washed over her. She stumbled forward, but Jonah's hands wrapped around her waist, locking her into place.

"Sorry." His voice was a low rumble along her cheek, he hovered over her so close.

"It's okay." More than okay, she thought, delighting in the feel of his warm hands on her skin. She was glad she'd worn a shirt that left a little skin exposed at the waist.

Deja's laugh reached her again, strengthening the relief she'd felt upon first hearing it, and she broke away from Jonah's hold to find her daughter.

Malaika stepped into what appeared to be the living area, Jonah just a step behind her. They paused at the entrance to observe Deja playing a card game with the vampire who'd welcomed them to his home. Like the rest of Christian's home, the room had been carved out of the earth. Wooden boards were nailed into the ground to form a floor, and boards surrounded the room in place of walls. Thick hooks were mounted into the walls and from them hung lanterns to provide light. Above them, a ceiling was formed by more wooden planks. What kept it all from falling apart, Malaika didn't know, but the overall effect was actually quite nice.

The furnishings in this room were comprised of a long couch and a comfortable looking armchair surrounding a coffee table, and a chaise off to the side. Along the far wall, Malaika noticed a counter area with a sink, and a small dorm-sized refrigerator. Her stomach did a little roll at the thought of what a vampire would keep in there. A vampire! Despite spending a good length of time with them, the shock of it had yet to completely wear off. Along with the shock of being a witch.

To her left, Deja and Christian occupied two of the six available chairs encircling a round, wooden table. Deja emitted another series of giggles as Christian made a funny little face indicating his defeat, and playfully slammed his cards on the table. "You win again. You're just too good at this."

Deja laughed wholeheartedly and raised her little fists into the air. "Yay me!"

"Yay, you," Christian agreed, and scooped the cards up. "Morning, guests. Sleep well?"

Malaika started forward, not realizing the vampire had been paying them any attention. Jonah patted Deja's head, and pulled out a chair for her as they reached the table. Malaika eyed him warily, but when he only raised an eyebrow in response, his mouth tugging slightly at the corner, she took the offered seat. Accepting the seat he offered was no big deal, she told herself. It didn't mean things would lead anywhere near the vicinity of where her dreams had traveled the night before.

She noticed Christian's expectant gaze, and recalled he'd asked her how she'd slept. "Oh, sorry. I slept, fine, thank you," she answered, deciding no one needed to know about the heated dreams she'd had, dreams she shouldn't have been having considering the immediate danger her daughter was in. "Thank you for allowing us to stay here." *And not sucking us dry.* She studied the vampire, taking in his youthful, innocent appearance. Thanks to her psychic—apparently witch—abilities, she could tell the man was extremely powerful, but if she were to judge by looks alone, she'd have no clue. He was tall and lean, his face clean-shaven, so smooth she suspected it had never hosted any stubble at all. His eyes were warm and innocent-looking. They had the ability to invoke a person's complete trust. His lips were thin, and despite the lack of lines around them, he appeared to be a man who smiled often.

He beamed one of those smiles her way before tilting his head in the direction of Jonah, who'd taken a seat on the other side of Deja. "And you? You were not where I expected you to be this morning."

"Yeah, it got kind of stuffy in here after a while, so I slept on the floor in the girls' room."

"In here?" Malaika glanced around the room, again only noticing the chair, couch, and chaise.

"The chaise is actually pretty comfortable," Jonah stated. "But the air is kind of thin through here. The floor was fine. After all the stake-outs I've done, floors aren't bad at all. Beats being stuck in a cramped car for hours on end."

"I'm sorry," Christian apologized, rising from the table. "I have limited sleeping areas down here since it is so important I keep my private residence a secret. My sleeping quarters are nearly devoid of air, and the other good room was for Nyla and your brother. I figured with her being with child—"

"No need to explain or apologize, man. I'd beat my own ass for taking a bed if it meant a pregnant woman went without it."

Malaika's heart did a little flutter at Jonah's display of consideration. As she recalled, Craig hadn't been exceptionally considerate when she'd carried his child. He hadn't bothered going to the grocery store with her, cooking, cleaning the apartment every once in a while. Hell, she couldn't even remember him calling to see if she needed anything. If he'd called, it was to ask for something. Craig, the energy-sucking monster.

Her heart twisted as she remembered the way Deja had looked the night—morning?—before. Drained. Lifeless. Now she was bright-eyed and full of life. The way she should always be. Damn Craig to hell and back. She took a deep breath to fight off the emotion clogging her throat and rubbed a palm along Deja's braided hair. "Where is Seta? I'd like to thank her for helping my little girl."

Deja frowned and she remembered she'd been asleep or unconscious for most of the time they'd been around Seta. She had no idea what all had happened.

"Seta had to attend to some personal business," Christian answered, crossing over to the counter area. "Can I get you all something to eat?"

Malaika blanched at the thought of what a vampire would offer in terms of nutrition, and Christian caught the expression. "I keep regular food upstairs for my..." He glanced at Deja. "I have guests from time to time who do not match my particular nutritional needs. I have cereal, fruit, sandwich items... and I might have some lasagna left." He reached into the small refrigerator, but the door blocked Malaika's view of the contents. He pulled out a cereal bar and inclined his head toward Deja. "I brought this down last night, figuring she'd be hungry upon waking. Do you mind?"

"No. Thank you," Malaika answered, giving him permission to give the cereal bar to Deja. "I'll probably just grab something for myself later. How often do you have guests?"

"Unfortunately, too often. Of course even once is too often, really." Christian sank back down into the chair he'd occupied at Malaika's right side. "I offer a place of refuge for runaways, and those who fall into the wrong hands."

"Oh." That was awfully nice of the vampire. Unless he fed off the guests. Her eyes narrowed on the friendly looking vampire. Looks could be so deceiving, and she knew better than anyone. Craig had appeared to be a stand-up guy. Look how he'd turned out. "How do they pay for their stay?"

Christian studied her, and smiled. "Not how you're thinking. I get my nourishment from bags, and hopefully they repay me by doing something to help someone else in need."

"You bring them here and trust them not to tell anyone about the secret door?"

"They stay upstairs. You noticed the cot where Deja rested. I have a few rooms up there. Rarely do I allow anyone down into my private residence."

"But you allowed me."

Christian glanced at Deja, his mouth curving into a grin as he watched her chew her cereal bar. "Seta was kind enough to cast spells of protection over my home after I first built it. No one can step inside unless I want them to. I thought it the safest place for the child."

"And you trust me not to tell anyone of it?" A little ray of warmth sparked in Malaika's chest. Just the day before she'd felt persecuted by these people. Now she was being accepted.

Christian looked at her in grave seriousness. "Seta gave me a guarantee that would not happen."

Just as quickly as it had sparked to life, the little ray of warmth fizzled out as the cold truth sank in. "Meaning, she wouldn't allow me to tell."

"No." Christian replied with no emotion displayed on his face or in his tone.

A warm hand covered her own and she glanced up to see compassion in Jonah's hazel gaze. Her breath caught and she was sucked in by his gaze, her mind suddenly full of his image. Laughing, yelling, sleeping... Image after image of him filled her, like little lost pieces of memory. Then she saw him hovering over her, sweat dripping from his brow as he joined his body with hers in the most intimate way possible, whispering words of love...

"Morning, people. Everyone rested and ready to snuff out some fuglies?" Jake asked as he entered the room.

Jonah pulled his hand away and the images escaped with the loss of his touch. Malaika tried to pull them back, but they were good and truly gone. Still, the odd sense that she'd seen the images before lingered.

Malaika rubbed the spot where Jonah had touched her, and watched Jake cross the room to join them at the table, where he turned a chair around and straddled it, resting his elbows before him on the table. He wore a black T-shirt and jeans, his short hair wet from the shower. He glanced between Jonah and her, frowning slightly before asking Christian of Seta's whereabouts.

"She's with Rialto and Aria. After I told her the news of Malaika's vision, she thought it best to bring them here."

"What vision?" Jonah asked, turning curious eyes on Malaika.

Before she could answer, Christian took Deja's hand and helped her down from her seat. "Once they arrive, you'll have much to discuss. I'll take Deja and see if we can't scrounge up any crayons, and perhaps a coloring book." He smiled down at Deja, his hand smoothing down a frizzy braid, before turning his gaze back to Jake. Concern flared behind his eyes. "Jacob, if you need any—"

"I'm fine," Jake said quickly, "and you know my name."

"Of course." Christian grinned, then nodded sharply. "Seta will be here soon with the others."

"Sooner than you think," the curvy vampire-witch announced as she entered the room, followed by a tall, muscular man with golden skin, dark eyes, and black hair secured at the nape of his neck. At his side was a gorgeous, light mocha-skinned woman with dazzling emerald green eyes and long, wavy brown hair. Malaika's eyes traveled down to her belly, round with child.

"Is this the couple you saw in your vision?" Seta asked, her voice parlaying her fear with a slight tremble. It was then that Malaika noticed the subtle similarities between Seta and the man. They could be brother and sister.

"Yes," she answered, recalling the vision, and again feeling the sense that she'd had the vision long before she'd been accosted by the vampire at the abandoned building. That, along with the images she'd just had of Jonah, images she knew she'd seen before but somehow suppressed, unnerved her. Why would she forget these images? She turned her head toward Jonah to see him looking at the couple with his mouth hanging open.

"Come, Deja. Let's go find some way to amuse ourselves." Christian touched Deja's shoulder and led her out of the room.

"We have much to discuss," Seta announced, her voice shaky. The powerful vampire-witch placed a hand on her stomach while directing the two newcomers to sit at the table. The two sat in the vacant chairs between her and Jonah, and Seta sat at her right, between her and Jake. "Something strange is going on."

"Yeah, like a vampire being pregnant," Jonah said, blinking out of the shock he'd seemed to have fallen into. "You said he turned her." He swiveled his head toward Jake. "How in the hell is she pregnant?"

Malaika studied the pair again, noting the strength rolling off of them, similar to the energy she felt from Seta and Christian. They were vampires. She was going to help a pair of vampires have a baby? The male vampire placed a large hand over the woman's smaller one and sent a quelling glare Jonah's way. Malaika frowned, wondering at the odd gesture, then understood as she took in Jonah's stiff shoulders and felt the anger, mixed with a trace of jealousy, he emitted. He was envious.

Malaika studied the female vampire again, her eyes growing hot. Damn Jonah. She so did not need a man in her life to be jealous about.

"Normally, vampires can't reproduce," Jake clarified. "Rialto and Aria are... special."

"How so?" Malaika asked, curious. If she was supposed to be there for the birth, she should know all the details.

Jake took a deep breath and glanced Seta's way. "There's this story—"

"Prophecy," Seta interjected. "The Blood Revelation."

The name rang a bell in Malaika's mind. She'd heard it before, she knew, but couldn't place where.

"To sum things up," Jake continued, "three sets of... special people were chosen forever ago to mate, and create even more special children. One of these children, the Child of Light, will save the world from Satan's wrath."

"My son, Rialto, and his wife—" Seta nodded her head in the direction of the vampires—"are one of the chosen sets. The child Aria is carrying will be one of the three special children."

"Your son?" Malaika gasped, studying the man again. He grinned and nodded.

"I was nineteen years old when I was changed into a vampire," Seta explained. "He had just been weaned. I turned him many years later."

"And now I'm supposed to help deliver your grandchild."

"According to your vision, and the one I recently had, yes. And somehow the vampire who attacked you knows, which means we are all in danger."

Jonah alternated his gaze between Malaika's paling face, and Seta's frown, acid churning in his gut. Slowly, he turned his head toward his brother. Jake quickly cast his gaze down, unable to meet his eyes. "There's more, isn't there? Why else would all of us be in danger?"

"Tell him, Jake." Seta's tone was firm, assertive. A warning that if he didn't, she would.

Jake glared at her and licked his lips. He took in a deep breath and released it slowly before at last meeting Jonah's gaze. "Nyla and I are one of the other sets."

The bottom of Jonah's stomach seemed to fall right out onto the floor. Jake was a slayer, a fact he'd advised him of the prior day. He had some kind of a psychic radar to help him find supernatural creatures and kill them. No big deal. He was still human. But as for the other piece of the set.... "What is she?"

"She's my wife," Jake all but growled, his hand clenched into a fist, "and her name is Nyla."

"You know what I mean, Jake. You said these chosen people were special. How special is she, and don't say 'very' or something else to avoid answering the question."

"She's a shape-shifter with vampiric traits, and your nephew might be, too."

Jonah blinked, running Jake's words through his head again. Vampiric traits. Okay, he could deal with that. It probably meant she had an allergy to sun and drank blood. So did Christian and Seta. He kind of liked Christian, and although Seta was the last person on the planet he'd ever cross, he did trust her to a point. Shape-shifter? Those beasts who'd attacked his partner and put her in the hospital, unable to even talk, were shape-shifters. They were animals. Beasts. And his brother was married to one? He'd had sex with one? Was going to have one as his offspring? "Tell me you're screwing with me, Jake."

"I'm not." A nerve ticked in Jake's jaw. "You're the only family I really have, Joe. I need you to accept this."

A wave of guilt swept over Jonah, but all he had to do to get rid of it was remember the damage done to Ronnie's throat. "Accept that you've decided to procreate with the same kind of beast who nearly killed my partner?"

"Nyla isn't that type of shape-shifter!" Jake's bellow reverberated off the walls. "She's not some filthy lycanthrope."

"She still turns into an animal, correct?"

"I know mortals who are more of an animal than her."

"Nice way of avoiding a direct answer. What is she? Tiger? Wolf? Hyena?" He knew the hyena mention was a low blow, but something propelled him to say it anyway. Just to be mean. His brother, his own flesh and blood, had ignored him for months, gotten married without so much as a notice, aimed a gun on Malaika just for being a witch, but all the time he'd been with a shape-shifter? Unbelievable.

"Actually, I'm a Pantherian."

Jonah, along with the others at the table, turned their heads toward the entry way to see Jake's wife approach. She was beautiful. Even though he now knew what she was, Jonah couldn't dispute that fact. He could see why his brother would be attracted to the violet-eyed woman with the long, flowing black hair. Despite the rounded belly she currently had beneath the black, snug-fitting T-shirt and leggings she wore, he could tell she probably had a nice figure. But still, knowing she could turn into an animal...

"Our animal form is the panther," she announced as she crossed the room to stand behind Jake, placing her hands on his shoulders. Jake visibly relaxed a little, and Jonah remembered him saying something about her having empathic abilities. "But, we can also take on the appearance of a black cat."

She narrowed her eyes on him, and tilted her head to the side as if awaiting a challenge. She blinked those big, violet eyes and realization slammed into Jonah's gut. Jake had a cat that'd followed him around since he was just a kid, since the night his best friend had been killed in an alley by a pack of vampires. He'd always joked with his brother about how jealous the cat was, scratching any woman who got close to him. A black cat with big violet eyes. "Holy—You're Alley!"

"That's correct," she said, "and you've held me in your lap and petted me in my animal form. Do you still find me a threat?"

He looked between Alley—Nyla—and Jake, remembering the damned cat who always seemed to know just what they were saying. And no damn wonder! "This is too much. I can't deal with this right now." Jonah scooted his chair back, ready to leave.

"Stay right where you are, Jonah Porter." Seta's tone warned him he would regret disobeying her direct command, so he stilled. "As I stated earlier, we have much to discuss. The Blood Revelation tells of these special pairings. It also tells of how every evil thing on this earth will try to stop these special children from being born."

Jonah looked at Nyla, let his gaze travel down to the bump encasing his future nephew, and swallowed hard. The baby growing inside her might well turn into a freaking panther, but it was still his brother's child. That made it his blood, regardless of how screwed up the child was. And Aria... He glanced at her rounded belly, too, not giving a damn that Rialto narrowed his eyes on him. He'd liked the woman a lot, had ended up pinned on a wall and beaten while trying to protect her. He wouldn't wish to see her child harmed, either. "What do I have to do with any of this?" he asked in honest curiosity. "I'm just a homicide detective."

"A homicide detective who just happens to know four very sought-after people," Malaika said in a near whisper, and wiped a tear from her eye. "Jonah, I think we're the reason why the vampires and were-hyenas are killing people. They're doing it to draw us out, and lead them to the chosen mates. If these babies don't make it to birth, it's because of us."

TEN

Every set of eyes in the room focused on her. Malaika wiped away another tear, feeling extremely uncomfortable under the weight of so many gazes.

"Why do you believe that?" Seta asked softly, and Malaika turned toward her.

"Because I... I'm remembering things."

"Such as?"

Malaika cast a glance at Jake, noted she had his full attention despite his obvious turmoil over Jonah's reaction to finding out the truth about his wife and unborn child. "When I was accosted by that vampire, he demanded I tell him where the child was at, and I had this image in my head of helping Aria give birth. It was such a familiar vision. I know I've had it before, a long time ago."

She looked back toward Seta and caught the frown marring the beautiful woman's face. "And just today... I've caught images, more like flashes, really, of Jonah." She looked forward, catching Jonah's gaze. "They were images I'd had before but somehow suppressed because until this morning, I had no idea they'd ever occurred."

"Malaika, I need full access to your mind."

Malaika turned her head toward Seta again. "All I blocked from you last time was Craig's existence and my suspicions that he was at those crime scenes. I've admitted all that to you now."

"Yes, darling, but you may have inadvertently kept me from finding out what he did to you to make you suppress important information."

"What do you mean?"

"Craig may have just recently become a prannie," Jake jumped in, "but he would have always been psychic. The fact that you never knew, and now you're having these flashes confirms a theory I've been hashing on since last night."

"What theory is that?"

Jake looked at Seta, receiving a nod from the vampire-witch. "I think he always knew what you were, and because you didn't know what you were, you were easy prey for him. He milked your mind for all it was worth, and did one hell of a mind-jack on you."

"A mind-jack?" Malaika trembled with anger, unsure whether it was directed at Craig or herself for being so stupid.

"He stole important information from your mind and suppressed that information deep in your psyche so you'd never know," Seta explained.

That bastard. Malaika fisted her hand until her short nails bit into her flesh. "But I'm remembering now."

"You're beginning to accept the enormity of what you are. You've acknowledged yourself as a witch, which has strengthened you. Once I tutor you in basic magic, your power will increase even more." Seta sighed, the sound full of desperate hope. "Malaika, if I can delve into your psyche and find the information lost to you, it would save us valuable time. It could save lives."

Two innocent little lives. Malaika looked at Aria's belly once more, swallowing against the fear climbing her throat. How was she supposed to help the woman—vampire—give birth? Sure, she'd had a baby herself, but that had been in a hospital with a team of professionals while drugged on an epidural. But she had to. And she had to do whatever was necessary to make sure that child—and Jake's child—made it safely into the world. "I'll do it, and then I want you to teach me how to fight against that vampire, and Craig."

"We will."

Malaika wheeled her head around at the sound of her grandmother's soft, withered voice. The older woman stood two feet away from her in a long, loose brown dress, a multicolored scarf wrapped around her head. "Grandma Mahdi."

She nodded, a serene smile spread on her lips. "It is time I taught my granddaughter what she should have always known."

"And I will help." Seta rose from her chair and gestured for Malaika to stand.

"You see my grandmother, too?"

"Yes, dear, and together she and I will help you to find out just what has been done to you."

Malaika turned toward the others to see them looking in the direction of her grandmother, but not really seeing. Jonah gave her a curious look before turning his face away and running a hand through his hair. He'd clearly had more of the supernatural than he could wrap his mind around for one day, but she knew he was going to have to suck it up and deal with it. "My grandmother warned me that Craig intends to kill you," she announced, regaining his focus. "I suggest getting over your unease with this situation and working closely with your brother. He loves you, and he'll protect you."

With that, she turned and followed Seta and her dead grandmother out of the room.

"What happened in Hicksville?" Jonah asked after a long, uncomfortable silence had proven too much for him to take.

"Joe."

"Answer the damn question, Jake. I had to worry about you for nine damn months after the FBI went down there and found the whole town bathed in blood, and you didn't so much as call and tell me you were alive." His voice rose with each word. "Now you just throw it in my lap that you've married a Pantherian, whatever that truly is, and you're having some child that will be hunted, unless the forces of evil keep it from being born, and I'm just supposed to smile and accept everything, but you can't answer a few fucking questions?"

Rialto stood and helped Aria out of her seat. "Ladies, maybe the two of you can get to know each other a little better in a less hostile area."

Jake reached up and twined his fingers with Nyla's. "It's okay, baby. Go on with Aria and chat."

Reluctantly, she let go and, with a warning glare aimed right for Jonah, stepped away from the table to leave the room with Aria.

"You are brothers by blood and by love," the Spanish-Italian vampire said in a disapproving tone. "Resolve whatever this is that lies between you so we can figure out just how bad this situation is and protect our loved ones."

"You don't know—"

"I know every cell of your brother's body is programmed for killing my kind, but instead of following through with his natural instinct, he walked side by side with us to save you from that demon's clutches last year. For that alone, you should show him more respect."

Jake looked curiously at the vampire.

"That's right, slayer, I gave you a compliment."

"Well, don't expect my undying gratitude," Jake replied. "I still remember the feel of your boot against my head."

"I believe that was for threatening to kill my mother. You very well deserved it."

Jake shrugged, nonchalant.

"I just want to know the truth," Jonah cut in. "I'm tired of all the secrets."

"I just told you the truth, and now you look at me like the rest of the family does," Jake said slowly, as though measuring each word. "You're all I have, Joe. You, Nyla, and my son. I need you to accept them."

Jonah closed his eyes as hot guilt lanced through his chest. His own parents had practically abandoned Jake, embarrassed by his odd behavior as a child, his talk of vampires and other imaginary creatures. They'd sent him to shrink after shrink, and when that failed to work, they'd just given up on him, doting on Jonah instead as their one chance for a normal family. They'd showered him with gifts on his graduation, set him up with dates, supported him in everything he did, but had totally ignored Jake's existence. He'd finally had enough last year, and told them not to speak to him until they could show his brother the same amount of love. He'd never seen his mother cry so hard.

Yet, through everything, Jake never held it against him that he was the favored son. There wasn't a single trace of envy. Jake loved him unconditionally, and he should repay his brother with the same consideration. The younger man deserved it, after all the love he'd never received from their parents.

"I'm sorry, Jake, but you gotta admit, that was one hell of a bomb you dropped on me."

"I know." He ran a hand through his short hair. "Trust me, it was the last thing I wanted to happen, but... Nyla's not an animal, Joe. She's nothing like what attacked Ronnie. Surely you know I wouldn't be with something like that."

Jonah considered his brother's words and nodded. Jake wouldn't be with something as vile as those were-hyenas. Hell, he wouldn't tie himself to one woman unless she was absolutely remarkable. "Who the hell would have figured you to be the one to get married first, let alone have a family of your own?"

"Sure as hell not me." Jake grinned.

"Well, now that that's settled," Rialto interjected, "I'd also like to know what happened in Hicksville, particularly the part where you killed Curtis Dunn. You did kill him, did you not?"

"Actually, no."

"No?" Rialto's one word was spoken in a low voice, but with enough power behind it to come out as a roar. "He watched as your brother was hung on a wall, and my wife nearly drained of every drop of blood in her body."

"Which is exactly why I hunted his ass," Jake said.

"Then why have you not come back here with his blood on your hands?"

"Surely your mother told you that he saved me."

Rialto's deep brown eyes darkened to a near black. "That does not mean you had to spare his life."

"He's proven valuable, so I spared him. If he ever slips up, don't worry. I'll kill him without hesitation."

"Will you now?"

"Do you think a day goes by I don't see my brother beaten and bloody, hung on that wall?"

Rialto and Jake stared each other down, silently challenging the other until finally, Jonah broke the silence.

"Curtis Dunn saved you?"

Jake broke off the stare-down to look Jonah's way. "Yes. I finally found the vampire who killed Bobby, and that same vampire would have killed me, if not for Curtis's interference.

Jonah sucked in a breath. "You found the vampire who killed Bobby? Did you kill him?"

"Yes."

"Good." Relief flooded through Jonah. The image of his best friend's murder had haunted his brother since he was just a kid. He'd found and killed a few of the vampires involved, but the main one had always been just out of his grasp. "Now you have closure."

Jake shrugged. "Closure doesn't really mean shit, bro. I can still hear Bobby screaming."

"I'm sorry."

Jake nodded. "You know, that's the night Nyla entered my life. She saved me from the vampires, and got bit in the process."

Jonah frowned. "Are you saying what I think you're saying?"

Jake nodded. "The vampire who killed Bobby was the same vampire who gave Nyla her vampiric traits."

"I thought a bite couldn't infect."

"Nyla is a Therian, and an empath. Something in her physiology reacted to the bite, and she gained some vampiric attributes. The vampire also took some of her race's traits."

"This stuff just keeps getting crazier and crazier." Jonah shook his head. "And now, the two of you are going to father children who will grow up to help save the world from Satan?"

Rialto and Jake looked at each other, and nodded.

"Could one of them be this special child, the Child of Light?"

"Possibly," Jake answered. "But we haven't yet come across the third mated set. There should be three children in all."

"You have no idea when the third child is supposed to be born?"

"For all we know, the child could have already been born," Jake answered. "But the fact that the evil powers that be are after us, makes me think the third set of mates have not found each other yet."

"Or could already be captured," Rialto added.

"Well, aren't you a bucket full of sunshine?"

"Honesty is always best when dealing with such matters," Rialto replied, holding Jake's gaze. "We must think of every possibility."

"Do you really think these murders have been occurring because of me?" Jonah took a deep breath, helpless as guilt coursed through his body.

Jake scratched his head. "I think Malaika's boyfriend took valuable information from her mind without her knowing about it. And I think the pranic vampire who changed him over, found that information and realized what he'd stumbled upon. Knowing you were a homicide detective, it would make sense to stage murders in this area, knowing you would show up at the scenes, and that I'd come after you if you were captured, but..."

"But, what?"

"I don't really know if that's it at all. If Malaika had a vision of helping Aria give birth, then that means she was already predestined for that role. She was already pre-destined to meet them with or without these murders happening. Even if she'd had visions of you, we don't know if there was enough from those visions to indicate you were related to one of the other chosen sets. We need to know what was taken from her before we make any assumptions."

A dull ache throbbed at Jonah's temples. This was all entirely too much to think on. "You said that witches who feared water did so because of the Salem witch trials. Because they were evil. Do you still believe Malaika is untrustworthy?"

Jake sighed deep, flexed his fingers. "I don't know. There were a few instances when completely normal people were put on trial, so who's to say an innocent witch didn't get tried? Just be careful with her, Joe. Innocent or not, it is her boyfriend who tried to kill you."

"Ex-boyfriend."

"Are you sure about that?" Jake held his stare, despite the heat of anger Jonah could feel behind his eyes. "She knew all along that he was involved in some way, followed his trail to every site, but she kept that from us."

Jonah looked down, unable to dispute those facts. Though he'd seen the desire in her eyes when she looked at him, she still protected Craig. "Still..."

"Don't go in blind, Joe. That man gave her a child, and that's a powerful bond."

Jonah buried his head in his hands, the dull headache gaining in pressure. How could he explain to his brother the depth of his feelings for Malaika? The instant attraction, the way he'd seemed to sense her at the crime scene before they'd even met. Yes, there'd been a split second when Aria had walked in, her belly round with Rialto's child, and he'd been a little jealous, but not of them. He'd had the image in his head of Malaika carrying his child. What he felt was too strong for a woman he'd just met, but it didn't feel as though he'd just met her. That was the strangest thing. The more time he spent around her, the more he got the feeling that he should have known her for years.

With Grandma Mahdi at her back, and Seta to her side, Malaika focused on the candle burning in the center of the table.

"You control the elements," Seta said softly. "Gather the wind, order it to obey you."

Malaika squinted her eyes, focusing harder on the flame. Her head hurt from the strain. The damned wind wasn't listening to her, and why would it? It was wind.

"You are trying to control the elements with your brain, not from your heart." Seta made a clicking noise. "I made the same mistake when coming into my powers."

"I don't understand."

"Love the wind, Malaika. Love its graceful dance, its freedom and purity. Love the earth for its fertility, the water for its beauty and clarity. Open your heart to the elements, and they will obey you."

Malaika closed her eyes and thought of the wind. She thought of the way it blew her hair, made the leaves dance on a fall day. She thought of how powerful it could be, building the force to tear roofs off houses. It was a beautiful thing. Full of grace one moment, but a powerful warrior the next. She opened her eyes, focused on the candle, and silently asked the wind to blow out the flame. It did.

Malaika gasped, and the two witches with her clapped.

"Now, move the candle."

Malaika looked at Seta, and the vampire-witch nodded her head in the direction of the candle. "Pick it up from the table and hold it, suspended in the air."

With a deep breath, Malaika focused on the pillar of wax, conjuring images of the wind in her mind. The image of a tornado entered her thoughts, and gave her an idea. Focusing her mind and heart on the power of the wind, she created a small, clear tornado and sent it to the table, where it lifted the candle and held it in the air while it spun.

"Good work."

Malaika let the tornado wind down and set the candle back on the table. Sweat beaded along her brow. She'd mastered fire, water, and now air. All that was left was earth, but Seta said earth was the easiest of all the elements, once the others were learned.

"The more you use your powers, the stronger they will become," Seta advised her. "The spells we have taught you and the power of the elements will protect you."

"Now we must find out what exactly we are protecting you from," Grandma Mahdi said, stepping out from behind her. "Lay on the table, child."

With a sweep of Grandma Mahdi's hand, the candle flew from the table, allowing room for Malaika's body. She lowered herself onto the table and stretched out.

"Close your eyes and relax."

Closing her eyes was easy. The relaxing part proved difficult with the knowledge that she was soon going to find out whatever dark truths Craig had kept from her. Craig, the man she'd loved. The man who'd given her the most beautiful child.

"Relax, Malaika." Grandma Mahdi's fingertips rested at her temples.

Seta started a chant, something strange in a language Malaika didn't understand, but at the same time, she felt an odd familiarity. An unsettling warmth spread through her limbs, rendering her immobile. She tried to open her eyes, but found the lids too heavy. She was frozen in place, unable to escape.

Grandma Mahdi joined in the chant, the strange words seeming to come from farther away as Malaika felt herself drifting down a dark hole...

"Witch! Witch!" The children screamed after her as she ran through the woods, branches cutting at her skin. She ignored the sharp needles of pain, doing her best to see past the tears coating her eyes and run to freedom.

Where am I? What's happening to me?

Malaika hid behind a large Oak, squatting down and wheezing, greedily sucking in large gulps of air. She looked down at her body and noticed how small it was. And what was she wearing? The dingy dress she had on looked as if it were constructed out of a flour sack. And what awful boots.

Oh, shit. This must be a past life.

A twig snapped in the distance behind her, and fear froze her breath. Those kids had called her a witch. What had she done?

"Bertrina!"

"She's not going to come to you, stupid."

Bertrina? Was that her name?

"She might as well. It'll be dark soon, and she'll be lost."

"The dark should not matter to her. You saw how she made fire in her hand."

Oh, hell. *Malaika listened to the two girls, both around thirteen years of age, and tried to figure out why she was having this particular memory. Seta and Grandma Mahdi were supposed to have worked a spell to show her what Craig had taken from her.*

"You know, in Salem, they burn witches."

"How do you know she's a witch? My mother says all that is a lie."

"She made fire in her hand to light the candle."

"I know."

Their steps came closer.

"So what else would explain it?"

"Demon possession."

There was a loud gasp, and Malaika shook. They were nearly on her.

"If Mother knew one of her servants was demon-possessed, she would order Father to kill her immediately."

"We must go back and tell."

"No! She may escape. We must kill her ourselves."

"No! What if we are wrong?"

They were right behind her. Malaika could barely hear over the pounding of her own heart.

"You know the rule. Demons hate water."

"They do?"

"Of course they do. They are made of fire. We will throw her into the lake."

One more step and they would be on her. Malaika took off at a run.

"There she is!" The girls cried in unison, and raced to catch her. It didn't take long before they were on her.

Malaika fought them off the best she could, but they grabbed her hair and dragged her through the woods, sticks and stones cutting through her dress and scraping her skin.

"Leave me alone! I'm not a demon!"

"Of course you deny it," one of the girls, a homely-looking child with red ringlets replied.

"Maybe she tells the truth," the chubby brunette said.

"She is a demon, Katherine. She lies."

Malaika struggled until her energy was spent. The sky had grown dark some time ago, but she barely noticed, her eyes shut so tight against the pain of rocks grinding into her flesh.

Finally. They let go of her.

"Are you sure about this?"

"Of course. My mother has told me all about demons and witches. If we do not destroy her while she is weak, she will smite us, our families, and our whole bloodline."

"We are doing a good thing?"

"Yes, of course."

"Then let us hurry before I lose my nerve."

Two sets of hands gripped her shoulders, and Malaika knew this was her last chance for survival, but she couldn't do anything to save herself. After all, this was her past life. It was already over.

So she let them drag her into the lake and let go.

She was running, her usual jog through the park. She'd jogged every day of her life until she'd met Craig. Soon after they'd started their relationship, he'd insisted she get a gym membership, claiming the park was too dangerous for her to run. In the image, she ran quickly, the wind whipping past, coating her hot skin with refreshing coolness.

"Hey! You're pretty fast."

She glanced back. It was Jonah! He was gorgeous, with those warm hazel green eyes and his dark hair curling up at the ends from sweat. She slowed her pace and smiled at him, wishing she didn't look so sweaty and unappealing. Then she felt a wave of guilt. She was with Craig. She shouldn't even notice other men. But then again, she'd been thinking of telling Craig to step, anyway. She had her suspicions of what he was really doing when he claimed to be working late. She sure hadn't seen the extra money he should have coming in.

"What's your name?"

"Malaika."

"Beautiful name, for a beautiful woman."

She rolled her eyes, and he laughed.

"Sorry. I usually don't hit on women like this. I just saw you and couldn't resist. I'm Jonah, Jonah Porter."

"Nice to meet you, Jonah Porter."

"Tell you what. I'll race you to the fountain and if I win, I get to buy you lunch."

"What if you lose?"

"I'll buy you dinner."

Malaika smiled. "That doesn't seem right. Whether you win or lose, you're still buying my meal."

"So you accept?" His whole face brightened. Man, when had been the last time Craig looked at her like that?

She glanced ahead at the fountain. "Yes, but if you win, the dessert is on me."

She lunged forward, thinking up all kinds of things she could do for "dessert" with this man before intentionally lagging behind to let him win.

"I love you, Malaika."

Malaika struggled to catch her breath as she looked up into Jonah's dark, lust-filled eyes. She'd never known sex could be so good. She'd actually screamed. What would the neighbors think? Did she actually care? "You don't have to say that just because we had sex."

His dark eyes narrowed, his brow creased. "I mean it. I love you, and sex has nothing to do with it."

Malaika bit her lip. Maybe he really did. He'd shown her nothing but kindness. And he'd invited her to dinner with his parents. No other man had ever done that. Hell, he'd even put up with her mother's rudeness, and had actually seemed to win the woman over, though she'd never admit it.

His mouth came down on hers, hot and greedy. Just like that, her entire body lit with fire again.

"Marry me."

"Wh-what?" She grabbed his face in her shaking hands. "What did you just say?"

"Marry me, Malaika. Please."

Malaika turned before the full-length mirror, admiring herself in the long, white gown. It was very simple and plain, but very elegant. With a deep breath, she smiled. She was going to become Mrs. Jonah Porter today.

"You look beautiful."

She turned to see her mother standing in the doorway. "Thanks, Momma."

Helen Jordan smiled and closed the door behind her. "Honey, I know I've been kind of hard on you about certain choices you've made in your life, but..." She reached out and smoothed a piece of Malaika's hair back. "I've always wanted the best for you, because I love you. I think you've found yourself a good man, even if he is white."

Malaika laughed. "I'm glad you agree with my decision."

"When I'm wrong, I say I'm wrong," Helen said, her tone serious. "That Craig was all wrong for you, and not just because he was a white man. Truth be told, I'm not much into the whole interracial thing, and I have my reasons, but Jonah Porter is a good man. That Craig... Baby, he was just wrong."

"Jonah!"

Jonah marched forward and stepped into the elevator. Malaika had barely made it through before the doors closed.

"Jonah, honey, talk to me."

"Just leave me alone, Mel."

"Baby, it's not that bad."

"Not that bad?" He glared at her, his eyes dark and hot. "Not that bad? I might as well be a fucking eunuch."

He turned his face away, but Malaika had already seen the sheen of tears he desperately fought to suppress. What could she do to help him through this?

"I love you, Jonah. We'll get through this."

"You want a baby. I can't give you that. How in the hell are we supposed to get through that?"

Malaika sighed in defeat. They'd tried for a year to get pregnant, and finally had went to see the doctor to find out if something was wrong with her. They'd never suspected Jonah to be sterile.

"We can adopt."

"Why? So every time I look at the kid, I can be reminded that I don't measure up as a man?"

The elevator doors opened and he stormed out, as if he couldn't wait to get away from her.

"Jonah. Jonah!"

He kept on walking.

The door burst open and startled Malaika awake from her nap on the couch. She looked up to see a tall, sandy-haired man holding a gun on her.

"Who the hell are you?" he asked.

Malaika worked her mouth, but words wouldn't come out.

"Are you my brother's wife? Are you Malaika?"

She nodded.

"Son of a bitch. Why did you find him? To get to me?"

She shook her head, holding her hands up to show she was unarmed and not a threat. "What the hell are you talking about? Jake?"

She'd never met Jonah's brother, but had heard about him. He was the black sheep of the family and a self-proclaimed vampire hunter.

"You know who I am, witch."

"Witch?"

He frowned. "Where's my brother?"

154

"*Right here.*" *Jonah stepped through the door and looked between the two of them, his gun in his hand.* "*Jake, what the hell are you doing holding a gun on my wife?*" *He raised his Glock and aimed it at Jake.*

"*What the hell am I...? What the hell are you doing holding a gun on me?*"

"*Put it down, Jake.*"

"*Put yours down.*"

"*No, not until you put yours away and quit scaring my wife.*"

"*Your wife is a witch.*"

Jonah closed his eyes for a fraction of a second and sighed. "*Jake, you need some help.*"

Jake's eyes darkened. "*Now, you too. My whole family is against me when I'm telling the truth. I've killed hundreds of vampires and witches, but you won't believe me.*"

"*Jake...*"

"*No! I lost Bobby and I won't lose you, whether you believe me or not!*"

Jake turned toward Malaika and started to pull the trigger. Instinctively, Malaika reached inside herself and brought green fire into her palms. She flung the balls of power at the younger Porter brother and knocked him into the wall. His gun went flying.

"*Malaika?*" *Jonah looked at her, wide-eyed.* "*What the hell did you just do?*"

"*I don't know!*" *Malaika looked at her palms, stupefied by what had just happened. She'd done it once before when a boyfriend had tried to hit her, but she'd convinced herself she'd imagined it.* "*How did I do that?*"

Jonah crossed the room and examined her hands. A groan behind him alerted them that Jake was coming to. Jonah turned and shoved her behind him. "*Stay behind me, no matter what.*"

"*Why?*"

"*Because... maybe my brother's right, and you do have some kind of powers. He'll try to kill you, but he'll have to get through me, first.*"

"*Jonah!*" *Malaika gasped as she saw her bruised and battered husband lying still in the hospital bed. His eyes cracked open as she rushed to his side.*

"Mel?"

"Jonah! Oh my god, Jonah."

"I'm gonna be good," he said, his words a little slurred. "It's alright."

"What happened to you? They said you were found inside a serial killer's home." He could have been killed there. Malaika's heart seized in her chest. They'd had their troubles, first with his difficulty dealing with being sterile, and then with his brother, but if she lost him... She couldn't imagine what she would do without him.

"I was following Aria Michaels, the girl whose mother was murdered."

Malaika sucked in a breath. Jonah had spent entirely too much time following that woman. "And?"

"And I was grabbed out of my car by..." He strained to lift his head from the pillow, but couldn't. "Are we alone?"

She glanced at the door and saw only the cop standing guard outside, customary when one of their own was hospitalized, and thought to possibly still be in danger.

"There's a cop standing guard outside."

"Come closer."

She leaned forward so he could whisper what he wanted to say.

"Jake was right. There are vampires, and demons, and... witches."

She jerked straight up, surprised by his words. "Jonah, honey, I think that's the morphine talking."

"No." The word came out strangled. "Demon almost killed me," he whispered. "Jake and the vampires saved me. They can help you."

"Help me what?" The poor man was bonkers, but she could play along. He'd probably forget everything he said to her once he came out of the drug haze.

"Your powers, Mel. You're a witch. They can teach you what to do."

His eyes drifted shut and he fell into sleep. Malaika replayed his words through her mind, the sincerity with which he spoke, and she trembled. It was crazy, preposterous... but deep inside, it just felt right.

"Push, now," Malaika directed the vampire.

Aria groaned and pushed against the pain wracking her body. A small head started to emerge.

Malaika smiled and let healing energy flow from her fingers and into Aria, easing the vampire's pain. Behind Aria, Rialto held his wife's shoulders, supporting her while waiting anxiously for his child to be born.

"It'll all be over soon," she said in a soothing tone and prepared to grab the baby, one of three special children born to immortals.

Malaika sat upright, gasping for air.

"Relax, darling, and just breathe." Seta patted her back.

Malaika looked at her surroundings. She was on top of the table in one of the rooms in Christian's church. Seta and the ghost of her grandmother were with her.

"What did you see, dear?" Grandma Mahdi asked expectantly.

Malaika swiveled her head around to face Seta. "I thought you were going to go in with me. Didn't you see everything?"

"No." Seta frowned. "Magic does not always work the way you intend, especially when it comes to spells. I could not mind-meld with you."

"What did you see?" Grandma Mahdi asked again.

"I saw myself die in a past life," she whispered, a tremble coursing through her limbs. She hadn't been killed during the Salem Witch Trials like Jake suspected, but had been murdered by children. Children! All because she'd lit a candle using her powers.

"I'm sorry, dear." Grandma Mahdi smoothed a hand over her hair to sooth her. "What did you see about Craig? Do you know what he suppressed from you?'

"He took my life," Malaika said bitterly. "I used to go jogging, and he must have seen that I would meet Jonah one morning during a run."

"Let me guess," Seta interrupted. "He made sure you never met."

"He told me to join a gym, said the park was unsafe. I should have met Jonah. We should have been married."

"So Craig saw your future with Jonah and prevented it so he could keep you to himself."

"Yes."

"What else did he see? Would he know anything of the Blood Revelation?"

Malaika thought back over the images she'd just seen. "Yes. There was the vision of me helping Aria have her baby. In my head, I thought of the child as one of the special three born to immortals."

"So that's how he knew about you having access to one of the special children." Seta wrung her hands nervously. "Does he know about Jake and Nyla's child?"

"No." Malaika shook her head. "But he would know that Jonah has a brother who is a slayer. And the vampire who changed him would know that if he read his mind." Malaika shook. "Can he still get in my mind?"

"No." Seta shook her head adamantly. "Part of the spell we just worked on you will ensure that he'll never get in your head again. And the fact that you were starting to regain images on your own indicates that what he had done to you was wearing off. His power over you only worked when he stayed in close proximity to you."

"I just don't understand. He willingly followed that siren away, and who knows what else he did with other women. He couldn't have loved me, so why did he want so badly to keep me?"

"Because he wanted to control you," Grandma Mahdi said on a sigh. "That's his type. He saw power in you and it made him feel better to control it by controlling you. In that sense, he felt he held all the power."

"And he never let me know what he was."

"Of course not," Seta said. "He wanted you completely unaware of what he could do to you."

Anger surged anew. Malaika looked at her grandmother. "You said Craig would try to kill Jonah."

"Yes." She nodded solemnly. "He still considers you and Deja to be his property, and the thought of you being with the man he did so much to keep you from is like a slap in the face to him. He will try to take that man out of the picture."

"I can't be with Jonah." A heavy weight settled in Malaika's chest. "For his own good, I can't be with him."

"That's the stupidest thing I've ever heard," Seta muttered. "Craig is going to try to kill Jonah whether you're with him or not. Even if you send Jonah away, you won't stop loving him. You can't. That is why Craig will kill him."

"So what do I do?"

"Kill Craig first."

The door opened and in stepped Jake and Jonah. Jake's face was grim, and Jonah wouldn't even look her way.

"You got her all witchified yet?" Jake asked, looking at her curiously.

"If you mean, has she been shown how to protect herself," Seta asked, "then the answer is yes."

"Good, because if we're going to end this and protect these babies, we gotta get moving. We're going to go with my original plan to draw these bastards out."

"What would that be?" Seta asked.

Jake looked at Malaika, and swallowed hard. "We use the junior witch as bait."

ELEVEN

"Everyone know the plan?" Jake looked at the group assembled in the room, his eyebrow raised.

Malaika stood in her living room with Jonah, Seta, Rialto, and Deja. She knew her daughter was safer back at the church, but couldn't bare saying goodbye to her there. She wanted to hold on to her as long as she possibly could, unable to shake the feeling she might never get the chance to see her again.

"Malaika and I stay here and see if Prince Charming shows up," Jonah stated, bitterness generously lacing his words. Malaika looked at him out the corner of her eye, her heart breaking for him. He should have been her husband. She'd allowed another man to control her and take away something so precious from both of them. Her hands squeezed on Deja's small shoulders. But she'd never have had her sweet Deja if not for Craig. For her alone, she couldn't completely hate Craig for what he'd done. He'd given her a child. A little girl with his eyes and her smile.

"You wait close outside to protect these two," Rialto added, "while Seta and I protect the expecting mothers. Christian will..." He glanced down at Deja, who, fortunately, was oblivious to the danger of the matter they were discussing, "baby-sit Deja."

Deja smiled, her eyes lit up with joy. She'd grown to really like the vampire. Malaika smiled to herself, running a hand over Malaika's head, feeling the frizzy braids under her palm. She needed to fix her baby's hair, but right now, protecting her life was more important.

"Right. And if anyone sees Prince Charming, we destroy that mother-fu—"

"Jake!"

"What?" Jake snapped, glaring at his brother.

"The F word."

Jake blinked, shook his head. "The F-word? What are you, like five?"

"No, but she is." Jonah jerked his head toward Deja and Jake followed the movement, sighing in frustration.

"Fine. If anyone sees the doody-head, pop him. That better?"

"Much. You're going to do such a good job with your own kid."

Jake rolled his eyes in annoyance and clapped his hands together. "Daytime doesn't last forever, and the newly turned creep at night. Let's get it done, people."

Good-bye time. Malaika leaned down, encircling Deja in her arms, smelling her sweetly scented hair. "Mama loves you, baby girl. You be good for Christian."

"I will, Mommy. I love you bunches!"

Reluctantly, she let her little girl go, and watched as she joined Rialto and Seta at the door. They smiled at her, waved goodbye, and took her daughter to safety.

Jake stepped before Jonah, his serious eyes level with his brother's. "Remember everything I've told you about these things."

"I will."

"Be on guard."

"I will. Of course, if you're the super-slayer you're supposed to be, I shouldn't have to worry about anything," Jonah teased.

"Yeah, well, regardless of my utter awesomeness, just be careful."

Jake looked at Malaika. "As for you, witchy-woman, I expect you to fry anyone who gets too close to my big brother, here."

Malaika grinned, knowing that simple statement was probably the closest she'd ever get to a "Hey, you're alright with me" from the slayer. Seta had told him about her past life and for some reason, he'd been a lot less hostile with her. "I will."

He narrowed his eyes on her, doubtful, before turning back to Jonah. "Kick ass and spill blood, bro." He extended his hand and Jonah clasped it in one of his.

They shook firmly, then quickly, so anyone who blinked would miss it, gave each other a quick one-armed hug and backed away from one another.

"Alright, pussy-boy, don't screw up," Jake mumbled as he headed toward the door.

"Yeah, you just watch yourself, jerk."

"Bitch."

"Ass-wipe."

Jake paused at the door, looked at his brother with a slew of raw emotions twisting in his eyes. His jaw clenched so hard enamel was probably being ground off his teeth. He looked at Malaika, silently pleading with her to not fail his big brother. She nodded, and he returned the gesture before pulling the door closed behind him.

"Interesting way you brothers have of saying goodbye," Malaika commented after they could no longer hear his footsteps pounding down the stairs in the hall.

Jonah grinned, nodded his head before turning it to look down at her. "You all right?"

"As good as I can be, half scared out my mind." Her stomach grumbled in protest of not having been fed, and she rubbed it with her hand. "Did I mention half-starved, too? I never did eat anything today."

"Afraid to eat whatever a vampire might provide?"

Malaika laughed. "I know it's silly, and he made sure Deja had plenty to eat, but..."

"I know." Jonah patted his stomach. "I'm running on empty too."

"I'll cook you something." Malaika walked into the little kitchen area and started sifting through the refrigerator. "We still have some time before dark sets in, and we'll both probably do better with some food in our bellies tonight."

"If you don't mind."

"I don't." She glanced up as Jonah took a seat among the stools at the counter which separated the kitchen area from the living room, and found herself lost in the beautiful, warm depths of his eyes. Heat flushed over her skin. She was going to cook for her man, something she should have been doing for years now.

Tears formed in her eyes, unbidden, and she turned her face toward the refrigerator. She swallowed hard, tried to get past the surge of emotion clutching her chest. All the times she'd cried because Craig hadn't thought her worthy enough to propose, but Jonah had... or would have, if she hadn't been so stupid to let Craig get inside her head and change the order of events in her life.

Strong arms wrapped around her waist, and pulled her back against a solid wall of security. "I saw the tears in your eyes," Jonah said softly, his breath fanning across her cheek. "What is it?"

She rested her head against his chest and let out a sigh which twisted into a strangled sob before she could control it. "I'm just tired."

"You don't have to cook."

"Yeah, well, I'm more hungry than tired, and I want meat." She stepped out of his embrace, fighting against the urge to just stay there wrapped in his arms for the remainder of whatever length of time they had until Craig showed his face, and grabbed a few meat patties out of the refrigerator. "Hamburger or cheeseburger?"

"I'll take cheese," Jonah answered softly, stepping back to give her room to work.

She grabbed the necessary components to make cheeseburgers and closed the refrigerator door. "Fries?"

"Sure."

Malaika chuckled softly. "Are you sure Deja hasn't worn you out on fries yet?"

"I'm a thirty-one-year-old man, Malaika. I can put away fries and other assorted fast foods with the best of them." The smile could be heard in his voice. "I won't start eating healthy until I get a wife ordering me to, I imagine."

Malaika placed the frying pan on the stove top harder than she'd intended, the weight of it half-falling out of her suddenly weak hand. "You should take care of yourself anyway. You're a good man."

"And you know this after having just met me?"

"I shouldn't have just met you," she couldn't stop herself from saying as she pulled out a bag of frozen french fries from the freezer and dropped a healthy amount into the pan of grease she'd started heating on the stove.

"Malaika?"

"Yes?" She didn't turn around, didn't dare to see whatever emotion he held on display in his gorgeous hazel eyes.

163

"What aren't you telling me? And why the hell do I feel like I already know?"

She did glance back at him then, saw the hope and confusion twisted in those green-brown gems that so effectively melted her into a puddle of need. "What do you mean?"

He closed his eyes for a brief moment, shook his head. "I can't kick this feeling that... that we've met before, or if we haven't, we should have."

Malaika felt her eyes grow wide. And she'd thought she was the one with the psychic powers. But Jonah had surprised her before, as well. The way he'd known there was a woman involved in the murders, the way he always seemed to pick up on little tiny things no one else would. Maybe he was a tad psychic himself, or just really sensitive to other psychics. "It's understandable you would feel that way."

She heard his intake of breath as she turned to flip the hamburger patties over and cover them with cheese. "Why?"

"Because." She checked the fries. "We should have met about seven years ago while jogging in the park."

It was her! Jonah's mouth hung open in shock as the image of Malaika running in little pink shorts and a sport bra flooded his mind. He'd watched her for what seemed an eternity all those years ago, taking in her graceful strides, the toned body that glistened in the sunlight, begging to be tasted. She'd been sex in sneakers, a vision of perfection he woke up every morning just to catch a glimpse of. Then she'd disappeared, just as he'd worked up the nerve to approach her.

"You were the park goddess."

Malaika laughed, her eyes gleaming with amusement as she turned her face to glance at him. "The park goddess?"

Jonah shrugged, embarrassed. He hadn't meant to let the name he'd used when thinking of her slip out. "I didn't know your name, so I called you what you were to me."

"Wow." She put the food onto two plates and handed them to him. "I don't think I've ever been called a goddess before."

He smiled, taking the plates from her to deposit on the bar while she quickly cleaned the dishes she'd used to prepare dinner. "Thirsty?"

"I could take a sweet tea."

Jonah fixed the drinks and joined her at the bar, sliding onto the stool next to hers. He bit into the cheeseburger she'd cooked and flavor flooded his mouth. "Damn, girl. This is good."

"I prepackage them individually with special seasoning."

Jonah swallowed the delicious meat, followed with a few more bites, and turned toward her. "You said we should have met seven years ago. Why didn't we? Why'd you disappear when I finally worked up enough courage to introduce myself?"

She chewed on a fry, looking thoughtful, and swallowed, her eyes sad. "Seta and my grandmother worked a spell to show me what Craig had taken from me. Apparently the bastard could read my future and he knew I would have met you if I continued to run in the park. He convinced me to join a gym and effectively altered the rest of my life."

She popped another fry into her mouth, chomping harder than needed to chew the strip of potato. Jonah's breath stuttered, hope and a bit of satisfaction filling him as he deciphered her words. "You were with him then, but you would have left him."

"Yes."

"For me?"

"Yes." She turned her face toward his, her eyes hot and angry. A little bit needy. "And I would have married you within the year."

She should have been his wife. The familiarity that struck him at the crime scene, the need to protect which he hadn't been able to fully shake, not even when Jake had told him she was a witch, suddenly made sense. She was supposed to be his. His wife. The one thing that could fill the void he'd been feeling for the past several years.

He kissed her. He gave no thought to words. Forget questions, explanations. She should have been his wife. That's all he thought of as he pressed his lips against hers, stood from his seat and pulled her small body against his. She was his, should have always been. He swept his tongue inside her mouth, claiming his property, determined that when he was through she'd be so full of his taste, she'd forget that bastard, Craig, had ever existed.

Reality slammed into him, cold and harsh. Craig was still out there, determined to keep him separated from this woman by any means possible. He had to stay focused on her protection, and Deja's. White-hot anger rolled through him at the thought of another man giving Malaika the child he should have created with her, but he suppressed it. It didn't matter. Despite the child's paternity, Deja was an extension of Malaika, had been created in her womb. He loved her for that alone and would lay his life down for the little girl just as he would for her mother. Forcing himself to break away, he pulled back and gently rubbed a thumb over Malaika's kiss-swollen bottom lip.

"What—" She sucked in a breath— "was that for?"

"Making up for lost time," he responded with a smile, his whole body straining to start it over again. He bit into his lip, the small stab of pain helping to clear his lust-filled brain. "But I shouldn't. I have to stay clear-headed and focused. I have to make sure that bastard is good and truly gone before we can really explore what we've both been missing."

Her eyes glazed over with heated desire, killing him softly. "If that was just a taste, I don't know if I can wait for the rest."

She licked her lips and his whole body hardened. "Shit, Mel. You're killing me here."

He dipped his head, brushing his lips over her warm, inviting ones again. Jake was near in case anything happened. He could do this and somehow keep part of his mind focused on the danger lurking in the darkness of night. Surely. His tongue met Malaika's and they both trembled. She was worth dying for, he rationalized as her hands gripped his shoulders with the ferocity of a tigress. In fact, there was no better way to go out than melded with her.

The sound of keys jingling at her door drew him out of the lusty thought, and they turned their heads just as the lock twisted and the door opened, allowing entrance to an attractive light-skinned black woman with bright green eyes, whose scowl upon seeing Malaika and him wrapped in an embrace was darker than the black silk pantsuit she wore. "Well, look what the cat finally dragged back home," she said, her scolding eyes crawling over every inch of Jonah.

"Mom." Malaika released her iron grip on him. Her greeting held a warning tone.

Mom? Well, if there was anything to make a man's hard-on turn into a limp noodle, it was being interrupted by a parent. He stepped away from Malaika, giving his flaming hormones a chance to cool down.

"I've been calling all day," Malaika's mother went on, stepping into the apartment fully and shutting the door behind her. "Imagine my surprise when police questioned me about your whereabouts. And who the hell is this?" She pinned Jonah with a lethal glare. He actually swallowed hard, feeling the brunt of her distaste.

"This is Jonah Porter, a detective with the Baltimore homicide department, and a close friend," Malaika all but growled, clearly unhappy with her mother's rudeness. "Jonah, this is my mother, Helen Jordan."

"Nice to meet you, Mrs. Jordan," he greeted her out of obligation, despite the way she looked at him. As if he were dirt soiling her daughter.

She looked him over, her nose turned up in snooty disgust, and ignored him to focus her full attention on her daughter. "Homicide detective, huh? And you have the police department looking for you, too. What is going on? Where's Deja?"

"I'll call Granger and let him know you're with me," Jonah announced, stepping away from the two women while he turned on his cell phone and walked down the hallway. There were sparks flying in every direction from the women and he didn't want anywhere near them when they blew.

He'd turned his cell off once he'd found Jake at the church, and hadn't felt any need to turn it back on. Jake was the only person whose call he'd been awaiting anyway, and if Granger could get a hold of him, he could question him about Malaika. Something he hadn't wanted to deal with. The man had trouble accepting the fact Malaika was a psychic. He sure as hell wouldn't understand her being a witch, not that he had any inclination to tell him that. He wasn't surprised to see several messages from Granger on his phone.

He braced himself for the inevitable ass-chewing and dialed his boss's number.

"I asked you a question, young lady."

"I'm not a child," Malaika snapped and collected the plates of half-eaten dinner. She had the sinking feeling the food would be completely cold by the time her mother finished interrogating her and left. "I'm not in any trouble with the police." Just some crazy creatures.

"Then why are they looking for you?"

"I'm helping with a case, the murders you've been seeing on the news."

"The mutilations?" Horror rent Helen's pretty features into a mask of fear. "How could you possibly be helping them with that mess?"

"Because..." Malaika threw away the remains of dinner and braced her hands on the kitchen counter. "I see the murders before they happen."

"Oh, not this again!" Helen threw her hands in the air, shaking her head. "What? Did you call them, claiming to be some kind of psychic?"

"No, I didn't. I sensed the murders and followed the sense to the scenes of the crimes. Jonah saw me there and—"

"Oh, you stupid, stupid fool! They think you're the killer!" Helen looked down the hall in the direction Jonah had went before turning those hot, angry eyes back to her. "They're going to pin these murders on you."

"I am not stupid," Malaika managed to get out through the tears struggling to break free. "And Jonah knows I'm innocent."

"Jonah? Jonah." Helen laughed, and it was the ugliest sound Malaika had ever heard. "Oh, well, if Jonah believes you, you're just fine. It's not like he's a homicide detective who might enjoy using you before slapping on the cuffs."

"He's not using me. You don't even know him!" Malaika tightened her shaking hands into fists, felt the fire warming her palms as she stepped before her mother.

"*You* don't even know him! Just like you didn't know that other white excuse of a man who used you, impregnated you, and left you alone to raise his half-breed daughter."

Malaika slapped her mother's face out of pure reflex, and didn't feel a twinge of remorse. "Don't ever speak of my daughter as if she's some sort of mongrel."

Helen backed away in surprise, her hand covering the skin which was now red from the weight of Malaika's hand slamming into it. "I didn't... I ..." She shook her head from side to side, tears spilling from her eyes. Her green eyes. "I love Deja."

"But you'll never get over the fact she has a white father, just like you'll never get over the fact that you have a white father." Helen's eyes widened, and Malaika shook her head in disgust. "Come on, Mom. Anyone with common sense can look into those bright green eyes of yours and tell you're biracial. How can you hate what you are?"

"I don't." Helen's voice was dark. "I hate what that man who fathered me was, and I hate that man who used you. I've learned the hard way what they're capable of."

Malaika frowned, her head hurt from trying to understand her mother's bigotry. She'd never known her grandfather. Even Grandma Mahdi wouldn't speak of him. He had to have been an awful man. "What did my grandfather do to you?"

"He used me, just like the rest of his kind do."

"How?"

Helen shook her head. "You'll learn the hard way like I did. Don't say I didn't try to protect you."

Annoyance and sheer exhaustion of the issue gave Malaika an idea. "Tell me or I will make you tell me."

Helen laughed. "How? With your magical powers? You and your grandmother, I swear. If magic existed, my mother would have saved me."

Malaika frowned, wondering what her mother was talking about. Saved her from what? Grandma Mahdi appeared then, tears falling from her eyes, but Helen couldn't see her.

"Tell me."

"Figure it out yourself while you're in prison."

"I'll just figure it out now." Malaika reached for the power inside and pinned her mother to the wall. She ignored the wide-eyed look of fear on the woman's face and touched her palm to her mother's temple. She closed her eyes and inhaled, snatching her mother's memories just like Seta had shown her. She wasn't prepared for the darkness she found.

Helen had been molested, repeatedly, by her own father. Her entire childhood was spent in hell, awaiting his nightly visits. Malaika struggled to stay inside her mother's mind despite the hideous cruelty she found there. She had to know why her mother hated white men so.

Yes, she'd been abused by her white father, but that shouldn't have made her hate the whole race, just the evil demon in question. She swallowed past bile, skimming over the images. She couldn't see her grandfather's face, just his tall, lean build as he hovered over her mother's bed, his arousal evident against the strain of his pants.

The images ran past, one horrid image after another, and she saw Grandma Mahdi shoo Helen away when she tried to tell her what was happening. Blinded by love, she didn't even listen to her young daughter's cries. Malaika frowned, unable to believe Grandma Mahdi would do such a thing. It was as if the woman had been mind-controlled to ignore what was happening.

She saw her mother run from the small apartment she'd grown up in, her nightgown bloody and tattered. Saw her run into a group of men outside a liquor store, a group of drunk white men. She saw the way they looked at her as if she were trash and handed her right back to her father. She was trash to them, and no concern of theirs. Now, if she had been white, they would have helped her. Malaika saw it clearly in their eyes, and so had Helen.

The abuse continued and no one came to her rescue. Not even Grandma Mahdi, until eventually something happened to break the spell cast over her. She charged into the bedroom after years of the abuse had been spent, and pulled the rutting man off her daughter. Malaika watched as Grandma Mahdi fought her surprised husband—No, they'd never married—until they reached the other room. She watched as with magic, Grandma Mahdi forced the window open, and invoked the wind to carry her grandfather out the window and drop him three stories to his death in the dark, filthy alley before packing up and leaving with Helen.

But the image didn't stop there, despite the fact her mother couldn't have possibly known what happened next. Malaika watched the rain beat down on the lifeless shadow of the man in the alley for what seemed like hours. Then she saw him sit up, heard the crunch of bones as he twisted his neck, realigning his body, and she gasped as she finally saw his face clearly in the rain. She'd been wrong when she'd thought of him as a demon. She'd had the wrong creature in mind. Her grandfather was no demon. He was a pranic vampire, the same one who'd attacked her less than twenty-four hours ago.

Malaika's knees buckled as she withdrew from Helen's mind, but she was caught by two bands of steel before her rump could hit the floor.

"Malaika?"

The concern in Jonah's voice helped still some of the tremors wracking her body, but it couldn't completely chase away the coldness. She looked between her grandmother's sorrow-filled eyes, and the angry eyes of her mother, and couldn't speak.

"Tell her I'm sorry," Grandma Mahdi managed through deep, wracking sobs. "He controlled me for so long."

Then she was gone. But Helen remained, her body rigid as she was lowered to the floor. "You..." The word came out as a growl. "You invaded me."

"I had to know," Malaika gasped out on a whisper. Guilt chewed at the edges of her conscience but she knew deep inside her mother would have never told her what had happened to spark the bitter hatred inside her.

"Well, now you know." Helen's dark gaze cut to Jonah. "They're all the same. They won't help you. They'll only take."

"No." Malaika shook her head adamantly, and placed her hand over Jonah's as she felt him stiffen. "My grandfather didn't abuse you because he was white. He abused you because he was evil, as were the others who you sought help from."

Helen closed her eyes and shook her head sadly. "My stupid, stupid daughter. I've failed to teach you." She threw up her hands in defeat and broke down into deep sobs as she crumpled to the floor.

"Malaika?"

She turned in Jonah's arms and saw the confused bewilderment in his eyes, in the crease of his brow. What must he be thinking? She could delve into his mind and find out, but she didn't want to do that with him. Nor did she need to. He, she could trust enough to just ask. "Just hold me for a minute."

He obliged with no questions asked, surrounding her with love and warmth as she rested her head on his chest, trying to clear the jumble inside it long enough to think straight. Her grandfather was a pranic vampire? Did Grandma Mahdi know? She knew Helen didn't. When had he been changed, and why was he in her life now? How had he and Craig come together? It was all too coincidental for her liking. She should talk to Jake. She rose her head from Jonah's chest to ask him to call his brother, but before she could speak a single word, the lights went out.

Everything happened so fast. Fear spiked. Windows burst. The door crashed open. Her mother screamed. Jonah cursed. They were torn apart from each other by unseen forces, and had to fight with no idea where the blows would come from. With the windows and door gone, light should have found a way to filter in, but this darkness was unnatural, not caused by the electric having been cut. This was a magical darkness cloaking them. Hampering their chance of defense.

Malaika formed fire in her hands, but each time she formed a ball of it, she had to use it against an attacker. There was no time to use it to help her find Jonah in the darkness. She felt him though, somehow felt he was alive. So was her mother, who didn't stop screaming. But the attackers, and there were many of them, paid her no attention.

She struck again and again with the fireballs, hoping Jake would burst into the room at any moment to save them, but if he had, she couldn't sense it.

There was a loud cracking sound behind her and alarm slit through her heart. Jonah was hurt. Bad. She felt the darkness closing in around him as if it were her own body succumbing to unconsciousness. "Jonah!"

"I'm afraid your boyfriend can't respond now," came a dark voice from before her. Tremors danced over her skin at the familiar sound. It was the voice of the vampire who'd attacked her in the abandoned building. The vampire who'd abused her mother for years, destroying her innocence.

She judged his distance by the sound of his heavy breath, and spit into his face a second before pain exploded against her temple.

TWELVE

Coldness invaded Malaika's senses first, followed by stiffness. She cracked open her eyelids but couldn't see a thing through the haze of pain.

"She's awake."

She tensed at the deep gravelly sound of a male voice, her only relief the fact that it didn't sound like the voice of the vampire who'd attacked her before. Her grandfather.

"Should we tell Xander?"

"We were only instructed to watch them."

Them? Malaika narrowed her eyes, straining. About six feet before her stood two tall, blurred forms. One lean and lanky, the other pretty beefy. As her eyes focused, she saw the gleam of the men's eyes. One was focused on her. The other man's head was directed toward her right, where a soft groan rumbled. She followed the sound and found another man, bent over, on his knees. His arms were raised up, his wrists bound with thick rope to a post at his back. He slowly, as if the mere action heightened his pain, looked up until their eyes met. Despite the deep gash over his right eye, he was the most beautiful sight she'd ever laid eyes on.

"Jonah."

"Mel." His head lowered, another groan escaped him. "I feel like I just went toe-to-toe with a truck."

The men before them chuckled, obviously proud of the beating they'd subjected them to. Anger rekindled itself in Malaika's chest. "Were either of you bastards the ones who knocked us out?"

"Maybe," came the amused reply from the lanky one. "Why?"

"Oh, I'd just like to know who to kill slower."

Both men laughed. "And how are you going to do that?" Beefy asked.

Malaika smiled, slow and deadly as she reached inside for her power, and came up with nothing. Looking down, she discovered why the men were so amused by the thought of her doing anything. She was wrapped in another witch's net.

"Don't provoke them," came a warning from her left, and she turned her head to see an older man tethered to a post just like Jonah. "They'll only hurt you more, the monsters."

Familiarity struck and Malaika frowned, trying to place the voice. The man was in or around his fifties, with long, gray hair and a hook-like nose. He looked up then and despite the swollen condition of his eyes, she recognized the lower portion of his face. "You're the fisherman I saw in my vision."

His eyes widened, but just barely due to the condition they were in, before he nodded. "You are psychic too?"

"Yes."

"Then they'll probably kill you slowly as well, making sure you're completely drained first."

Fear clogged Malaika's throat as she twisted her head around to look at Jonah. His head was raised, his eyes locked on hers.

"No one will hurt you," he promised. "I swear with my life."

The men guarding them laughed. "Listen to the mighty warrior. Tell me, human, what do you plan to do to protect your woman while your hands are tied above you?"

Jonah glared at the lanky man who'd spoke the taunt, his eyes parlaying his dark threat. The man heckling him actually swallowed, clearly unnerved by Jonah's intent. "The last man who tied me up and beat me was just as cocky as you until my brother and his friends burst through the door and blew his ass apart."

"Your brother will not save you this time." The lanky guard smiled, showing deadly teeth. He was one of the were-hyenas. "Xander is smarter than the man who last held you captive."

"That's why you're enslaved to him?"

The men bristled at Jonah's comment. "We are not slaves."

"Please. You're were-hyenas. Filthy, stupid creatures who can't even exist on your own. You have to be baby-sat by higher life forms so as not to totally screw yourselves." Jonah shook his head. "It's actually quite sad. All that brawn and not an iota of brain power to back it up. That's probably why it was so easy for me to kill two of your pack."

The beefy guard took a step forward, but was held back by the lanky guard. "Xander will take care of him."

"Xander?" Jonah laughed out loud. "What a bunch of pussies. Yes, let Xander take care of me, the weak human. Hell, I don't even think you things come with dicks."

Both men rushed toward him and Malaika's breath caught in her lungs. What the hell was Jonah doing? She surveyed the room, looking for something, anything to help him, but the room they were in was a basic cell. Hard floors and walls. No décor, no furniture. Besides the table far in front of them which held the weapons Jonah had carried on him before they were taken. She fought against the witch's net and found it gave a little, but not enough for her to do much. Like incinerate the beasts rushing at Jonah. Now that would have been useful. She couldn't call fire. Or wind. The earth was easiest, she remembered, and was hit with a brilliant idea. She was interrupted before she could put it in action.

"Stop!"

Malaika jerked toward the powerful man standing at the room's only door, and recognized him instantly. After all, she'd had a child with him.

The two beasts stopped, growling as they backed away. Jonah paid them no attention, completely focused on the vampire entering the room. The man who'd stolen what was rightfully his.

He'd jumped up as the beasts rushed him, and found though he was tethered to the pole sticking out of the ground, he could still move most of his body. Now his arms were at an awkward angle, but his hands were hidden behind his body, out of view. He half-squatted, half-stood and worked at the rope binding him as the vampire approached Malaika.

"The human is not to be killed yet," Craig stated firmly, his eyes never leaving Malaika. He reached out and caressed her face with the back of his hand, ripping a roar of disapproval from Jonah.

The vampire turned his gaze toward him then, his eyes dark and full of hate. Jonah quit working the rope as he approached, unsure how observant vampires were, if he could tell his hands were moving behind him. He rose to his full height, knowing doing so would further hide his hands behind his body, and ignored the pain shooting through his arms.

"I should peel your skin from your bones," the vampire said, stopping in front of him so they were face to face. "You should have never touched what is mine."

"I could tell you the same."

Craig's eyes narrowed. "Malaika has discovered the truth then?"

"That you saw our future together and screwed with her real fate? Yeah, she knows you're a lying, cheating dick."

A grin tugged at the corner of the vampire's mouth, but his eyes remained dead. "I gave her what you never could. And you'll never take it from me."

Jonah frowned, wondering what the vamp was talking about. "The only thing you gave her was pain and heartache. Distrust. Abandonment. Danger."

Craig grinned fully now. "She hasn't told you everything."

"Craig, don't." Malaika pleaded with the vampire, distraught. Jonah turned his face toward her to see tears glistening in her eyes. "Please."

What the hell had she seen?

Craig threw back his head and laughed before turning his gaze toward her. "How sweet. Stand by your man, and all that. Except you forget, I am your man."

"You stole me from my man and you damn well know it. Haven't you hurt us enough?"

Craig's body tensed, his eyes warmed with rage. "You did not mind. Every time I tasted you, filled your body with—"

White-hot rage filled Jonah and he jumped, ignoring the pain threatening to tear his arms apart as he brought his legs up and kicked the vampire with all the strength he had.

Craig went flying backward, a grunt of pain torn from him before he regained his footing, turning lethal eyes on Jonah. "You miserable waste of flesh."

"Craig, don't!"

Malaika's cry went ignored as the vampire charged, ramming his fist into Jonah's stomach hard enough to steal the breath from his lungs. Jonah bent forward, reacting to the blow, and fought back bile. He wouldn't give the vampire the satisfaction of throwing up, even though doing so on the bastard's feet was tempting.

"Craig! Stop!"

The vampire backed away, and Jonah pulled himself back up, discreetly tugging at his restraints. They gave a little slack. Not long now, and the bastard was his.

"Leave us."

Malaika watched as the were-hyena guards followed the command, sniffing at her as they passed. She cringed at the realization they probably wanted to chew on her like they had the bodies of the victims she'd seen in her visions.

Craig stepped toward her, his gaze unwavering. A predator stalking his prey. A cold chill trembled up her spine, but she ignored it, looking past Craig to study Jonah. Craig had delivered a hard blow, one that could have killed a lesser man, but the Porters were made of strong stuff. Which Jonah proved by simply being able to stand. He didn't look at her, but at Craig, the promise of death in his eyes.

"I do not understand you," Craig said, his tone genuinely laced with confusion as he knelt down to her level. "I gave you everything he could not, yet you still feel such strong emotion for him."

Malaika met the gaze of the man who'd raided her mind for information without her knowledge, changed her fate for his own personal gain and then preceded to harm the daughter he'd claimed to love. Her stomach churned with self-disgust. How could she have been so blind? "Jonah can give me love. I don't think you even know how to do that."

His eyes widened. "I have always loved you, Malaika. I wouldn't have changed the course of your life if I did not love you."

"Wanting to control someone is not the same as loving them," she all but growled. "If you saw my future, you saw my love for him. You took that from me."

"I gave you something he never could." He grinned. "Do not tell me you would trade that in in order to have him in your life?"

"What the fuck is he talking about?" Jonah asked, irritated.

"I'm talking about you not being a man," Craig stated, sparing a glance in Jonah's direction to gauge his reaction. "You could never give her a child, but I could, and did."

Malaika sucked in a breath, bracing herself for Jonah's reaction. Her visions had already shown her the pain he'd endured with the knowledge he couldn't give her a child. He looked at her now, mouth open, eyes questioning.

"Malaika?"

She closed her eyes, fighting back hot tears. She didn't want to have this conversation. Not now, not here with the father of her child taunting him. "It doesn't matter, Jonah."

"Yes, Jonah. It does not matter that you are not even half the man I am," Craig taunted him further. "I was nice enough to fill her womb with a child, something your useless, sterile dick could not—"

Malaika kicked out and found the witch's net had weakened enough to allow her to move that much. Her foot found Craig's chest and propelled him backward. He landed on his rump with a look of surprise. The surprise grew as she stood and shook off the silvery remnants of the net. "Leave him alone. He is more of a man than you will ever be, and I loved him, even without a child. The only good thing I can say about you is you gave me Deja. I'll always be grateful for that, but even giving me a child could never make me choose you over him."

Applause erupted from her right, and Malaika turned to see her grandfather standing in the doorway, his smile lending no warmth to his eyes. They were cold and dead. Evil. "I must say, it does fill my chest with pride to have such a powerful witch in my get. That net should have contained your physical movements longer."

Malaika's stomach rolled again, this time with the knowledge she was related to the beast crossing the room toward her. She waited for him to approach so she could spit in his face again, then remembered what she'd been doing before the attack. And what he'd done to Helen all those years ago. "Where is my mother? What have you done with her? And how the hell did you get into my apartment?"

He waved a hand dismissively. "The wonderful thing about apartment buildings is that once you gain permission from a landlord, you can get inside any apartment you like, and your mother is of no importance. I left her there."

Malaika studied his face, tried to gauge whether he was being dishonest with her. After all, the man had enjoyed torturing her mother during her childhood. "I saw what you did to her, you sick bastard."

He grinned. "She may have been of no importance, but I cannot deny she was a tasty morsel. The scent of her fear as I invaded her was like ambrosia."

Malaika swung her arm, determined to slap the grin off his face, but her wrist caught in his steel grip. "Now, now, little witch. Did your mother not teach you to respect your elders?"

"How the hell did you father her?"

He chuckled, letting go of her. "It's simple birds and bees, my dear. And, obviously, I didn't take the leap into immortality until after she'd been conceived."

"You're not immortal," Jonah stated. "Just harder to kill."

Her grandfather—who she now realized was the Xander the were-hyenas had mentioned—looked at Jonah in amusement. "And I presume you think you'll be the one to prove that?"

"I don't see why not."

Xander chuckled again. "Your human amuses me."

"Too bad we're going to kill him once we figure what it is about him that makes him immune to our mind-hold," Craig interjected, now standing.

Xander shot him a look of annoyance. "I'm not so sure of that. A man with such a strong lock on his mind could be a powerful warrior for our cause."

"He's the brother of a slayer. He'll never take the change," Craig argued.

"You are far too new a vampire to have any idea what you speak of," Xander snapped, "and a mad vampire can be very worthwhile if properly controlled. Unlike those bleeding hearts who saved him once before, I care not how many innocents my creations destroy."

"What are you talking about?" Malaika asked, her palms growing clammy. She couldn't let them change Jonah into what they were. "What do you need an army for?"

Xander's eyes gleamed as they fell upon her. "You already know of the Blood Revelation. Why else would you have a vision of helping a vampire couple give birth?" He narrowed his eyes on her and his mouth split into a smile. "Don't deny it. I've overheard enough of you and Craig's little chat in here to know you've regained what he took from you. Imagine my surprise when, while hunting, I found a new psychic to induct into my army, and raided his mind, only to see images of my own flesh and blood."

Malaika cast a glance at Craig and he looked away, his face coloring. Out of shame? Did he actually have a fragment of conscience left?

"Not only did I see you, my granddaughter, a powerful yet untrained witch, but I saw the man you were supposed to have been with before Craig here got a little greedy and changed your course." He cut Craig a glance, and gave him a nod of approval. "You see, I've seen your human before." He chuckled at Malaika's surprise. "There was a man who tried to invent an immortality serum by experimenting on vampires. He tried to catch me, but failed. My curiosity was, however, piqued, so I followed his doings. Your human was abducted by him and rescued by a slayer and a group of vampires, along with the woman—now a vampire—you envision giving birth."

Malaika shook her head, trying to clear it. "I don't understand. Jonah and I have nothing to do with this Blood Revelation. We're not the chosen."

Xander rolled his eyes, displeased with her. "No, but you know who the chosen are, and can lead me to them."

She swallowed hard, and carefully sequestered all thought of Rialto and Aria behind the silver wall in her mind. She shoved Nyla in there as well, for safe measure. "Craig changed my future. Those visions don't mean anything now. Changing the events of my life changed everything."

Xander laughed. "No, my dear. You can play with fate but what is predestined has a way of happening no matter what anyone does to obstruct it. You did meet the man you truly desired after all, did you not?"

Malaika looked at Jonah, her heart racing. He had a point, and was too clever for her to pull a bluff on him. Shit. "We found each other because of the murders. You led us to each other."

"No, I did not. Fate led you to one another."

"Then why the murders?" She shook her head, confused. "Why did you leave the bodies behind, knowing we'd follow? You knew what you were doing."

"I told you, I was—and still am—building my army for the upcoming war between the light and the dark. My siren snares the psychics, bringing them to me. If they are strong enough to take the change, I turn them into pranic vampires, as I did with Craig. If they aren't, I kill them and let the were-hyenas feed." He shrugged. "It keeps them from running loose, killing senselessly. As annoying as they can be, they are good guard-dogs, and we need all the force we can acquire. You sensing Craig during the attacks and following him was not planned, but a rather convenient bonus. I must say, I'm rather pleased with the way it worked out."

Malaika turned toward the fisherman, who was watching in silence. "What about him?"

Xander turned toward the fisherman. "Him? Caught him trying to warn some of our prospects away from the siren. He knew too much to be allowed to remain free so I've kept him for sustenance. We'll use your human in much the same way until we tire of him."

"Put your mouth on me and I'll rip your fucking heart out," Jonah promised.

Xander chuckled again. "I do like his bravado. Hopefully, you'll comply with my request so I don't have to kill him."

"What request?"

"Have you not listened to a word I've said?" Xander turned his gaze back to her, his eyes displaying his exasperation. "You will take me to the child."

"There is no child. I don't know the vampires you're talking about."

Xander closed in, invading her space. "You've had the vision, and it will come to pass. Once it does, you will give me that child to kill."

"To hell I will."

His eyes narrowed. "You either give me the child to kill, or I kill Jonah."

"I thought you wanted to keep Jonah," Malaika challenged.

"I want the child more."

"Don't tell him anything!" Jonah yelled.

"Ah, your boyfriend seems to think you might know something," Xander said softly, his tone full of menace. "I wonder why. Maybe you have already met the vampire couple since you've met their friend."

Malaika cursed inwardly. "The vampires may have saved Jonah from that madman, but it doesn't mean they've stayed in touch with him. They could be anywhere."

"But they're not." He jerked his head in the direction of the fisherman. "Why do you think we kept Samuel for our own sustenance instead of letting the hyenas have him?"

Malaika looked at the fisherman and burned with anger as he looked away, unable to meet her eyes. He was psychic, and had been helping the vampires. "How could you help them?"

"Wait until they torture you a little bit," he said gruffly. "You'll break, too."

"I know you've met them," Xander said. "We can wait around for the baby to be born, however many months that may take, and kill it." He paused, staring her in the eye. "Or we could do this the easy way and kill the woman before she gives birth so you don't have to hear the baby's screams."

However many months? Aria was about to pop. Either Samuel wasn't very good in the psychic department or he'd made sure he'd only "helped" enough to spare his life, without endangering anyone else's.

"Will it be option A or option B?"

Malaika took a deep, calming breath, unsure what to do. She had to stall him for as long as possible. Give someone—and she hoped there was someone, namely, Jake—enough time to rescue them. "I think I'll go with option C."

Xander frowned. "Option C?"

"Yeah, the one where you kiss my big, black ass and go to hell."

Xander's eyes widened and in the next second pain ripped across Malaika's face. The son-of-a-bitch had backhanded her! She hit the floor the same time a roar ripped out of Jonah's throat. She looked up in time to see him plow into Xander. He'd somehow worked himself free of the binding and was going to get himself seriously hurt—or killed—defending her.

"Jonah!" She leapt to her feet and summoned fire. By the time the first ball formed in her hand, Xander had thrown Jonah off and sent him crashing against the wall. She threw the fireball at Xander, but the lightning-fast vampire ducked out of the way before she could fry him. Craig hit her from the side before she could get another ball fully formed.

They went down and Craig shifted to take the brunt of the fall. "Don't provoke him," he whispered as they hit, but it was too late. A roar of rage rent the air and the room shook with it.

"Confine her," Xander ordered, pointing a shaking finger in her direction before stomping over to Jonah.

Malaika started forward, but Craig clamped his hand on her forearm and yanked her back. In his other hand, she caught sight of silver dust. Another witch's net. If she allowed herself to be trapped in another one, she'd be no help to Jonah.

Craig pulled back his arm, ready to throw the net. Desperate, Malaika kneed him in the groin, figuring racking a vampire hurt just as much as racking a human. They still had balls. Craig bent forward in pain, and Malaika brought up her knee again, connecting it with his face. He fell back and the witch's net poured from his hand.

She started to cross the room, but halted as she caught sight of Xander. He'd forced Jonah to his knees and held his head at a hard angle. One twist of his arm and Jonah's neck would snap. "Let him go, Xander."

"Xander? Shouldn't you call me Grandfather? The title holds a higher level of respect." He smiled at her, enjoying her fear. She didn't bother hiding the emotion. One wrong move and Jonah was dead. The evil beast looked down at the man he tortured. "Of course, he could probably tell us where to find the chosen."

"Fuck you," Jonah rasped. "I'd rather you kill me."

"If you kill him, I'll never help you," Malaika cried.

"Is that so?" He cut a glance toward Craig, who was rising to a stand behind her. "I could always take your daughter."

"No!" Craig bellowed. "That was not the deal."

"You forget who the master is here," Xander snarled. "The child has no power. She is expendable."

Malaika choked back the fear climbing her throat. She used her anger to keep it at bay so it wouldn't hinder her. She had to get out of this, if only to save those she loved. "Deja is well-protected. You'll never get to her."

"Protected by whom? The slayer?" His mouth twisted into a mocking grin. "Don't you realize I would plan for him if I took his brother?"

Jonah's pain-filled eyes widened in fear and connected with hers across the room. Dread filled Malaika's stomach. Jake should have come to their rescue by now. Surely he wouldn't allow the vampires to take his brother from the apartment without being hot on their heels.

"Where is Jake?"

Xander laughed. "Where all good little slayers go when their time ends, I suppose."

Jonah jerked and was roughly restrained by Xander's tightening grip. Hot tears of hopelessness fell from Malaika's eyes. "He's not dead. You're lying."

"Check and see." He nodded his head toward Samuel.

Malaika looked between Xander and Craig, saw that neither appeared ready to tackle her, and crossed the distance to the fisherman. She placed her fingertips to his temple as Seta had taught her and filtered through his mind for images of Jacob Porter. She hit some sort of wall and frowned, but continued to travel along it until images fell through.

The fine hairs along the back of Jake's neck stood on end as magic stirred in the air. Dark magic, black and unnatural. He tightened his grip around his blade and exited his car, his gaze scanning the alley as he made his way toward the front of the apartment building.

Glass shattered and he looked up to see shards of it raining down from the windows of Malaika's apartment. Ropes hung from the roof. The brazen hyenas had traveled by rooftop and swung through the windows.

But they weren't alone. The sense of magic hinted at something else entirely. Some sort of witch, and it wasn't Malaika emitting the dark power. Her power was more earthy and natural.

He barreled through the front doors of the apartment building and raced up the steps toward the sound of screaming, but came face to face with the source of the dark power before he could reach the apartment. He stopped, a breath away from the busty brunette in the flesh-colored gown. The shade matched her skin so perfectly, she looked naked. She opened her mouth and the most beautiful sound he'd ever heard came out, drifting onto the night air. She reached out and touched his face, licking her lips, promising him with her eyes that though he might die tonight, he would enjoy it. Maybe even beg for it.

He sensed evil behind him and realized the pranic vampire who'd attacked Malaika had been a busy little soul-sucker, fathering more prannies. They closed in on him, but allowed room on the stairs for him to back down, or as it turned out, follow the siren down.

She passed him, pressing her breasts to his chest, letting them rub against him as she passed, singing that strange, intoxicating little melody. He turned and followed, aware of the prannies and hyenas following close on his heels. They were going to kill him, he knew, but thought nothing about it. He only followed the woman before him, allowed her to lead him back into the dark alley until she stopped and turned toward him.

Her smile was cunning, a promise of death, and he smiled in response. "Do you want me, Jacob Porter?" She lowered the thin straps of her gown, revealing heavy, round breasts topped with dark, pebbled nipples.

"Oh, yes," he whispered, his palms growing sweaty.

"Good. I want you to do something for me," she said, the words coming out as part of a lilting song. She smelled of the sea and Jake could actually smell the ocean breeze on her breath.

"Anything."

"Take your knife and kill yourself."

"Okay." He raised the blade and brought it down hard into his gut, falling to his knees with a smile as his blood poured out to coat the alley. The last thing he heard before his heart ceased beating was the loud maniacal laughter of the were-hyenas.

— ❦ —

Malaika pulled out of Samuel's mind and let out a cry of anguish. Behind her, Jonah growled in rage and Xander laughed. They were doomed. If a slayer couldn't fight a siren, how in the hell could she and Jonah fight off pranic vampires and were-hyenas? And there'd been so many surrounding Jake. She could only imagine how many were outside the cell Xander held them in.

"I take it you just witnessed the vision Samuel shared with me before the two of you regained consciousness. You know there is no one strong enough to save you, no one to come to your rescue. The vampires helped Jonah when one of their own was in trouble. They will not put their lives on the line to help either of you now."

Malaika slowly turned, glaring at the evil vampire, and wished looks really could kill. She'd love to rip the cockiness out of Xander before destroying him completely.

"You must help yourself, Malaika. Give me the child and I will release Jonah."

"Don't," Jonah managed to get out, his voice heavily strained.

Malaika looked at him, her heart twisting. His brother was dead and the siren was still out there, finding more psychics for Xander to recruit for his evil army. They would kill Jonah eventually, no matter what she did, and they would eventually kill Deja. Even if she managed to escape and take Deja into hiding, there would be a war and innocents would be killed. There was no way for her to win. God help us, she pleaded silently, her soul weighed down with hopelessness.

Loud maniacal laughter rent the air from beyond the room, the sound of the hyenas calling to one another. All heads turned toward the door and heard the sound of gunfire.

"What the hell is going on?" Xander released Jonah to the floor and strode forward. "Did Rema return?"

Craig shrugged. "The siren hasn't been heard from since she took out the slayer."

The two vampires rushed toward the door to check out what was happening as screams and gunfire grew more plentiful. Now was the only chance she'd get. Malaika remembered the idea she'd had earlier when the hyenas had rushed Jonah, and called upon the earth just as Xander and Craig reached the door.

The ground rumbled as it shifted and the vampires lost their footing, falling down. The floor cracked and divided into two sections, divided by a ten-foot wide, and twice as deep, canyon. The left wall crumbled and the roof caved. Malaika summoned the wind to carry the pieces away from her and Jonah, but wasn't as kind to the vampires. Stone rained down upon them, cutting their flesh. They let out howls of pain and fury as they dug themselves out from under the debris.

She stumbled toward Jonah, too new in her powers to perform so much magic at once, and knelt at his side. "Jonah?"

"Jake's dead? Really dead?" Tears dripped down his face, leaving tracks in the grime and blood he'd collected since they'd been attacked.

Malaika released her own set of hot tears and gathered Jonah in her arms, kissing his head. "I'm so sorry," she whispered against his temple. "The siren snared him."

"But he's a slayer." He frowned. "He kills vampires and demons."

"But he was also a man. He gave in to the siren's pull." She swallowed down bile. At least he hadn't really fantasized about the siren in the same way Craig had, but still... she was disappointed in him. She'd thought he was a much more honorable man. Poor Nyla. How would she tell the woman that the father of her child had succumbed to the siren? She'd been in her place, and it was an awful place to be.

Laughter pulled her from the thought. "Stupid witch. Do you really think this will save you?" Xander squinted at her while the gash above his brow bled into his eyes, and picked up a large chunk of the roof. With a growl of rage, he threw the stone at them. Malaika gasped and found herself rolling out of the way, Jonah's arms wrapped tight around her. The chunk of ceiling skimmed over them and hit the wall, shattering on impact.

"Hey! Quit throwing shit at my brother, you fugly bastard!"

Malaika's head jerked up and she froze, taking in the scene before her. Jacob Porter stood in the doorway, living and breathing. Xander turned toward him and stood in open-mouthed surprise as Jake swung his arm, a long, silver blade in his hand, and effectively sliced the vampire's head clean off his body.

"Nothing like the element of surprise," Jake quipped and turned for Craig, but Craig had already seen what happened to those who stood still for too long in front of Jake Porter. He took off at a run and leaped across the magically-created canyon, landing right next to Jonah.

Malaika let out a yelp and backed away, pulling Jonah with her. Jonah shrugged her off and stood as Craig's boot came down toward him. He sidestepped it, and threw a punch, connecting his fist to Craig's head, knocking the vampire back.

"I've waited for this, bitch." He taunted.

"Likewise, mortal."

"We're all mortal," Jonah spat back, ducking a blow. He punched Craig in the ribs before rising to a full stand.

"Um, Malaika," Jake called from across the canyon. "Not that I don't like what you've done with the place, but how the hell am I supposed to get over there now? I'm awesome and all, but I can't leap like a damn vampire!"

Still surprised to see him standing there, and not in spirit form, Malaika didn't have a response. She heard the sound of flesh pounding flesh and turned her attention back to the fight. Craig held Jonah down on the ground, his hands wrapped tight around his neck and sucked in air until his face turned blue. "Why can't I drain your energy?"

Jonah landed a strong punch in Craig's face and was released. "I guess I'm just special." He kicked Craig off and started to stand, but Craig quickly recovered and had him slammed back down on the ground in a heartbeat.

Malaika called upon fire, and after much strain, had two fully formed fireballs in her palms, but as the men twisted on the ground, she had a hard time releasing them. It would be too easy to accidentally hit Jonah.

Craig held Jonah down with one hand and punched him repeatedly with the other. Jonah was a good fighter, but Craig had the strength of a vampire behind him. That, mixed with the fact Jonah had suffered other beatings already, gave him the upper hand. Malaika raised her hands, but the fireballs fizzled out, her magical strength waning from the excessive use.

"Malaika!" Jake shouted her name and a long blade whizzed past her face, embedding itself in the wall. She glanced his way and he made a slicing motion over his own neck.

She swallowed hard and grabbed the handle of the blade, yanking hard to retrieve it from the wall. With trembling legs, she carried its surprisingly light weight toward the men.

Too busy pounding his fists into any part of Jonah he could find purchase, Craig didn't notice her until she hovered over him, the blade raised, ready to strike. When he looked up, his eyes grew wide with shock. "Malaika, baby, what are you doing?"

"I'm not your baby," she said, her voice a low threat of danger. "You hurt our baby, your own flesh and blood."

"I'd never hurt Deja."

"You drained her energy."

His face diffused with color, shame flushed his cheeks. "I needed energy, but I never took much. I just wanted to see her, to let her know her daddy was alright, that I didn't leave her."

"You did leave her," Malaika snapped. "You left both of us for that siren. You saw us clearly in your mind, but followed her anyway, thinking what I didn't find out wouldn't hurt anyone!"

"You saw that?"

"I saw it all, Craig. You disgust me."

"Baby, I couldn't help it," he pleaded, rising to his knees, releasing his hold on Jonah, who lay limp and unconscious. Fear tugged at Malaika's heart.

"But I still love you, both of you. Xander wanted me to get the information out of you and kill you, but I refused. I've played him all along. I know you found those vampires. I can follow Deja anywhere, and I know those vampires are in that church watching over her. I could have let Xander know anytime, but I didn't. I wouldn't have until I knew the two of you were safely out of his grasp."

"You'd lead him to a baby so he could slaughter it?"

"If it meant protecting our child, yes." His eyes darkened. "I'll do anything to protect what is mine."

Malaika glanced down at Jonah, then remembered the way her daughter looked so natural in his arms. "So will I."

She brought the blade down in a fast arc, and sent Craig's head rolling, surprise still showing in his dead eyes.

THIRTEEN

Jonah sucked in air and massaged his throat. He felt like he'd just gotten into a fight with a bulldozer and lost. The sound of gasping and deep sobs roused him, and he sat up to see Malaika bent over Craig's decapitated body, her back heaving with the exertion of her crying fit. "Mel?"

She looked at him, her face wet with tears. Her eyes beseeched him of understanding. "I had to, Jonah, I had to. He could have found her at any time, no matter where we went." She broke down into another heavy round of sobs and Jonah worked his way toward her, his battered body protesting the effort. Finally, he reached her and cuddled her against his chest, understanding what was happening. She might have done what was necessary, but being the good person she was, she'd always carry the guilt of the kill.

Headlights cut through the night, visible beyond the crumbled left wall, and Jonah heard the familiar rumble of Jake's engine. Jake. Relief swamped his body as the Malibu rolled to a stop and his brother stepped out.

"Next time your girlfriend causes an earthquake to get you away from the bad guys, make sure she leaves a strip of land for me to cross over," he said as he approached. "It was a ten-minute drive until I found a place I could cross over to get to your side. How's she doing?"

Jonah stared at his brother, taking in the ripped T-shirt that sported a large amount of blood. "As could be expected for a woman who just killed a man and witnessed another come back to life."

Malaika pulled away from him then, and looked up at Jake. "I saw you die." She stood and reached for Jake's T-shirt, lifting up the hem.

"Whoa, there, girlie." Jake backed away. "You're pretty easy on the eyes, but I'm a married man, and my brother has a claim on you. I'm not sure you should be checking out the goods."

"I saw you die!" Malaika said more forcefully. She looked toward the fisherman, who was still bound to a pole, watching the scene before him. "You showed me him dying, bleeding from a self-inflicted stabbing."

"Yes, I did", the psychic, Samuel, said with a nod. "But I blocked the vision of him rising from the dead and all that happened afterward so Xander wouldn't know."

"Rising from the dead?" Jonah rose to a stand. "What's he talking about, Jake? Malaika was absolutely sure you'd died."

"I did," Jake responded, his face devoid of expression. "I've been known to do so from time to time."

Jonah stared at his brother, baffled, then remembered the way he'd been aloof with his responses to the questions about Hicksville. He remembered his reason for not killing Curtis Dunn. "Sonofabitch. Curtis Dunn created the immortality serum and injected you with it."

"Yup. I'm like the Energizer Bunny, but far manlier," Jake answered with a grin. The amusement disappeared as he looked into Malaika's fear-stricken eyes. "I'm sorry if I scared you, but I had no idea there was a psychic with you who could see me die." He turned toward Samuel and frowned. "Speaking of which, do I need to kill him or let him go?"

"He's fine," Jonah answered. "He's the fisherman Malaika saw in her vision, one of the good guys. So you're saying you can't die?" He tried to wrap his mind around that fact and all it meant.

"Apparently not, at least not for long."

Disgust slithered into Jonah's stomach. "Do you have to drink blood?"

Jake looked away. "I eat very rare steak now."

"Gross."

"I know."

"But no human blood?"

"No." The word was a growl, and Jake's eyes held a definite warning not to continue the course of questioning. "Look, Malaika kind of created a natural disaster here, so despite the fact this place is in the boonies, you can bet news teams are on their way, as well as the police. I left a ton of dead bodies on the other side of that wall over there so it's time we haul ass and get out of here."

Jonah sprang into action, untying the fisherman from the post, and helping him to Jake's car. He let the man have the passenger seat so he could sit with Malaika in the back. She was still shaky from what she'd done, and Jonah knew a part of her guilt came from hurting a man she'd cared for.

"Why did you kill yourself?" he asked as Jake wound his Malibu through trees, eventually finding a road to pull onto.

"Dude, I was surrounded by prannies and were-hyenas in a cramped stairwell. My best bet was to draw them away from where you two were and get them to a place where I could maneuver better. I faked the snaring and killed myself, knowing they'd let their guard down and close in on me. I stabbed myself in the gut so my hand would be close to my inner jacket pocket when I went down. The moment I came to, I reached in and grabbed a UV bomb, taking out all those prannies at once."

"And the were-hyenas?"

"Element of surprise is a handy trick. Most of them just stood there scratching their heads in confusion as I sliced and diced them. Then I went up to the apartment and saved Malaika's mother." He glanced at Malaika through the rear-view mirror. "Not that she was appreciative at all. That woman is a trip."

"What about the siren?" Malaika inquired, her tone holding a trace of hostility.

Jake grinned as he glanced back at her. "First of all, I don't know what psychic-dude over here showed you, but that thing never had me snared. I could see the real creature behind the facade and that bitch was fucked up. Unfortunately, she got away while I killed the hyenas."

Jonah let out a deep breath and asked the question niggling at him since Craig's first attack. "Jake, why can't the prannies get in my head and suck out my energy?"

His brother glanced at him and grinned before returning his eyes to the road. "We might not have shared a womb at the same time, but we did share one. I'm a slayer. I guess some of my natural-born awesomeness rubbed off on you."

"But I was born first," Jonah commented, confused.

"Dude, the thing with magic and supernatural crap is that try as you might, you will never completely understand it. Some stuff is just too weird to even try to figure out. Just be thankful you've got the mind-block."

"Wait. What about my apartment?" Malaika asked. "Surely someone called the police with all the commotion."

"I'm sure they did," Jake commented. "I got your mother and got the hell out of there before they arrived, but I left some blood on the carpet. Probably on the walls, too. Then there's the bodies."

Jonah groaned. "How the hell do we explain that? Granger was already looking for us after they discovered the body you found last night. I said we'd stop by the department and speak with him, but after this? I'm going to prison. Both of us are."

Malaika tensed beside him and he wrapped an arm around her shoulders, trying to comfort her despite knowing they were both screwed.

"Relax, bro." Jake chuckled. "I called in Seta before I left. The woman is a one-woman cleanup crew. However, Malaika will need a new place to live."

"Why?" Malaika sat up straighter. "I thought Seta cleaned it up."

"Oh she cleaned it up, alright. Mind-controlled all the residents outside and torched that sucker."

Malaika gasped, and Jonah held her closer. "At least we're alive."

"You're right," she said and lay her head on his shoulder. "And the children will be safe." She jerked up suddenly. "Jake!"

"What?!" Jake jerked, swerving the car, and shot her a look of annoyance through the rear-view mirror.

"Step on it! The babies are coming!"

Jacob Porter could not die, but he sure could sweat. Malaika grinned, watching the macho man tremble in fear as Nyla pushed. She cried out and Seta spoke the incantation to relieve her pain.

"One more push," Malaika coaxed her, surprised with the ease she felt helping to deliver the babies.

Aria and Rialto's baby had come first, a beautiful caramel-colored girl with a thick mass of dark hair and green eyes. They'd named her Njeri, which meant Destiny, and Malaika had watched in wonder as the little girl suckled at her mother's breast, drinking both milk and blood.

Then Nyla's contractions kicked into overdrive and she'd switched over to help Seta deliver her baby. "Come on, Nyla," she said softly as the head crowned. "One big push and you're done."

Jacob Porter's son came into the world screaming for all he was worth. Malaika wiped him clean and looked into his gorgeous eyes, a deep, dark amethyst ringed with chocolate-brown, and was amazed by the power she sensed from him.

"Can you shift now?" Seta asked after the placenta had been delivered. "It will help your healing."

Nyla was there one second, and the next, a large panther stood on the bed she'd rested in. Just as quickly as she'd shifted into the cat, she shifted back into human form.

"Wow," was the only thing Malaika could think to say, and Jake laughed.

"Let's hope Jonah can get used to it," he said, and sobered, a look of worry on his face. "Little Slade will probably do the same thing."

Malaika handed Nyla the baby, and glanced down at the gorgeous, dark-haired boy, now suckling at his mother's breast, and smiled. "Jonah will adore him."

She looked at the two couples and sighed. The love in the small room Christian had put them in for the deliveries was so abundant, a tear of joy escaped her eye. She excused herself and left Christian's private quarters, taking the stairs to the church sanctuary.

She found Jonah there, watching over Deja as she napped in a pew. "You have a gorgeous new nephew. His name is Slade."

Jonah smiled. "That's great."

"You want to see him?"

"I'll give Jake and Nyla some time to bond with him," he answered, and sighed, ramming his hands into the pockets of his jeans. "Malaika, can I ask you something?"

"Of course." She swallowed past the ball of worry in her throat. Jonah's tone was serious, in the probably-about-to-say-something-not-so-good-serious-way.

"About what Craig said back there..."

Oh, no. "It doesn't matter, Jonah."

"Is it true? Am I sterile?"

She sighed. "I had a vision of our life together, and we'd visited a doctor after a year of unsuccessfully trying to get pregnant. The doctor told us you were sterile, but I don't know why, or what caused it." She placed her hand on his arm. "But it doesn't matter. I loved you in that vision, and I…"

He looked her in the eye, hope bright in his. "You really do?"

"I love you, Jonah Porter. It may seem sudden, or just strange, but despite Craig keeping us from meeting… I saw those visions and I felt the love in them. I know what a wonderful man you are, and I love you for that."

He nodded his head and looked down at Deja. "I'm glad Craig did what he did."

"What?" Malaika realized she'd nearly shouted and checked Deja. She still slept, as did Helen, a few pews down. Samuel glanced at them from where he sat far away in the last pew and closed his eyes, nodding back to sleep.

"He was right." Jonah pulled her closer. "He gave you what I couldn't, and I'm glad you have such a beautiful little girl to call your own."

"It doesn't matter to me that you can't give me a child."

"Good." He took in a deep breath and let it out. "So marry me, and let me adopt Deja."

Malaika's jaw went slack, and Jonah grinned. "Well?"

She blinked, shaking her head. "Did you just ask me to marry you?"

"That's what it sounded like to me," he answered. "I love you, woman, everything about you, and that includes Deja. She needs a daddy and I need you. What do you say?"

"I say I need you, too." She laughed, relief and joy flooding through her chest. She kissed Jonah, long and hard, then remembered her mother. "Who gets to tell Helen?"

Jonah looked toward her sleeping mother. "I'm the one that gets to come up with something to tell Granger about these murders and your burnt-down building, and suffer through another round of psychiatric evaluations in order to keep my job. You get to deal with your mother."

"Chicken."

"Witch." He grinned and dropped a kiss on her nose.

"Damn straight," she said cheekily, "and proud of it."

The Blood Revelation continues with Siren's Snare, available now.

About the Author

Crystal-Rain Love resides in the South with her three children and enough pets to host a petting zoo. When she's not writing she can usually be found creating unique 3D cakes,hiking, reading, or spending way too much time on FaceBook. Slightly obsessed with David Cook and Supernatural.

Read more at https://crystalrainlove.com.